Praise for *The Escape*

"An excellent thriller with well-drawn characters and the suspenseful start to Harris's new US Marshals series."

Booklist

"There are so many unexpected twists and turns that I was engaged from beginning until end. I can't wait for the next book in the series."

Relz Reviewz

"This story gripped me from the very beginning and didn't let go. Of all the Lisa Harris books I have read, I would easily say this is my favorite and one I recommend to readers who like a high-thrill ride with characters they can relate to and a story that will keep them on the edge of their seat late into the night."

Write-Read-Life

Praise for *Traitor's Pawn*

"Harris presents a fast-paced adventure that balances intriguing clues, complex suspects, light romance, and messages of forgiveness to create an excellent, entertaining read."

Booklist

"Lisa Harris never fails to bring an action-packed, adrenaline-filled romantic suspense to her readers."

Interviews & Reviews

Praise for *Deadly Intentions*

"A story of corruption and greed, but also a story of romance and healing."

Compass Book Ratings

"Lisa Harris never fails to amaze me with her high-intensity, adrenaline-fueled, action-packed plots and beautifully crafted characters racing against time and enemies to find the solution to a looming threat."

Interviews & Reviews

THE CHASE

Books by Lisa Harris

A Secret to Die For
Deadly Intentions
The Traitor's Pawn

Southern Crimes

Dangerous Passage
Fatal Exchange
Hidden Agenda

Nikki Boyd Files

Vendetta
Missing
Pursued
Vanishing Point

US Marshals

The Escape
The Chase

US MARSHALS · 2

THE CHASE

LISA HARRIS

Revell

a division of Baker Publishing Group
Grand Rapids, Michigan

© 2021 by Lisa Harris

Published by Revell
a division of Baker Publishing Group
PO Box 6287, Grand Rapids, MI 49516-6287
www.revellbooks.com

Printed in the United States of America

Library of Congress Cataloging-in-Publication Data
Names: Harris, Lisa, 1969– author.
Title: The chase / Lisa Harris.
Description: Grand Rapids, Michigan : Revell, a division of Baker Publishing Group,
    [2021] | Series: US Marshals ; 2
Identifiers: LCCN 2021006620 | ISBN 9780800737313 (paperback) | ISBN
    9780800740016 (casebound) | ISBN 9781493430413 (ebook)
Subjects: GSAFD: Christian fiction. | Suspense fiction.
Classification: LCC PS3608.A78315 C47 2021 | DDC 813/.6—dc23
LC record available at https://lccn.loc.gov/2021006620

This book is a work of fiction. Names, characters, places, and incidents are the product of the author's imagination or are used fictitiously. Any resemblance to actual events, locales, or persons, living or dead, is coincidental.

The author is represented by Hartline Literary Agency, LLC.

21 22 23 24 25 26 27   7 6 5 4 3 2 1

ONE

Madison James burned through the final sixty seconds of her workout on the stationary bike, then released a slow breath. Rain had kept her inside this morning, but the forecast was calling for a break in the bad weather later today. It felt good to have things back to normal again.

She headed to the bathroom, then stopped at the dresser where she'd set her Deputy US Marshal badge and picked it up. Today was her first day back on the job. It had been twelve weeks since she'd been shot.

And she still had no idea who'd pulled the trigger.

The doorbell rang, and she hesitated for a moment before grabbing her Glock off the bedside table and heading to the front door. She looked through the peephole, then smiled.

She unlocked the bolt and the handle before opening the door. "You're early."

Her partner, Deputy US Marshal Jonas Quinn, held up a paper bag. "I thought you might appreciate breakfast on your first day back. And since I didn't know what you might be in the mood for, I brought you a bit of everything." He headed to the kitchen, set the bag and two coffees on the counter, then turned back to her.

"Okay." She let out a low laugh. "My interest is piqued. What did you bring?"

"Let's see . . . raspberry vanilla croissants, an apple Danish, and *pain au chocolat*." Madison's stomach rumbled as he pulled the baked goods out of the bag one at a time. "Or if you'd prefer something savory," Jonas continued, "I've got a couple smoked salmon croissants, two more with bacon, and one with spinach."

"I don't recognize the name of the bakery on the bag." She grabbed a couple plates from the cupboard and set them on the counter. "Where did you find this place?"

"Apparently they just opened a couple weeks ago. Michaels recommended them to me."

She wasn't surprised. Their boss, Chief Deputy Carl Michaels, and his wife, Glenda, were always searching for the best places to eat in Seattle.

She glanced at the options, then picked a raspberry croissant. "Not that I'm complaining, but it looks like you were expecting to feed an army."

Jonas laughed. "No, but I did assume anything that didn't get eaten here, we could always take into the office."

She took a large bite of her croissant, savoring the flavor. "Nice way to win brownie points with the boss."

He winked. "Oh, and there is one more thing." He pulled a little box from the bottom of the bag and held it up. "Chocolate mocha cheesecake."

"It's six thirty in the morning."

"This is for later. I know it's not Friday, but I thought we might need to celebrate your first day over dinner. Unless you're busy tonight."

"No. I'd like that."

Somehow over the past three months, they'd made Friday nights a standing "date" between the two of them. Though she'd never officially call it a date. It started with Jonas coming by with takeout as an excuse to check on her after she got out of the hospital. She'd tell him the boring details of what she'd done that day in physical therapy, then she'd probe for details on whatever case he was working. Eventually, they ended up starting one of the DIY projects in the house she'd bought after the attack. With his help, they'd managed to paint her bedroom, redo the floors in the living room and kitchen, and update the tiles in the guest bathroom.

Once, instead of their normal takeout fare, he'd made her shrimp linguine that was so good, she told him he might have gone into the wrong business. Boy, the man could cook. Their time together was something she'd come to look forward to, like Sunday dinners with her father and her sister's family. Except with Jonas, she could talk about things she couldn't talk about with them.

Her sister had teased her that there was more going on between her and her partner than just friendship, but Madison ignored the not-so-subtle hints. They'd only officially worked together two times. The first time was five years ago when she trained under him at a shoot house in Nashville, and the second was just before her accident. The two of them had tracked an escaped felon across the country. But the bottom line was that they were friends, nothing more, and that's how things were going to stay.

"This is delicious." She took another bite of the croissant.

"You can feel free to stop by with breakfast any morning of the week. I promise I won't complain."

He laughed at the comment and picked up one of the bacon croissants. He took a bite. "Did you run this morning?"

She glanced out the window, not surprised it was still raining. "I chose to bike indoors over getting soaked."

"I don't blame you." He wiped his mouth. "How was your last day in physical therapy?"

She turned back to him. "Worried about my overdoing it?"

"Maybe." He took another few bites of his croissant, finishing it off quickly.

"I passed, Jonas. I even did a ten-minute mile."

"Not bad. You've worked hard these past couple months." Jonas grabbed a second croissant. "How are you sleeping?"

She avoided his gaze, focusing instead on her breakfast. "Why the twenty questions?"

"Just making conversation."

Right.

"I know I slept, because I dreamed a lot." She kept her voice even, not wanting him to worry about the nightmares that woke her up most nights. Or the memories that refused to surface.

"The memories will come back eventually," he said, reading her mind. "Just give yourself some time."

Except she'd given herself time, and three months hadn't been enough.

She waved her hand like it didn't matter. "Stop worrying about me, Jonas. I'll get through this. It's part of the risk we take every day."

Ironic, though, how she could chase a convicted felon halfway across the country and end up with barely a scratch, and then turn around and get shot in her own home. The place where she was supposed to be safe. It was part of the reason she'd put her old house on the market and snatched up the property she'd been eyeing in a different neighborhood. All new locks and double bolts on the doors had helped ease her anxiety. Running scared wasn't something she was used to. She was the one who went after the criminals. Not the other way around.

But what she did know about the accident terrified her. Whoever had shot her had also murdered her husband.

"I just wish whoever shot me wasn't still out there," she said.

"We'll find them," he said.

"How? We have nothing." She grabbed a napkin from the bar, wiped the sticky sugar residue off her fingers, then eyed the spinach croissant before picking it up. "No forensic evidence. No DNA or fingerprints. Even our one eyewitness—yours truly—doesn't have anything, and we know I was just a couple feet from the shooter."

At least that's what she'd been told from the ballistics report.

"You're putting yourself under too much pressure."

"No." She shook her head while Jonas grabbed another croissant and started eating it. "I need to remember. Luke has been dead for five years, and I'm no closer to finding his killer than we were the day he was murdered."

She'd told Jonas some of the details of the day her husband died. Luke had just finished a twelve-hour shift in the ER. He'd called her on his way to the parking garage like he did almost every day. He said he would pick up some takeout and meet her at home once she got off. She expected him to be there when she pulled into the driveway. Instead, two officers from her district office were waiting to give her the news that Luke had been shot twice in the chest in the hospital parking garage.

For her, life was never the same again.

Madison ran her hand automatically across the four-inch scar on her stomach, trying to focus on the spinach croissant she'd been nibbling.

She hadn't told Jonas how many hours she spent going over every scrap of evidence the authorities had collected on both Luke's death and the attempt on her life. But all she'd found were dead ends. The only evidence they had was a black rose left at the scene—mirroring the cryptic message someone left on Luke's grave every year—confirming in her mind that whoever had shot her was the same person who'd killed Luke.

But she had no idea what they wanted. Or when they might strike again.

"I got your text last night," she said, shoving away the memories that haunted her. "You said Felicia's back in town?"

"Changing the subject?"

She shot him a smile, needing to ease the tension that had surfaced between them. "I'd always rather talk about your drama than mine."

"There's no drama," he said, reaching for his coffee.

"If you say so."

"Her grandmother Hazel texts me every once in a while. She just said that Felicia's been having some problems with her prosthetic leg and came to Seattle to see a specialist."

"Are you going to see her?"

"I'd like to. If nothing else, for some closure. But according to Hazel, she still doesn't want to see me."

She caught the lingering hurt in his expression and wished she could take it away. But some things, she'd learned, couldn't be repaired.

"I'm sorry," she said.

"Me too." He took a sip of his coffee. "How's the croissant?"

"Delicious, but you know as much as I do that I need to get back to work." She held up what was left of the spinach croissant. "If you keep spoiling me like this, I might not pass my next fitness test."

"I doubt that, and on the upside, your new house is looking amazing. I see you hung up that new copper light."

She turned to admire the new wall fixture she'd installed the night before. "I hope you don't mind that I didn't wait for you. I woke up in the middle of the night and had this inspiration to hang it in the kitchen instead of the dining room."

"No. I like it," he said. "It adds a lot of light to the room."

"That's what I thought."

Jonas's phone buzzed and he pulled it out of his pocket. She could see his expression sour.

"Everything okay?" she asked.

"It's a text from Michaels. A federal warrant finally went through for a suspect involved in a string of bank robberies."

"Great. What are we looking at?"

Jonas hesitated. "*Me*, not we."

She caught his gaze. "Jonas—"

"I'm serious. Give yourself time to ease back in. Michaels wants you at the office this week."

She thought about arguing with him, then bit her tongue. She was going to have to find a subtler way to convince him she was ready to be out in the field. "Remind me about the case."

"There's been a string of bank robberies across the state. I think I've mentioned it to you. They've managed to steal over two million dollars and the Feds still don't know who's behind it."

"And the warrant?"

"We were able to trace a fingerprint back to a Ben Galvan from a getaway car that was abandoned."

"Who is he?"

Jonas moved to the sink to wash his hands. "Not sure. Except for a couple minor speeding infractions in college, the guy has a clean record. He's an accountant with a large firm in town."

"And now he's robbing banks?"

"That about sums it up. At least that's what we think."

"I want in on the raid," she said, no longer beating around the bush. "If Michaels isn't convinced, you can vouch for me."

Jonas reached for a dish towel, avoiding her gaze.

"Wait a minute." She moved around the bar and stopped in front of him. "Is that the real motivation behind the croissants? You're the one hesitating?"

"No, it's just that—"

"It's been three months, Jonas. I'm more than ready. My doctor has signed off, my psychologist has signed off."

"I know." He dropped the towel back onto the counter.

"You don't think I'm ready." It wasn't a question, as far as she was concerned. It was a statement. She knew him well enough by now to read him.

"You're the only one who really knows," Jonas said, "but I know how hard this has been on you emotionally. And on top of that, you have the added stress of your father's recent diagnosis. Alzheimer's is a devastating disease."

Madison frowned. "So you're saying that my father has a legitimate reason to forget who I am, but you're questioning my ability to do my job because I can't remember who shot me."

"I'm not questioning your ability. You're the best marshal I've ever worked with."

"But?" she prodded.

"I'll admit, the fact that you still can't remember does worry me. Michaels and I think it might be best if you start back slow. Spend some time getting readjusted before you get back into the field."

"I'll call Michaels, and—"

"He left it up to me."

Her jaw tensed. "You can't leave me stuck behind a desk."

She didn't want any tension between them. Their job required complete trust in each other. But if he couldn't completely trust her, where did that leave them?

She picked up her coffee and took a long sip. She'd been told that she likely had dissociative amnesia stemming from trauma. In other words, she couldn't remember who shot her because of the psychological trauma to her brain. Typically, a victim lost personal memories, but she lost something of even more importance. She needed to remember who'd pulled the trigger.

"I want you back," he said. "Trust me. It hasn't been the same working without you."

"So?" She popped the last bite of her croissant into her mouth, then swallowed.

"Are you sure you're ready for this?"

"I am."

He hesitated, then nodded. "Okay."

"Okay?"

"You're in. Just don't prove me wrong."

"You don't have to worry about that. How much time do we have? I need to shower."

"Five minutes."

She nodded, then felt a surge of adrenaline shoot through

her. Her sister had never understood Madison's need for that rush, but it was the fuel that kept her going. She needed to get back out in the field. Because if she didn't, then she let whoever shot her win. And she wasn't going to let that happen.

TWO

Jonas pulled on his bulletproof vest and tugged it into place, glad that the early morning rain had finally stopped. He knew he'd upset Madison with his concerns, but he'd had to make sure she was ready. She'd been quiet on the ride over to the sleepy waterfront community where they were preparing to do some investigating, but maybe she was just focused on the job ahead. On the other hand, he knew he shouldn't have made it sound as if he doubted her. Because he didn't. He'd first learned how competent she was when they'd met in Nashville a few years back, and then again just over three months ago when they'd worked together for the first time as partners. He trusted her with his life.

He glanced at her profile as she checked her service weapon and adjusted her gear. Dark brown hair with a few scattered highlights hung just past her shoulders and her expression was completely focused. He'd missed her input out in the field the past three months. The time they'd spent together had proved that not only was she smart, able, and beautiful, but at times, vulnerable as well.

He'd make it up to her tonight over dinner.

And maybe tell her what he should have told her weeks ago.

He checked his own weapon and felt his mouth go dry. Setting up a raid on a fugitive was one thing. Telling her how important she'd become to him, and how almost losing her had made him realize his feelings toward her were far from simply professional, was a completely different thing.

"You ready for this?" he asked, pushing his feelings aside.

"I'll admit to having a bit of nerves under the surface, but the adrenaline is good for me. It keeps me focused and on my toes."

"I agree. And Madison . . . I hope you didn't take what I said at your house the wrong way. I really am glad you're back."

She pulled on her raid gear that was marked with both POLICE and US MARSHAL. "It's a job with high risk, and I understand your hesitations. You just need to know that I'm mentally ready for this, and I've got your back."

"I've got your back."

The thought hit him from out of the blue. Felicia had always said that to him every time they went out on a raid. Was that the problem? He'd allowed his feelings toward Madison to cross the line and now he was worried that the same thing was going to happen to her that had happened to Felicia.

He forced himself to ignore the thought. Whatever he felt for Madison didn't matter right now. The two of them had a job to do, which meant he had to stay as focused as he expected her to be. He shoved his weapon into the holster then slammed the trunk shut. He'd gotten used to compartmentalizing his personal and career lives in order to keep the two separate. It was the only way to function because distractions could be deadly. And now definitely wasn't the time for a distraction.

He finished securing the rest of his gear, his focus now

razor-sharp. This raid, like most of those he planned, was the culmination of days of surveillance and started early in the morning to help with the element of surprise. That surprise was their ace up the sleeve. But no matter how much they planned and how many details they ironed out, when tracking down fugitives, they had to be ready for the unexpected.

As soon as the small task force made up of US Marshals, FBI, and local law enforcement was assembled, he started giving out assignments and ensuring they were all on the same page.

Jonas's jaw tensed as he rested his hands on his hips and glanced toward the line of houseboats. "We'll approach the house from the east. From the information we've gathered, this is the house of Ben Galvan's ex-girlfriend, Kira Thornton. We know that a man—who we believe is Galvan—has been staying here. A neighbor identified the photo we showed her and said she'd seen him around within the last twenty-four hours."

He glanced one last time at Madison before they started moving from the parking lot at the edge of the pier toward the house. No matter how many concerns he had, he knew she was right, and he didn't have to worry about her. This was their window of opportunity because another day and Galvan might be long gone. They had no idea what they were going to find on the other side of that door. It was always a risk. Always a gamble that something out of their control would go wrong.

The small waterfront community was made up of several dozen houseboats, all connected by wooden walkways. The additional touch of flower boxes had been added to the floating neighborhood.

Four deputy marshals lined up outside the front door, while the rest of the team fanned out, ready to proceed at Jonas's signal.

When they were all in place, he banged on the front door. "US Marshals with a warrant. Open the door."

He waited a few seconds then pounded again, ready to make a forced entry if necessary.

He was about to signal for the man behind him to break down the door when a young woman opened it. Clearly surprised, she took a step backward. Her long blonde hair was pulled up in a ponytail and she was dressed in shorts and a T-shirt. Jonas recognized her from the photo that had been distributed to the team earlier.

"Kira Thornton?" he asked.

"What's going on?"

"I have a warrant to search your house and a federal arrest warrant for Ben Galvan."

"Ben . . . No . . . Wait . . . Ben doesn't live here."

"Then I'll need you to stand back while we search the house."

"I'm telling you the truth." Panic laced her voice. "Ben isn't here. We're not even together anymore."

"Is there anyone else in the house, ma'am?"

"No . . . yes." She shook her head, clearly confused by the unexpected encounter.

"Is there anyone else in the house?" he repeated.

"I'm sorry . . . My brother. He's been staying here with me for a few days, but I don't understand what is going on."

"What's your brother's name?"

"His name's Brandon, but you're still not telling me what's wrong. What did Ben do?"

"I just serve the warrants, ma'am."

"Well, he's not here, and I have no idea where he is."

"You need to stay here while we search the house."

Jonas signaled two of the officers to stay with her while the

LISA HARRIS ———— 21

rest of them made a sweep of the house. He couldn't assume she was telling the truth, and he didn't want to be taken by surprise.

Assumptions. That was when things went wrong. He sent two more officers upstairs, then headed down the short hallway that was flanked by three doors in the back of the house. The first one opened to the bathroom.

"Clear."

A man in his midtwenties, with cropped blond hair, stepped into the hallway, immediately locking gazes with Jonas. From the photos he'd passed out to his team, he knew immediately that this wasn't Ben. Which meant it had to be Kira's brother.

Jonas held up his badge, keeping his gun in front of him as well. "I need you to put your hands in the air now and move into the living room in front of me."

The man hesitated for a split second, then did a one eighty and burst into one of the rooms at the back of the house.

Jonas spoke into his two-way radio. "We've got a runner. He's heading out of the south side of the house. I'm going after him."

The window was already up and the screen knocked out by the time Jonas entered the bedroom seconds later. He shoved open the window a couple more inches, then slipped outside and onto the three-foot-wide deck that ran the back of the house. Beyond that was the water. Brandon was sprinting toward the next house to the left.

Where did he think he was going?

One of their agents rounded the corner and ran toward them. Brandon hesitated briefly then slammed into the agent, knocking the man onto the deck. Jonas maneuvered around the downed agent, still managing to stay a few feet behind

Brandon as they neared the end of the deck. Brandon jumped the couple of feet onto the back of the next houseboat.

While the fronts of the houses were attached to a wooden sidewalk, the backs had varying widths of a narrow ledge. One misstep would leave one—or both—of them in the water. Jonas frowned. Not exactly how he wanted to start his day.

Jonas saw Brandon's feet slip as he jumped onto another deck, but he managed to catch his balance. There were only a few more houses until they got to the end, and after that, there was nowhere left to go. Brandon launched himself onto the back of the last houseboat, then glanced behind him as if trying to decide what to do, but the man was running out of options. Jonas sped up. There was no way he was going to let him get away.

Brandon jumped into a small boat tethered beside the last house on the row and tried to start the motor.

Seriously?

Jonas drew in a sharp breath of fresh air. The guy needed to know when it was time to give up.

A second later, Madison came around the corner, then stepped on the edge of the boat, her gun pointing at him. "I'm not sure where you think you're headed, but it ends here. Put your hands in front of you now."

Brandon halted, then turned toward Jonas, who was just a bit farther behind. Brandon looked at the gun Madison leveled at him and surrendered.

"Now that was impressive." Jonas walked toward the two of them. "Apparently three months of rehabilitation and you haven't lost your touch."

"Just doing my job." She shot a grin at him, then pulled out a pair of handcuffs and slapped them on the man's wrists before reading him his rights. She turned to Jonas. "And I didn't even break a sweat."

"I'm not sweating." He looked down at his shirt and vest and laughed. "Or I wouldn't be if I wasn't wearing so many layers."

At least he hadn't fallen in.

Madison smiled. "Why don't you go ahead and question him. I'll be right back."

Jonas turned back to the man. "I need to know why you were running, Brandon."

"I don't know . . . Maybe because seeing an armed man in the middle of the hallway before I'm even half-awake scared me. What would you have done?"

"I wouldn't run when someone showed me their badge," Jonas said. "People sometimes run when they're guilty."

"I told you, you scared me. That was all."

"Maybe next time, you should think twice about running." Jonas held up his phone. "Do you know this man?"

Brandon squinted his eyes while he looked at the screen. "Sure. It's Kira's old boyfriend."

"Her ex?"

Brandon nodded. "That's what she told me."

"When's the last time you saw him?"

"I don't know. A month or so ago. We weren't really friends. I don't think he liked me, which was fine, because I wasn't crazy about him either."

I wonder why.

"Why didn't you like him?" Jonas asked.

"Does it matter? He just . . . didn't seem good enough for Kira. In the end, she said she needed to get on with her life. Whatever that means. Why are you looking for him?"

"We have a warrant out for his arrest," Jonas said.

Brandon shook his head. "I never did like him dating my sister. And I was probably onto something if you've got a warrant out on him." He caught Jonas's gaze. "So what did he do?"

"I figured you'd know."

"To be honest, except for the fact that he likes skydiving and rock climbing, the guy's a bit of a bore. I mean he's an accountant." Brandon motioned toward his hands. "So I've answered your questions. Can we please take off the cuffs?"

"I don't think so. Both you and the cuffs are heading downtown."

Brandon held up his hands. "This was a mistake. I know I shouldn't have run—"

"But you did," Madison said, walking back up to them. "So I called in to see if there might be another reason for you to run. Looks like there are two open arrest warrants out on you for drug possession and distribution."

"That explains a lot," Jonas said, signaling to one of the officers. "Which means we're going to have someone take you down to the station and book you."

Jonas handed Brandon off, then headed with Madison back to the houseboat, where they were still searching. One of the officers hurried toward them.

"What is it?" Madison asked.

"A box of ammo." Officer Alexander held up the bagged evidence. "It was shoved back behind a stack of books in one of the closets, but it's the same caliber that was found in the bank robberies."

"Did you find a gun as well?" Jonas asked.

"No. Just the ammo."

"Let me take a photo before you file the evidence. My guess

is that Kira's trying to protect Ben," Madison said, turning back to Jonas.

"He could have stashed it here without her knowing it."

"Maybe," Madison said. "We need to talk to her. If he's involved in the robberies, there's a good chance she knows where he is."

THREE

Madison and Jonas approached the houseboat where Kira was standing in front, yelling something at one of the officers, clearly angry over her brother's arrest.

Jonas stopped at the end of the wooden planks leading up to the house. "Since your intuition has been right on target today, I'm happy to have you handle her."

Madison rested her hands on her hips. "Is this all a part of your plan to welcome me back to full-time duty?"

"Honestly, I'd hoped for something a bit more exciting, but I guess this will do."

She shot him a smile. "Very funny."

They walked up to one of the officers, who was just ending a call on his cell phone.

"What is she hollering about?" Jonas asked.

The officer slipped his phone into his pocket. "She's convinced her and her brother's rights have been violated."

"But there was a warrant out on Brandon," Madison said.

The officer shrugged. "She doesn't seem interested in that fact."

"I'll talk with her," Madison said, starting toward the house.

She walked up to the woman and forced a smile, flashing her badge. "Kira, I'm Deputy US Marshal Madison James—"

"I need to know what's going on. Now. You can't just take my brother, but no one will listen to me."

Madison held up her hand. "I know you're upset, and I'm here to listen to you, but I need you to stand out of the way while they finish searching your house. There's a bench—"

"No . . . you have no right to harass me and my brother."

"First of all," Jonas said, coming up behind Madison, "we have a warrant to search the premises. Second—your brother is under arrest for drug possession and distribution."

Kira crossed her arms over her chest. "That's not possible."

Madison tried to soften her expression. "I know this is up-setting, but the best thing you can do at this moment is let us do our job."

"How? By letting you take my brother away?"

"Brandon is being escorted to one of the district offices. As soon as a judge sets his bail, you'll be able to get him out, if that is what you choose. In the meantime, please cooperate so they don't decide to arrest you as well. I'm pretty sure you don't want that."

Kira's frown deepened as her phone rang. She glanced at the screen before shoving it into her pocket and then shifting her attention back to Madison. "I'm sorry. You're right. This . . . this just wasn't exactly what I was expecting today."

"How about we go sit down for a few minutes then?" Madison followed the woman to an iron bench overlooking the water and a row of houseboats, then sat down next to her while Jonas stayed standing. Madison decided to start with the nice-cop approach. "How are you feeling? No one expects their home to be raided, and I know something like this can be unnerving."

Kira's brow rose. "Unnerving? Terrifying is more like it. Do you know what it's like to be dead asleep, then hear people shouting at your door and ordering you to open up? All I could think about was that one of us would get shot by mistake."

Madison glanced at Jonas then back to Kira.

"You do know that this isn't the first time your brother has been arrested. He's in serious trouble."

Kira's expression darkened. "I know it's not the first time. Brandon's been in and out of trouble with the law since high school. I was just giving him a place to stay while he's between jobs. He's always between jobs, but he said he was clean. I wanted to believe him."

"Which is understandable. We want to believe those we care about." Madison watched as Kira's shoulders dropped slightly. She was starting to relax some. Madison took the opportunity to press further. "It's quite a place you have here. The houseboat and these views of the water and Mount Rainier are amazing."

Kira just shrugged. "It's my parents' place, actually. They're traveling through Europe right now."

"What do they do for a living?"

"My dad's semi-retired but is still part owner of a tech company. He still goes in to work three or four days a week."

"And I understand you work for him?"

"In the marketing department." Kira's frown settled on her face. "Listen, do I need a lawyer?"

"That is up to you, but you're not under arrest," Jonas said. "We're just hoping for information."

"About Ben."

Madison nodded.

"You said you had a warrant for him," Kira said, "but you still haven't told me what he did."

"He is the reason we have a warrant on your house. We have evidence that he's been staying here."

"He was for a bit, but not anymore. Like I told you, we broke up. I haven't seen him for weeks."

"When exactly is the last time you were in contact with him?"

"The day we broke up. Four, maybe five weeks ago."

"We have a witness that said they saw him here yesterday."

"Then they were mistaken. Maybe they saw my brother." Kira let out a puff of air. "So why are you looking for Ben?"

Madison hesitated, carefully studying Kira's expression. "He's wanted in connection with a string of bank robberies across the state."

"Bank robberies? Ben?" Kira let out a low laugh. "Yeah, you've definitely got the wrong person. Ben's an accountant. He spends his days crunching numbers, not robbing banks."

"That might be true, but we still need to speak to him. I'm assuming you can tell us where we could find him. From what we were told, he works from home."

"I have no idea where he's living now," said Kira. "When we broke up, I told him I didn't want to see him again, and I haven't."

"Did he normally work from the houseboat when the two of you were together?"

"Either that, or he'd hole up at a coffee shop. He had this weird habit of being able to focus better when there was more noise around him."

"Why did you break up?" Madison asked, needing to push her, but not hard enough that she completely shut down.

Kira scowled. "I don't see how that is any of your business." She turned away for a minute, looking out over the water. "But our relationship had gotten a bit . . . stale. When he wasn't working, his attention consisted of getting takeout, playing video games, and watching ESPN. And, I don't know. I guess I got tired of the rut. He worked fifty hours a week, which meant when he wasn't working, he was tired. I decided I needed a bit more . . . sizzle . . . in my life that went beyond work."

"So you never saw anything that implied he might be involved in anything illegal?" Jonas asked.

"If you knew Ben, you'd know it's just not possible. I mean, when would he have done it? Until recently, he was always either working or with me."

"And you have no way to get ahold of him?" Madison asked.

"Since you found me, I'm assuming you probably know more about him than I do and would have a better chance of tracking him."

"So no forwarding address or new telephone number?"

"I have one number for him. I don't even know if he uses it anymore. And like I said, I have no idea where he's been staying since he moved out."

"We'll need that number." Madison pressed her hands against the bench. "Are you dating anyone new?"

"Yeah, actually. I joined a dating site. Had a date last night, in fact."

"Think you'll see him again?"

"My first date made Ben look like James Bond, but last night's . . ." Kira shrugged. "I might see him again."

"My sister met her husband online," Madison said.

"I'm not surprised, though it all depends on what you want, I suppose." Kira shrugged. "And if you're lucky."

"That definitely wouldn't be me. I do have one last question for you, Kira."

"What's that?"

Madison pulled up a photo on her phone. "We found this box of ammo in your house but couldn't find a gun registered to your name. Do these bullets belong to you?"

Kira's brow furrowed. "I don't own a gun. Maybe they're my father's since this is his place. Where did you find them?"

"In the back of a bedroom closet," Jonas said.

Kira shook her head. "I've never seen them before."

"Does your father own a gun?"

"I don't know, to be honest. I know he does a lot of shooting at the range, so it's possible."

"We appreciate your talking with us," Madison said, slipping her cell phone back into her pocket.

"Not like I had a choice. And by the way, if you ever decide to try online dating, try Tally. It's discreet and they do a great job of matching interests."

"I'll think about it." Madison pulled out a card and handed it to her. "And in the meantime, if you do hear from Ben again, call me. It's in both your best interest."

Kira nodded.

"I think we need to see about putting more pressure on the brother," Jonas said as they walked away. "See if he isn't more willing to talk."

"Before his sister bails him out."

Jonas gave instructions to the team on finishing up, then headed toward the car with Madison.

"Your sister actually joined an online dating site?" Jonas asked.

She laughed. "Is that all you got out of that interview?"

"That was the most interesting part, though now I'm wondering if you've ever joined one."

Madison stopped next to his car. "I was just trying to connect with her. It felt as if she was trying too hard to convince me she was single."

Jonas unlocked the car. "So you don't believe her."

"No, I don't." She pulled open the passenger side door. "And for the record, I would never join a dating service."

"I'm just trying to imagine what your profile might say if you did. I've heard it's more important than even a good photo," he said, smirking at her from across the top of the car. "You have to put information out there that really gives insight into who you are. You know, things you're passionate about or who has influenced your life. As long as you're sincere—"

Madison groaned as they both slipped inside the car. "I got the information I needed. That's what's important right now."

"And what information would that be?"

"I saw her screen saver when she got that call."

"Okay. And?"

"It was a photo of her and Ben," she said while securing her seat belt. "On top of that, she seemed genuinely surprised when her brother was arrested. It totally set her off-balance. But when we talked about Ben, her body language changed."

"I'm not sure I follow," Jonas said, starting the car.

"It was as if she'd rehearsed what she needed to say in case she was questioned, including the entire bit about the dating site. She had all the right answers on the tip of her tongue, and more than likely a profile to match, but I'm pretty sure Ben is not out of the picture."

"She could be hoping they'll get back together," Jonas said.

"Maybe, but I think it's more likely that they never broke up in the first place."

"You're basing all of this on a screen saver?"

"You're the one who said I should take the lead because of my intuition."

"While we might have had enough for a federal warrant, Kira had a point," Jonas said, as he sped through traffic on the way back to the office. "From all we know about Ben Galvan, he doesn't exactly seem like the type who would rob banks."

"You don't think an accountant needs some adventure in his life every once in a while?" Madison turned toward him. "Maybe the risk is what fuels him, because it seems like it has to be more than just the money they're after."

"Money still has to play into motive." He pulled off the freeway.

"But not everyone commits crimes solely for the money," Madison said.

Jonas glanced at her, then flipped on his turn signal, merging into the next lane. "Whoever it is, they have to know that it will end at some point. Their luck won't last forever."

"Our only lead was Ben's fingerprints found in a stolen getaway car," Madison said. "How perfect of a match are the fingerprints?"

"The match was declared based on fifteen points in common."

"So there is a possibility they could be wrong?"

Jonas's fingers tightened on the steering wheel as he considered the theory. "I guess it's possible."

"It seems like the place to start is back at the beginning. We need to go through all the evidence again. Bank camera footage, witness testimonies, everything. Because something had to have been missed. These criminals can't be that good."

Jonas's phone rang and he answered, putting the call on speaker. "Michaels, what's going on?"

"911 just got a call. There's a robbery in progress at the bank on Hillside and Chapel Road. Three suspects all wearing black masks, which matches the MO of the previous robberies. Law enforcement is on the scene as we speak."

Jonas checked his mirrors, then made a U-turn. "We're on our way."

FOUR

J onas pushed down on the accelerator and headed toward the city. Normally, their job consisted of early morning raids, prisoner transports, and judicial security. Involvement in a bank robbery wasn't exactly in their job description, but today the rules had shifted significantly. If Ben Galvan was involved, Jonas was going to make sure this was the last time the man ever held up a bank.

"I've only got a few minutes to catch up on this case," Madison said, interrupting his thoughts. "All I know is what I've seen on the news and what you've mentioned to me over the past couple months. I want to make sure I'm not missing anything."

"Okay." Jonas turned down the news that had just come on the radio. "There are four of them, three who hit the banks and a fourth who drives the getaway vehicle. They wear black ski masks and are armed with automatic weapons. They are usually in and out in under five minutes. A bank employee was shot a couple weeks ago, but so far, no one has been killed. The fear, though, is that with the right mix of circumstances, that could easily change. They don't seem to have a problem intimidating tellers and customers or firing their weapons in the air."

"Hasn't security footage caught some of this?"

Jonas shook his head. "They do their research before they go in and always take out any lobby cameras. They've managed to never show their faces."

"What about any footage that shows them casing the banks before the robbery?" Madison asked.

"That has been looked at as well, but so far we haven't found anything. The only real lead we've gotten so far is a witness who was able to get a license plate number off the getaway car. Local police found it abandoned about ten miles from the bank in an old field. It had been stolen the night before and nearly wiped clean. That's where forensics found the fingerprint that led us to Ben Galvan."

She tapped her nails against the console. "Any hostages taken in previous robberies?"

"No." Jonas took a right turn. "They've always managed to get clear of the buildings before law enforcement arrives."

"So their execution is well planned out."

"Extremely well. According to witnesses, they carry back-packs and wear comm devices so they can talk to each other. We also can assume that whoever's in the getaway car is feeding them information from local police dispatches."

"Could they be getting their information from inside the banks?"

"Several leads were followed up on, but nothing came from them, though having an inside informer to so many different banks doesn't seem reasonable."

His hands gripped the steering wheel as he caught her expression. Her brow had furrowed like it always did when she was thinking over a problem. He knew she was thinking the same thing he was. How was it possible for someone to have hit so many banks without leaving a trail of evidence? There had to be something law enforcement was missing.

"And the customers and employees?" she asked. "What are they told to do during the robbery?"

"Each time they're told to lie on the ground, hands behind their heads, or they'll be shot. Apparently, the threat works."

He glanced at his GPS on the dash. They were sixty seconds out. So what had gone wrong this time? Why were the robbers still in the building when the cops arrived?

"You said a bank employee was shot in one of the robberies," Madison said.

He nodded. "In Yakima, one of the tellers disobeyed their instructions and tried to make a call. They shot him in the foot."

"So they aren't opposed to stopping anyone who gets in their way, and this time they're stuck inside the bank and desperate to get out."

"With detailed reconnaissance before each robbery, they're going to have an exit plan," he said.

Jonas felt his blood pressure rise as the bank came in sight. They just didn't have any idea what that plan was.

The lights on top of the squad cars flashed outside the bank that was already cordoned off by FBI and local law enforcement, who were setting up a mobile command center. It wasn't the first time Jonas had been involved in a hostage situation. Two months ago, he'd gone in with a team of US Marshals and a local task force in order to serve a warrant on an escaped prisoner who'd barricaded himself into the back room of his house, using his girlfriend as a hostage. He ended up walking out after five hours with no one getting hurt.

But situations didn't always end that way.

Upon exiting the car, they went directly to the commander in charge of the scene and introduced themselves. "I'm Deputy US Marshal Jonas Quinn and this is my partner, Deputy US Marshal Madison James."

"Special Agent Dean Osborne with the FBI." The man shook their hands, then tugged on his tie. "I was just notified that you were on your way and that you have a connection to the suspects inside."

"At least one of them, we believe. We executed a warrant for him this morning. Unfortunately he wasn't there, but we did interview his ex-girlfriend."

"Anything you know is more than what I have to go on. Witnesses outside the bank said that at least three shots have already been fired, but we don't have enough of a visual to see what's going on inside. We assume they must have everyone on the ground." He hollered at a uniformed officer to help hold back the growing number of spectators now crowded against the yellow tape. "Sorry. What can you tell me?"

"For starters, they always have a fourth man," Jonas said. "A driver."

"I've already got Seattle PD searching the area, though without the IDs of our suspects, it isn't going to be easy."

Jonas nodded, then asked for the man's binoculars. He zeroed in on the frosted glass windows on one side of the lobby that gave them a limited view of the situation. The agent was right. It was impossible to get a full picture of what was going on inside.

"How many hostages?" Madison asked.

"We're estimating between fifteen and twenty customers and five bank employees from a witness who left right before they locked the front doors."

"What about interior camera footage?" Madison asked.

Osborne shook his head. "That was the first thing they took out. They knew exactly what to do."

"They plan everything, down to the last detail," Jonas said, handing the binoculars back. "Bank layout, time of day, exit strategies, and alternative escape routes."

"So you think they have a plan to get out of this?" the agent asked.

Jonas nodded. "Definitely."

They just had to figure out what that plan was.

A phone rang behind them, and a second later another FBI agent stepped out of the mobile command center. "Sir, I've got them on the line."

"It's about time. I want the two of you to come with me." Agent Osborne motioned to the van that was set up inside with a long workstation, a conference area, computers, and phones.

Osborne took the phone from the other agent and put it on speaker. "I'm Special Agent Osborne with the FBI. I understand there were some shots fired, and I want to make sure everyone is okay."

There was a pause on the line and the sound of arguing in the background. "We're fine. Everyone is fine."

"I hope that's true because I'm concerned and want to make sure everyone stays safe. Who am I speaking to?"

"Just . . . just call me . . . Mike."

"Okay, Mike. I'm hearing some hesitation in your voice. Right now I just want to make sure that everyone inside is okay. Then I'm open to hearing what you need."

"The . . . the security guard was shot. He's hurt pretty bad."

"Thank you for telling me that, Mike. Can you tell me where he was shot?"

"On his side. There . . . there's lots of blood."

Jonas glanced at Madison and frowned. No matter how many scenarios their bank robbers had run through, this had to have been their worst nightmare.

"I need you to listen very carefully to me. You need to press something against his wound right now to stop the bleeding, but he needs medical attention," Osborne instructed. Jonas was impressed with the steadiness of the agent's voice. "And if he doesn't get any medical attention, you need to understand that there's a good chance he could bleed out in the next few minutes. I know you don't want that."

"This isn't my fault. If he just would have listened to me, no one would have got hurt." Mike's voice rose. "No one was supposed to get hurt."

"I understand, but you need to follow my instructions so he can get help. Can you send him out?"

"I can't do that. Not unless you guarantee us a way out."

Osborne's jaw tensed. "There isn't time for that, but if you'll let him go, I've got medics on standby who can give him the help he needs, and then I promise you and I can continue our conversation. You'll still have a room full of hostages, and we can come up with a solution."

There was a pause. "I don't know."

Jonas read the concern on Osborne's face as he spoke to the man on the other side of the call. They had all been trained in the importance of active listening in the middle of a negotiation, and of the value of gaining a rapport *before* trying to influence a suspect into a specific course of action. But waiting to get Mike to act could prove deadly in this situation.

"Listen, Mike. I know you have to be scared right now and I don't blame you," Osborne continued. "You probably have a job and a family and never imagined finding yourself in this place, but life isn't always black and white, is it?"

"So now you're trying to patronize me."

"Not at all. But I'm concerned about everyone in there. Including you."

"Yeah . . . I'm not stupid. You'll say anything you can to get me to do what you want. You'll empathize to get my trust. Tell me how you understand why I'm doing what I'm doing."

"I can tell you're frustrated, and I know . . ."

Madison pulled Jonas aside while the agent continued talking. "This isn't going to work. He *is* patronizing him, and the guy on the other end isn't responding to that."

"You have an idea?"

She nodded and started to tell Jonas, but he held up his hand and rushed back to the agent. They were running out of time and he was willing to trust whatever her gut said.

"Tell him you'll call him back," Jonas whispered.

Agent Osborne muted the call. "This isn't the time—"

Jonas met his gaze. "Tell him you'll call him back."

He shook his head, clearly irritated with the interruption. "I can't do that."

"Trust me."

Osborne hesitated, then tapped the mute button again. "Mike, I need to call you right back." He hung up the phone, his face reddening. "You'd better have an extremely good reason for cutting me off, because we've got a man dying in there."

Jonas nodded toward Madison.

"You're not going to talk them out of this," she said.

"What do you mean?"

"They planned every detail. They knock out cameras and use their weapons to scare people. You can hear the tension in his voice. They're arguing with each other in the background." She shook her head. "This wasn't part of the game plan. They've been on this winning streak, believing they're invincible, but now their luck has just run out. They're panicked because this is a situation they've never had to deal with before. You'll have to get him to do what you want him to do *without* taking away his control."

Osborne dropped his hands into his front pockets. "What are you suggesting?"

"They rob banks because it makes them feel like they're in control," she said. "They plan out their strategy, and they're in charge. And from what I've heard, it's not just about money. But while they want to be in control, they also don't want anyone hurt. Problem is, they just crossed that line."

"Sounds like a game."

"It is. But the problem is, they're losing, and they know it."

Osborne stared at one of the command center's screens that showed the front doors of the bank for a few long seconds. "Then what are we supposed to do? We don't have a clean shot to take them down, which means we have to *talk* them down."

"We have a probable ID for one of the suspects," Jonas said. "Ben Galvan. From what we've compiled, he's a risk-taker. He's not doing this just for the money, like my partner told you. In fact, from what we know, he doesn't need the money. It's for the thrill."

"What are you saying? He's robbing banks because he's bored?"

Madison nodded. "Think of it this way, every time they rob a bank and get away with it, it's an adrenaline rush that empowers them. So every time they get away with a load of cash, they're fueled up to do it again."

"The last time they shot someone, they didn't miss," Jonas said. "Witnesses said they shot him in the foot on purpose."

They had Osborne's attention now. "So they have some standard of ethics, but they're not opposed to holding people at gunpoint, and even shooting if necessary."

Jonas nodded. "That's one way to look at it."

Osborne tapped the table with his fingers. "So anything I throw at them will sound like a challenge, and they will resist that."

"Exactly," Madison said. "We interviewed the ex-girlfriend of one of the suspects. The guy's smart. He works for an accounting department at a major firm. He's not just going to walk away from this because you talked him down. He will only leave when and if he wants to."

"I hear what the two of you are saying, but what do you want me to do?"

"Jonas and I need to go in," she said.

"Excuse me?"

From the look on Osborne's face, he clearly wasn't convinced. But Jonas was.

"Make him think that he's getting something," Jonas said. "A couple more hostages for the victim who was shot. We can wear earpieces so you'll be able to hear what they're saying. But we need to hurry because at this point, they don't want to get caught, and they have nothing to lose."

"We'll try your way, but you better pray this works." Osborne signaled to the officer handling their communication with the bank phone, then picked up the tapped line again. "Mike? I'm back. How's the guard?"

"He . . . he's still breathing."

"I'd like to arrange for a couple paramedics to come in and

stabilize him, then bring him out. That way, you and I can focus on negotiating an end to this."

Silence hung on the line at the suggestion. Jonas held his breath.

"Listen," Osborne continued, "I know this isn't what you want. For someone to get hurt. I can help you work through this, but we need to make sure the guard gets the treatment he needs. Please."

"If I let him go, I'll need something from you then."

"What is that?" Osborne asked.

"I need you to move your perimeter back another hundred feet."

Osborne shook his head. "I can't do that, Mike. There are rules I have to follow—"

"I told you what you have to do. If you want the security guard to get medical attention, then do what I say. Now."

Osborne nodded at the FBI agent standing on the other side of him and mouthed *do it*.

"I've just ordered that the perimeter be moved," Osborne said into the phone.

"Fine. They can come in, but if they do anything—anything at all to make me question your motives—then I will shoot another hostage."

"Okay. Give us a minute, and I'll send them to the front door."

"No cops," Mike said.

"They won't be cops."

Osborne hung up the phone, then started barking orders.

A few minutes later, Jonas pulled on a button-up EMT shirt someone had handed him over his T-shirt. "You sure about this?" he asked, turning to Madison.

"I might as well make sure my first day back is one I won't ever forget, though I'm starting to see a strange pattern to my working with you."

His gaze narrowed. "What is that supposed to mean?"

"The first time I trained with you, there was a murder during one of our tactical training exercises. The second time, a prison transport ended in a plane crash, and now you've somehow dragged me into a hostage situation—"

"I dragged you?" he started to say before catching the soft gleam in her eyes as she tried to downplay what was going on. But the lighthearted exchange between them quickly vanished as they walked up to the front of the bank with a gurney and medkit. They were each wired with hidden two-way Bluetooth comms so they could communicate. This was no game. The lives of everyone in the building were at stake.

A man in black wearing a mask opened the door and motioned them inside. "Try anything stupid, and you'll both get a bullet in your head."

FIVE

Madison pushed the gurney through the front entrance of the bank behind Jonas, then held up her gloved hands as ordered while a second masked man patted her down for weapons. She used the pause to study the large lobby. A couple dozen hostages lay on the white-tiled floor with their faces to the ground. The three captors were dressed alike in black jeans and jackets and all wore face masks that covered everything but their eyes. They each carried a semi-automatic weapon. The glass door clicked shut behind her, but she could still hear shouts as law enforcement continued moving their perimeter.

"Mike?" Madison asked, grateful they hadn't discovered her earpiece.

The man who had let them inside nodded.

"Where's the guard?" she asked.

"He's over there on the ground, but don't forget that you are here to make sure he lives, not play hero. We already put a bullet in his side. And we can do it again."

Madison nodded, then grabbed the medical kit off the gurney. "Jonas, if you'll evaluate the wound and staunch the bleeding, I'll check his vitals."

Jonas knelt beside her as they surveyed the guard. Blood pooled beneath their victim, and his skin was cool and gray. She'd done enough medical training to know the importance of a rapid evaluation in order to assess the situation. But the actual treatment couldn't be done here on the floor of a bank lobby. And with an abdominal wound, observation was not enough, as it was impossible to know the extent of injury on the inside. If the guard survived this, it would be a miracle.

Madison lifted the man's hand, then began taking his vitals. "Sir, can you look at me? Can you tell me your name?"

"Vin . . . Vincent."

"Vincent, good. We're going to get you out of here and to a hospital as soon as we can, I promise. Can you squeeze my hand?"

His thumb pressed lightly on the back of her fingers.

"Airway is open, breathing shallow. Reflexes are weak," she said.

Jonas pressed a compress against the wound. "I can't be a hundred percent sure, but it looks like the bullet is still inside the body."

"Vincent." Madison leaned closer to his face. "Vincent, I need you to open your eyes again and talk to me. We're going to get you out of here, but you need to stay with me."

"I need . . . I need you to talk to my kids for me." He took a long, labored breath. "They told me to retire, but I . . . I did that once, and I hated sitting at home. Tell them I'm sorry. If I would have listened to them, I wouldn't be lying here right now."

"We're going to help you get through this." Madison choked

out the words. "There is no reason to talk that way. I just need you to stay focused."

Jonas stood up and walked toward Mike. "We can't wait any longer. We need to get him out of here now."

Madison kept her hands steady as she put pressure on Vincent's wound, even as Mike shifted his weapon at Jonas. "Not until your people are done moving the perimeter back."

"They're doing it now—"

He leveled his aim at Jonas. "Get back over there!"

Jonas returned to Madison's side and made a show of relieving her of putting pressure on the compress. "I counted sixteen customers plus four with name tags," he whispered.

She took a quick glance at the suspects and noticed they were distracted by the commotion outside. "Osborne?" she whispered. "The guard needs serious medical help. Any advice?"

Silence.

She lowered her voice. "Are you receiving?"

Still nothing.

Madison turned to Jonas. "Are you getting any response on your comm?"

"Negative. They've got to be scrambling the signal."

"They really did think of everything." Madison chewed her lip. *Including a way out. But how?*

She looked to the front door, where a row of three backpacks had been set, then back to the hostages, trying to work through the suspects' options. Except for a young woman who was wheezing in the corner and the sounds of footsteps from the captors pacing the room, the lobby was quiet. Eerily quiet.

"What's their plan to get out of here?" she asked.

"I don't know." The compress Jonas was using was tinged

red, a reminder that they were running out of time. "Moving the perimeter has to be part of it, but even so, the building is surrounded and there are sharpshooters in place. If they step out of the building, they'll be stopped immediately."

Whatever their plan was, she and Jonas hadn't been sent in here to wait.

"We need to see if anyone else is injured," she said. "And we should check on the girl on the far left who's wheezing pretty bad."

"Something tells me that they won't be open to that idea, but stay here, I'll—"

"No. Let me do it. I'll be less intimidating."

Before Jonas was able to protest, Madison started to rise slowly, her hands in the air, deciding that action was worth the risk.

"What are you doing?" Mike turned to her.

"While my partner gets the bleeding stabilized, I'd like to make sure everyone else is okay. One of the hostages seems to be having an asthma attack."

Mike walked up to Madison and grabbed her elbow, wrenching her arm behind her back. "I already told you that you'll leave when I say you can leave."

"And if one of them ends up dying on your watch?" Heart pounding, she pulled away from him and started toward the counter without waiting for his response. "Does anyone else need any medical care?"

"That was not part of the deal," Mike shouted. "You came in to get the guard. That was it."

"Then let him go." She swiveled back to Mike, wishing she could read his expression behind the mask. "He's still bleeding out."

"She's right." One of the other captors spoke up. Madison noticed it was a woman's voice. "I didn't sign up for murder."

He took a step forward. "Are you questioning my decision?"

"I just know that this was never a part of the plan."

Madison turned, briefly catching Jonas's gaze. Was it possible that Kira was their third suspect? She couldn't be sure, but it was definitely a woman.

Madison turned back to Mike. "I'm assuming you don't want to add murder to your list of charges either. And it's our job to make sure that doesn't happen. You'll still have a room full of hostages, but at least you won't have anyone's blood on your hands. Let me take them both out of here."

"Please." A girl no more than sixteen was hunched over on her knees, her long red ponytail hanging over her shoulder. "I . . . I can't breathe."

Madison hurried over and knelt down in front of the girl. "Do you normally use an inhaler?"

She nodded, pressing her hand against her chest as she struggled to breathe. Asthma and panic attacks often went hand in hand. Sometimes all it took was a traumatic experience . . . like a hostage situation.

Madison rubbed the girl's shoulder lightly. "What's your name?"

The girl wheezed again. "Grace."

"Grace, where's your inhaler?"

"In my bag. It's . . . it's the red one."

Madison held up her hands and hurried to where they'd tossed everyone's bags and cell phones. "I need to find her inhaler."

She picked up the only red bag and dumped the contents onto the floor. The inhaler tumbled out.

"Madison, we're running out of time. We need to get him to a hospital," Jonas said as she rushed back to the girl and handed her the inhaler. "His heartbeat is slowing, and his blood pressure is dropping. He's still losing too much blood."

"Please," Madison said to Mike as the girl took her first puff from the inhaler. "Do it as a sign of good faith, if nothing else. He needs to go to a hospital. There is only so much we can do. But we need to get him out of here now."

"Fine." The man threw his hands in the air. "You want a show of good faith? I'll let all the hostages go except for your partner and the bank employees."

A flood of relief washed over Madison. "Let me call and tell them what to expect," she said.

Mike picked up the phone, dialed, then put it on speaker.

"This is Osborne. Mike, what's going on in there?"

"This is Madison. One of the medics," she said. "They are letting everyone go except for the bank employees and my partner. I'll bring our gunshot victim out on a stretcher along with a girl who's having an asthma attack in the front with me. The rest will foll—"

"The hostages will be instructed to walk out of the building," Mike cut in. "You are to stay back until they are all out. If one of them is shot by your agents, I won't be held responsible."

"Okay, Mike," Osborne said. "And thank you. You're making the right decision."

Mike pressed his finger into the receiver, then turned to the hostages. "I want all of the bank employees to stay on the ground, facedown in the middle of the lobby." He turned back to Madison. "Get the guard onto the gurney. You can take him out first, then the others will line up behind you." Mike raised his voice and looked around the lobby. "The rest of you will stay where you are, or you'll end up needing medical attention as well."

Madison rushed over to Jonas and quickly helped him get Vincent up onto the gurney. The older man groaned as she checked to make sure the gauze and bandages Jonas had applied were staying in place. The bleeding had slowed, but that wasn't enough. She could hear several of the bank customers sobbing in relief, but they weren't out the doors yet. She'd been in law enforcement long enough to know that the situation could change in an instant.

She took the car keys Jonas had handed her in case she needed them. "Promise me you'll come out of this alive," she said to him. "You owe me dinner tonight."

He smiled. "Don't worry. I wouldn't miss it for the world. And for now, your job is to get Vincent out of here safely."

She nodded, but she was worried. Mike shouted at Jonas to get on the floor with the rest of the hostages. Madison started toward the entrance, pushing the gurney in front of her. The other two captors pulled open the door so the hostages could leave, staying out of sight of any snipers waiting to take a shot. Her heart pounded as she crossed the threshold. The gurney clicked through the doorway, then out into the sunlight.

"Hang on, Vincent. This will all be over soon."

Lights from an ambulance flashed to her right. She could see officers standing next to their cars, ready to spring into action at the signal from their boss.

Special Agent Osborne walked toward the freed hostages. "I need each of you to keep your hands in the air. Please stay calm as our officers approach you."

There was a loud pop then smoke filled the entryway. Four more pops were followed by the earsplitting blast of an alarm system. Pain shot through her temples. Someone screamed. Smoke filled her lungs. She couldn't see anything anymore. Someone was shouting, but she couldn't understand what they were saying above the noise of the siren.

Several uniformed officers moved forward in order to control the scene, but chaos ensued. The smoke thickened. Someone pushed into her, almost knocking her over in their rush to exit the building.

She kept pushing the gurney down the sidewalk, knowing she needed to get Vincent to the ambulance, but also needing to be able to see where she was going.

The siren continued to blare, but the smoke was slowly clearing. Several of the hostages sat down on the sidewalk looking dazed. Several more were crying in a huddle to her right, including Grace, the girl she'd gotten the inhaler for. At least they were all alive. She headed toward the ambulance, her ears ringing from the noise.

This was their exit plan. They'd created enough chaos that they could slip out with the hostages. All they needed was distraction, and if they took off their masks and coats, the officers wouldn't be able to tell who were the hostages and who were the hostage takers.

Which meant now they just had to slip into the crowd and disappear.

"Jonas?" She tried her comm as she started toward the edge of the perimeter.

Nothing. The signals were still being scrambled. There was still chaos outside the bank as she spun around and searched the vicinity. The gray haze still lingered in the air, making it hard to see very far.

"Madison?"

She blew out a sharp breath at the sound of his voice. Jonas.

"Are you still in the bank?" she asked, pressing a hand over the comm in her ear to block out some of the noise.

"I'll check the interior then head out. They dumped their masks and coats. Do you see them? I wasn't able to get a good look, but I know that one was wearing a baseball cap and black boots."

"There's too much commotion. I can't see anything." She scanned the area to see if anyone was rushing away from the scene.

"Did you notice inside that one of them was a woman?"

"Yeah," Madison said. "I was thinking. . .what if it was Kira?"

A paramedic ran toward Vincent and her. "Hold on, Jonas," Madison said. "I've got the injured guard here. He needs to get to the hospital."

She left Vincent, then started searching the crowd. Most people would be running to the police. Their suspects would be running away. And like all the other cases, they would have a getaway car lined up. They couldn't have gone that far. Not yet. She'd exited the bank before they had. They still had to slip through the cordoned-off area, and more than likely, Agent Osborne had already set up roadblocks for anyone leaving the vicinity.

"Madison," Jonas spoke through his comm. "They have to be somewhere in this crowd."

"I know, but their plan might just work. I don't see them."

"Get the car and bring it around to the west side of the bank and pick me up," Jonas said. "They're not going to stick around."

"I'll meet you there."

"Deputy James?"

Madison turned around. Special Agent Osborne handed over the service weapon and badge she'd relinquished for the undercover operation.

"I heard your partner over the comm. What else can you give me?"

"We know that at least one of the suspects is a woman. We need to have roadblocks set up for their getaway car."

"We're setting one up at a ten-block radius as we speak."

"We can't be far behind them. I'm grabbing our vehicle and going to meet Jonas."

"I want to know what he saw," Osborne said. "I'll get his gun and badge to him."

She glanced at her watch as she ran to the car. The getaway vehicle would have had to be parked outside the initial perimeter around the bank. Far enough out that it didn't look suspicious. Leaving the scene separately would make them look even less suspect. She pulled out her keys and unlocked the car. It was time to tighten the noose and put an end to this.

SIX

The air was still filled with smoke as Jonas stepped out of the bank and into the sunshine. Figures sat along the sidewalk, coughing and crying, while officers and paramedics tried to bring order to the chaos. The suspects had managed to find their way out, but they couldn't be that far ahead of him. Despite the threat for those who had been left inside the bank to stay put, it had taken Jonas only seconds to realize that the plan had been for the suspects to leave with the hostages and then vanish into the crowd.

And so far they'd succeeded.

A uniformed officer approached him. "Sir, I need you to put your hands in the air and walk toward me slowly."

"I'm not a paramedic." He went to grab his badge, then remembered he'd left it with Osborne along with his service weapon.

"I have orders to check everyone."

"He's with the Marshals Service." Special Agent Osborne ran up to them and handed Jonas his credentials and Glock. The officer moved to the next person as Osborne asked, "Can you ID the suspects?"

Jonas shook his head. "All I know is that they ditched their masks and jackets before heading out, but there was too much smoke to see their faces. It's one woman, two men. I'm guessing they split up, but we need to search the surrounding neighborhood."

"I'm working on that now as well as roadblocks farther out, but it's going to take time."

"Time is something we don't have."

Jonas pressed on his comm button as he rushed toward the side street behind the bank where he'd told Madison to pick him up. "Do you see them yet?" he asked.

"No. Not yet."

While the smoke had dissipated farther from the scene, with no positive ID on the suspects, identifying them was going to be an issue. A misty rain started to fall as clouds moved in and covered up the sunshine. He started jogging west, where there were a number of side streets and the quickest escape to freeway access. He started going over the details of the last few minutes in his head. He'd seen the suspects' backpacks still lined up on the wall as he exited the bank, which left him to assume they'd found a way to take the money with them. Ten thousand dollars in hundreds could easily fit into a pocket and would be extra incentive to escape without getting caught.

About a hundred yards down one of the side streets, he saw someone wearing a baseball cap, their head down. Jonas picked up his pace.

"I've got a possible suspect in my sights," he said into his comm.

"Where are you?" Madison answered.

"Headed west on Downy Street."

"I'm on my way now."

"Osborne? Do you copy?"

Silence.

Jonas frowned. He must already be out of range.

Farther away from the bank the streets seemed eerily quiet. Movement to the right caught his eye. Two more figures emerged from an alley and were headed for a white van parked fifty feet in front of him.

Bingo.

He clicked on his comm again, hoping Madison could still hear him.

"I've got them in my sights," he said. "Three suspects running toward a white van on Downy."

"Roger that. I'm almost to your location."

Jonas picked up his pace and closed in behind them, knowing that any backup wasn't going to get there in time. "Stop where you are." He raised his gun and shouted at the strangers. "US Marshal. Drop your weapons and put your hands in the air now."

One of them spun and fired at Jonas. He ducked behind the engine block of a parked car, then took a double shot. The first one took out the back window. The second skimmed the back tire.

A crack of gunfire erupted from the van.

Jonas took a third shot. "Put your hands in the air now."

His demands were answered by another round of gunfire. A woman exited the building to Jonas's right, and he waved her back inside. Endangering innocent lives wasn't an option.

He turned back in time to see the damaged van skidding away.

"Jonas, I'm driving up behind you," Madison said.

"Be careful. Shots fired. I repeat. Shots fired."

She pulled in behind the car he had been using as cover and he jumped into her vehicle, bracing his hand against the dashboard as Madison pulled away from the curb and floored it.

"Go, go, go. We can't lose them," he said.

"I don't intend to."

Madison flipped on the lights and sirens, then swerved around a truck that had pulled over on the narrow street.

He called in to dispatch. "This is Deputy US Marshal Jonas Quinn. We're in pursuit of four suspects in connection with a series of recent robberies. Requesting backup immediately."

"Roger that. Can you give me a description of the getaway vehicle?"

"White van with a shattered back window." He leaned forward, then recited the number on the plate.

"I'm sending backup to your location now and tracking your cell phone."

"Be advised that suspects are armed."

"Roger that."

Madison's phone rang. He grabbed it off the console and answered. It was Michaels.

"I just got off the phone with the FBI," their boss said. "They told me the hostages were let go, but our fugitives escaped."

"I know. We have the four suspects in front of us. I just called dispatch for backup. You were my next call."

"Where are they heading?"

"Looks like toward I-5, but your guess is as good as mine after that."

"Were you able to make a positive ID of Ben Galvan?"

"Negative. I couldn't get close enough to any of them without their masks on, but check video footage in the area," Jonas said. "Maybe we can ID them that way."

"I'm working with the FBI for access to the bank's exterior security footage as well as cameras in the surrounding area. Be advised that there's a wreck on the freeway south of your location."

Jonas ended the call, frowning as he updated dispatch. Rush hour might be officially over, but in reality, it never really ended. The geography of Seattle, a city wedged between Puget Sound and Lake Washington, made it a natural bottleneck when going through downtown. There was simply no outlet for the heavy flow of traffic.

Madison pushed on the accelerator, then pulled in front of another car as she raced down the freeway, but the white van had managed to get three cars ahead of them. Jonas braced himself against the dashboard again. High-speed chases were always risky, but so was losing fugitives.

The heavy traffic gave them little room to get closer, but trying to force the other vehicle to stop at this point could endanger civilians. He glanced at Madison and caught the tension in her expression. Her hands tightened around the steering wheel as she worked to keep the van in sight with the near gridlocked conditions.

"He's taking the next exit," Jonas said.

She managed to maneuver her way across two lanes of cars and take the exit with only two cars between them. "They might be headed to Pier 52 where they could catch either the Bainbridge or Bremerton ferry."

"Agreed. The tunnel entrance is nearby, but a roadblock at the exit would be easy to set up. Maybe they're simply trying to lose us."

"I don't think so," she said. "They've had an escape plan every step of the way. I don't see why this would be any different."

Jonas nodded. "And it fits the profile we discussed regarding what fuels them."

"Exactly. They've played this all along like a strategy game, and their only way out of it is to ensure they stay one step ahead of the authorities."

There were a few pedestrians on the sidewalk of the one-way street with its downtown buildings towering over them and Elliott Bay in the distance. The van, still two cars in front of them, ran a red light. A Cadillac on its way through the intersection slammed on the brakes, forcing Madison to swerve to the right to avoid getting hit. Their car fishtailed and jumped the curb.

Jonas's body tensed as Madison checked both directions before pressing on the accelerator.

"They're turning right," he said.

"Keep your eye on them."

She plowed through the intersection, then took the next turn.

"This doesn't make sense." He shook his head. "They're heading away from the ferries."

Jonas tried to swallow his frustration and drummed his fingers against the console. If it were him, he would have stayed on I-5 and tried to lose the tail in the traffic. From there he would head toward Portland, or across 90 to Mercer Island and Bellevue, toward the mountains. Instead, they were heading north again, toward the aquarium, Pike Place Market, and the Space Needle. Maybe their plan was to ditch the van. Maybe they were betting they could easily vanish.

Jonas blew out a sharp breath. Their anticipated morning raid had turned into a bust, but Ben Galvan was in that van. He was certain of it.

A second later, the white van disappeared.

"Jonas, they had to have turned."

He leaned forward, checking every possible street, then caught the tail end of the van. He pointed. "There."

"Where does that street go?" she asked.

"Toward the parking garage for Pike Place Market."

Madison weaved her way through the traffic then followed. Seconds later, they were waiting for the yellow arm to let them into the garage. But by now the white van could be anywhere. Pike Place Market was one of the most popular destinations in Seattle. And it provided easy access to the bus system, light rail, and ferries.

"We could be looking at another hostage situation if we're not careful," Madison said, driving slowly through the garage.

"Yes, but they planned for this scenario. It would make more sense for them to get as far away as possible. They're not going to want to take any more risks. My guess is they dump the van and have a second car waiting, or they take public transport out of here."

But the problem was that there were too many exits. A few shoppers made their way to their car, a child's squeal echoed across the garage. None of them had any idea what was going on around them. Jonas considered the situation as he surveyed the area. Law enforcement couldn't just evacuate the building. That would only lead to panic and chaos. Neither could Jonas totally dismiss Madison's concerns regarding the possibility of a hostage situation. But his gut told him their suspects would stay under the radar and simply disappear. And he intended to find them.

She kept driving past rows of cars.

A few shards of glass caught his attention.

"Stop." He pulled open his door before she'd come to a complete halt. The white van with its shattered back window was parked beside an SUV.

He ran to the vehicle while she parked out of the way then started searching it, but it was empty. Nothing beyond some fast-food bags and a pile of clothes. No sign of their suspects. No sign of the money. They'd dumped the car and run.

He walked around to the other side of the vehicle, opened up the passenger door, then stopped.

There was a trail of fresh blood on the seat and floorboard. One of them had been hit.

SEVEN

M adison quickly scanned the parking garage for movement. A family was getting into a car four spaces
down, while another shopper, carrying half a dozen
bags, hustled to her vehicle. All were oblivious to the poten-
tial danger. But the suspects had just been here, which meant
they couldn't be far. They needed to find a way to track down
their fugitives without anyone innocent getting caught in the
cross fire.

"There's quite a bit of blood here," Jonas said, heading toward
her. "Enough that whoever was hit is going to need some kind
of medical care."

She walked toward the sky bridge that led to the entrance
of the market, then stopped and knelt down. "There's more
blood here, Jonas."

"Head to the market while I search the garage," he said. "I'll
catch up with you."

She nodded. "I'll call Michaels."

Madison pulled out her phone.

"We found the van," she said once Michaels had answered.
"At least one person was hit during the shootout with Jonas.

There's fresh blood in the van and on the sky bridge at Pike Place Market. That's where they parked. We followed them in and are checking the perimeter."

"Good job. I was just able to confirm that the vehicle was stolen two days ago."

She frowned. *Of course.*

"I'll distribute Ben's photo to market security so all their officers will be looking for him," Michaels said. "But without positive IDs on the other three, except for the fact that one of them is injured, you're going in blind."

"What about footage outside the bank when they left?"

"I've got Piper, our new intern, going through it now, but so far the smoke has made it impossible to see much of anything. From what I've been told, it's still a mess there as they try to interview hostages and witnesses."

"Keep me updated," she said, then disconnected the call.

Madison sprinted across the bridge that linked the parking garage to the market. To the south was the familiar view of the Bainbridge ferries and the Pier 57 Ferris wheel, but today she hardly saw it. There were a dozen ways out of the market. The suspects could have parked a second getaway car in the garage, or simply planned to run on foot. Close by was the metro bus route and the Link light rail station, and they weren't far from the ferries.

Jonas ran up next to her, matching her stride. "There's a good chance that they split up, but I think we need to start with the restrooms."

"I was just thinking the same thing," she said. "If one of them is hurt as bad as we think, they're going to need to try and find a way to clean them up."

The two marshals merged into the market, and just like

Madison remembered, the crowded space was packed. While the famous market had originally opened over a century ago to provide Seattle with local produce, today it was a hot tourist attraction that had expanded to nine acres and brought in thousands of visitors a day. She and her mother had come here at least once a year while she was still alive. The multiple floors were full of farmers, craft artisans, and mom-and-pop businesses. Restaurants, artwork, and toys filled the space. In addition to all that, there were hundreds of apartments, and even a hotel and a theater, making it the perfect place for an escape. Finding fugitives in the middle of thousands of shoppers was going to be a nightmare.

"There are four sets of public restrooms," she said. "I think we need to check them all."

Madison headed into the nearest restroom, quickly searching the stalls and trash. A couple older women were washing their hands, but there was no one matching a possible description of their fugitives. She stepped back outside where Jonas was waiting for her.

"Did you find anything?" he asked.

"Nothing."

"Me neither."

"We need to keep searching."

They pressed through the crowded market. A pianist was playing a tune in the background. Vendors sold flowers, food, and specialty items to the scores of visitors. The air smelled like fresh seafood. Fishmongers shouted to their customers as she hurried past the entertainment. To her it was nothing more than a distraction.

Their fugitives' plan had been clever. Disappearing into a pool of hundreds of locals and tourists, knowing that as long as they couldn't be identified they were essentially invisible. But unless they'd switched cars in the garage, they were here. Somewhere. They needed transport along with medical care. Getting shot wasn't a part of their plan, and it was unlikely they'd accounted for that variable.

The second set of bathrooms was just ahead of them. She stepped inside the women's, quickly clearing all the stalls, while a girl wearing acid-washed jeans and a sweater fixed her makeup in front of the mirror. Madison stopped by the trash can. She pulled a glove out of her pocket and put it on. Bloody paper towels lay just underneath the top layer.

Bingo.

Madison turned to the girl. "Did you see anyone come in here who was injured?"

The girl popped her lipstick back in her purse. "Nope."

"I'm sorry," Madison said, "but I'm going to have to ask you to leave. I need to close down this restroom."

The girl shrugged, clearly uninterested, and walked out. Madison followed behind her and found Jonas pacing outside.

"They were definitely here. I found bloody paper towels."

"And I found a sweatshirt with a bullet hole near the rib cage," Jonas said. "We need to find a security guard and close this area off until the forensics team can process everything."

She signaled at a uniformed security officer, then held up her badge. "I'm Madison James with the US Marshals Service. Can you assist us in shutting down these restrooms?"

"Aysha Larson," the security officer said, shaking their hands. "I just received the message about the fugitives."

"Did you see anyone who might have been shot?"

Aysha shook her head.

"Are you able to wait here until a crime scene team comes to make sure no one enters either restroom?"

"I can do that."

"Good. Thank you."

Jonas pulled Madison away from the guard. "I just got a message from Michaels," he said. "He wants us to go to the security office and look at video footage of the market and the parking garage. FBI is working on footage from the bank."

Once they confirmed that Aysha had the information she needed, they headed to the dispatch desk. Jonas presented Madison and himself to the head security officer, who introduced himself as Simon Hartman.

"I was told to do anything you asked," the balding officer said, shaking their hands.

"We appreciate your cooperation," Jonas said.

"All of my officers on duty are out there looking for your injured suspect, and we've activated our emergency response system."

"Good," Madison said. "We need to look at your video footage."

"Of course. What do you want to see?" he asked, motioning them toward the video monitor station. "We've got over a hundred cameras placed around the market."

Madison glanced at Jonas, then back to Hartman, who'd pulled up a chair in front of the monitors. "We can narrow down the time frame and the location to just before we arrived," she said. "We know they were in the parking garage, as well as the Soames/Dunn building and the restrooms there."

"Give me a second."

Madison stood over Hartman's shoulder as he ran through the footage. All they needed was one decent close-up of one fugitive's face. And if they could identify him or her, they might be able to track down the others.

"We monitor both the market and garage cameras pretty closely so we can respond to any incidents as quickly as possible." Simon tapped on one of the monitors. "Here's your time frame for the garage."

They watched as a white van pulled into the garage, then switched cameras as it pulled into a parking space. A second later, four people climbed out of the van. But their faces still were not visible. Two of them headed toward the market, while the other two headed on foot toward a street exit.

"So they definitely split up," Madison said. "We still need to try and get a look at their faces."

"I'm trying, but it's like they knew where the cameras were."

Madison frowned. Of course they did. Coming to the busy market had always been a part of their plan if things went south. Just like avoiding the bank cameras, they managed to evade detection here as well. But they no longer had masks on their faces, and one of them was injured. At some point, they were going to make a mistake.

"Try the restrooms now. Same time period."

Hartman scrolled through the video until he'd found the location that showed the restroom entrance and time frame they'd given him.

A couple walked up to the restroom. They slipped into the separate spaces, then came back out thirty seconds later.

"Stop, right there. Slow it down." Madison pointed at the screen. A man wearing a T-shirt and holding his side filled the freeze-frame. "That has to be them, and she just looked at the camera."

Simon backed up the footage again, then froze the photo.

It was clearly Ben and Kira.

"Your gut was right," Jonas said. "Kira not only lied to us about Galvan's participation in the robberies, she's involved."

Madison and Jonas stepped away from Hartman for a moment to make a call. Madison dialed Michaels, put her phone on speaker, then set it on the desk between them.

"We've got positive IDs on Ben Galvan and Kira Thornton," she said. "It looks like Ben was the one who was shot. We know there were two men in the bank as well as a woman."

"So either Kira was in the bank or was the getaway driver," Michaels said. "And the other two suspects?"

"We haven't been able to ID them, but it looks like they headed to the street level while Ben and Kira headed inside to the restroom," Jonas said.

"I think we can assume they didn't stay at the market." Madison sat down. "Which means they either left in another vehicle or used public transportation."

Jonas rubbed his jaw. "A second car would make sense."

Madison's head throbbed from the growing tension.

"Simon," she said, moving back to the set of security screens with her phone in hand. "I want you to check the parking garage exits and make a list of plate numbers leaving the garage."

Hartman nodded and grabbed a piece of paper and pen before starting to scroll through footage.

"I want the two of you to head back to the bank," Michaels said. "There are a couple people I want you to interview, including a hostage named Barton Wells. He might be able to help identify one of our fugitives."

"Copy that," Madison said, then ended the call and turned back to Hartman. "Thanks for your help. We'll leave our contact information with you to send us that list as soon as you can."

"This hasn't exactly been a dull start to your first day back," Jonas said as they headed to the parking garage through the crowded market.

Madison let out a low laugh. "Hardly."

They were heading to the sky bridge when her phone went off, and she pulled it out of her pocket. Danielle had just left a message.

> Just checking in on you and wanted to update you on dad's doctor appointment. Call when you can. No hurry.

"I need to call my sister," she said, quickly pulling up the number. Jonas nodded at her as she put the phone to her ear. "Danielle . . . hey. Is everything okay?"

"Everything is fine, but where are you? I can hardly hear you."

"Sorry. I'm at Pike Place Market, working on a case, but I have a second. What's the update on Dad? I'm sorry I wasn't there."

"Don't worry about it. One of the main things we talked about was his anxiety. It's not worse, but it's definitely there. The positive thing is that Dr. Wang believes the drug Daddy's been taking *is* slowing the decline in his memory."

"That is good news." Madison fidgeted with the zipper on her jacket, keeping up with Jonas as they entered the bridge. "Just because I'm back at work and can't come by as often doesn't mean I still won't be as involved."

"You're fine, Madison. We're fine. Please know that. What you're doing is important."

She tried to push away the guilt, but it had become a persistent companion. "I forgot to tell you. I spoke to my friend

Carrie about cleaning your house once a week. She can do it Thursday afternoons if that's okay with you—"

"You don't have to do that."

Madison stared out at the view from the sky bridge, past the Ferris wheel to Elliott Bay, trying to push back the emotions roiling inside her. "You have three kids and now Daddy. Hiring a housekeeper is the least I can do. Please. I want to do this."

"I'll let you, because it truly will help, but we're in this together."

"I know," Madison said, as she and Jonas crossed the garage. "Which is why I want to be there for you."

"And you are. I'll talk to you soon. Stay safe out there."

"I will."

Jonas unlocked the car. The evidence response team had already showed up and blocked off part of the garage. The investigation would be handled by the Feds, so there was no reason for them to stay. Their job was to hunt down the fugitives.

"Is everything okay?" Jonas asked as they slid into the car.

"My father had a doctor appointment today. I had been taking him while I was off work. It's just . . . it's hard when you need to be in two places at the same time."

"He knows you're there for him and so does your sister."

"I know." She snapped on her seat belt.

"But you still feel guilty."

"It's hard not to. I don't want Danielle to be stuck with the brunt of the responsibility, and yet in so many ways, there's nothing I can do."

Jonas pulled out of their parking spot, then headed for the exit. "I'd say you're already finding things to do. I heard what you said. Hiring a housekeeper."

"My sister has her hands full. It seems like the least I can do."

"I'm sure she appreciates it."

"I know she does." She stared out the window, her senses still on high alert. "I want to keep Daddy home as long as we can, and yet at some point, I know Danielle won't be able to handle things on her own. But we're moving in that direction."

"You're thinking about a memory care facility?"

She breathed in sharply. "Do you think that's a terrible option?"

"I think it can be a very positive option." Jonas paid the parking fee, then pulled out of the garage. "My grandmother lived in one before she died, and it turned out to be a huge help. We could visit her as often as we wanted, while knowing she was getting the care she needed."

"I think Daddy still has a while before we need to make a decision on getting additional help, but at some point . . ."

Thoughts of the way Alzheimer's had already affected her father flooded her mind. The hardest part was watching the man she'd looked up to her entire life struggle to remember words or complete familiar tasks. And it was only going to get worse.

Her phone rang.

"Michaels"—she put the phone on speaker, then held it up between them—"what have you got?"

"Possible good news and also bad news."

Madison sighed. "Let's start with the good."

"The Crime Scene Unit found a key in the van."

Madison glanced at Jonas. "What kind of key?"

"It goes to a high-security padlock."

"So maybe to a storage unit or a locker?" Jonas asked.

"Exactly."

"Okay," Madison said. "But we don't even know if the key belonged to our fugitives, or to the owners of the van."

"We talked to the owners," Michaels said. "The key isn't theirs."

Madison's mind worked through the information. "I think we can assume that they didn't just have a plan to get out of the bank if things went wrong, but out of the city at a minimum and possibly out of the country."

"Which means we need to find out what that key goes to," Jonas said. "If it was in that van, it makes sense it was a part of their escape plan, and in the chaos, they dropped it."

"Agreed," Michaels said. "We'll start at Kira's house and go from there."

"And the bad news?" Madison said, as Jonas pulled onto the freeway.

"I just got word from the hospital about the security guard."

"And?"

There was a short pause on the line. "He died on the operating table about twenty minutes ago."

Madison's stomach clenched at the news. They could now officially add murder to their fugitives' list of felonies.

EIGHT

I t was almost noon when Madison and Jonas stepped under the yellow tape surrounding the bank and headed across the blocked-off section of the parking lot toward Special Agent Osborne, who was talking on his cell. A few local cops and FBI agents were still working, and the Crime Scene Unit was now stationed on the northeastern corner, where its team had begun processing the scene.

The FBI agent ended the call and nodded at them. "I heard the two of you were able to confirm the identities of two of our suspects."

"Ben Galvan and his girlfriend, Kira Thornton," Jonas said.

"Well, that's a start. And I heard one of them was shot?"

Madison nodded. "We've got BOLOs out with updated information."

"Let's hope CSU can pull a rabbit out of a hat and get us something solid with that key we found," Jonas said. "We need to ID the other two."

"What about interviews with the hostages?" Madison asked.

"We're finishing up with the statements," Osborne said. "We'll do follow-up if necessary."

"We were told that we should talk to Barton Wells if he's still here," Madison said.

Osborne pointed to a slightly pudgy man wearing a blue suit who was talking animatedly to one of Osborne's fellow agents. "They'll be done talking in a few minutes, then he's all yours."

"I don't remember seeing him inside the bank," Madison said.

Osborne shook his head. "You wouldn't have. He was in the safe-deposit room and had direct contact with one of the bank robbers. Your boss thought it might be worth your speaking to him. He's actually running for mayor of Seattle."

"I knew his name sounded familiar," Jonas said.

Madison scanned the parking lot. Grace, the girl who'd had an asthma attack during the heist, sat on the curb, her knees pulled up to her chest again.

Madison signaled Jonas as she walked away. "I'll be right back."

She sat down next to the girl on the curb. "It's Grace, right?"

The girl nodded. "You were the paramedic who got me my inhaler."

"Yes, but I'm actually a Deputy US Marshal. I was sent in there to help everyone get out safely."

"Wow. That's cool. Thank you."

"Of course. How are you feeling?"

"Better, I guess. Still shaken up."

"Can I get you anything?" Madison asked. "Some water?"

"I'm okay."

"Have you already talked to the police?"

"Yeah." She wrapped her arms more tightly around her knees. "I called my dad, and he told me to wait for him to pick me up. He should be here any minute now. I . . . I don't think I can drive home."

"That was a good decision."

A moment of silence passed between them. Grace held up her trembling hand. "I can't stop shaking. It all just plays in my mind over and over. They didn't have to shoot the guard. He was just trying to help me."

"Do you want to talk about it?"

"I came in to get some cash," she said, staring out across the parking lot. "It's my dad's birthday this weekend. I started working at the mall a couple months ago, and I was excited to actually have money. Then . . . I don't know. It happened so fast. These three people stormed into the bank behind me, holding up their guns and shouting at everyone to dump their purses and phones in a pile on the ground, then sit down or they were going to shoot us. I just . . . I froze."

"I don't blame you at all," Madison said, attempting to reassure the girl. "That had to be terrifying."

"They started yelling at the tellers to give them money from their drawers. I could hear what was going on around me, but I . . ."

"You couldn't breathe," Madison said.

She nodded. "One of them came up to me and told me to lie on the ground or they were going to shoot me."

"Did you notice anything about them that would help us identify them?"

"Not really. They all wore black and wore masks, but . . ." Grace looked up at her. "I do know that it was a woman."

"You're sure?"

"She came right up to me and I could tell by her eyes. I remember being surprised. Her eyes . . . they seemed so cold."

"Do you remember what color they were?" Madison asked.

"Blue, I think. Yes. Definitely blue. I started crying. I didn't mean to, but I was so scared, and I couldn't breathe, and then . . ."

Madison remained silent, waiting for her to continue.

"The guard came up to me. He was trying to calm me down. Asking them if he could get my inhaler. I don't know what happened next. He went to get my purse, and then I heard a shot. Then he was lying on the ground and there was blood everywhere." She started crying again. "If he dies, it's my fault."

"No, Grace." Madison squeezed the girl's hand, shaking her head. "That's not true at all. This wasn't your fault. None of it."

A middle-aged man walked toward them, and Grace jumped up and ran into his arms.

"You must be Grace's dad," Madison said, standing. "I'm Deputy US Marshal Madison James."

"Thanks for sitting with her." He pulled his daughter against him. "I'm just so sorry, sweetheart. And I'm sorry it took me so long to get here. I was doing a job north of the city and got here as quick as I could."

Grace leaned against her father. "It's fine, Dad. I'm okay."

"I want you to tell your father what you told me, Grace," Madison said. "Will you promise me that?"

Grace nodded.

Madison pulled the girl's father aside for a moment. "It also would be good for your daughter to talk to someone who deals with trauma."

The man straightened. "Of course."

"Remember what I told you." Madison pulled out one of her contact cards as they returned to Grace. "And if you need someone to talk to, give me a call. Anytime."

"Thank you."

Madison was still standing along the curb when Jonas walked up to her a moment later.

"Barton Wells can talk to us now. He's waiting for us over by the lobby doors," he said, pointing to the bank entrance. He led the way toward the witness. "How is the girl, by the way?"

Madison blew out a deep breath. "The guard was helping her when he got shot. She's blaming herself."

"Wow." Jonas ran his hand through his hair. "That's a lot of misplaced guilt for a young girl to carry."

"It is, but I learned something else from her." She stopped beside Jonas and caught his gaze. "According to Grace, the fugitive who spoke to her was a woman with blue eyes. Kira has brown."

"So we're looking at two men and two women with Kira driving the getaway vehicle," Jonas said, as they started walking again. "Not exactly a typical date night."

"That's what I was thinking," she said as they walked up to the older man and introduced themselves.

"Call me Bart." He extended his hand to both of them. "I've already given my statement to the police. I'm still trying to wrap my mind around what happened. I understand these people already hit at least a dozen banks over the past few months."

"We believe this was the same group, yes," Madison said.

Bart shook his head. "Unbelievable."

"I understand you're running for mayor of Seattle."

"Yes, but trust me, I'd much rather be in the news for my policies than as a hostage in a bank robbery."

"You weren't injured, were you?" Madison asked.

"No, though I admit I'm still a bit shaken up. I've never had a gun stuck in my face."

"I know this isn't easy for anyone involved," Jonas said.

"I'm just grateful to be alive. I heard the guard was shot."

"He was."

"Did he make it?"

"I'm sorry, but we can't talk about that."

"I understand." Bart combed his fingers through his thinning hair. "I just . . . it still all seems so surreal."

"We understand you spoke directly with one of the bank robbers," Jonas said.

Bart nodded.

"Can you tell us what happened?"

"Of course. Like I told the other officer, I'd come in to pick something out of my safe-deposit box. An anniversary ring for my wife, actually. We're celebrating twenty-three years on the fifteenth."

Madison smiled. "Congratulations."

"Thank you. Anyway, I was in the room by myself and about to pull out the ring when I heard a loud commotion from the lobby. It startled me. So much so, in fact, that I knocked my cell phone off the table. I reached down to pick it up, but the noise just kept escalating, it unnerved me."

"What kind of noise?"

"Someone was shouting at people to shut up, and then I heard a couple gunshots. That's when I knew this had to be a robbery. There was nowhere to go and hide, but I thought if I just stayed quiet, they probably wouldn't check the room. I decided I should put the box back where it belonged. At least that way, if they found me, they wouldn't be able to get into my box. But before I could even grab it, one of them walked in the room. He told me to lay down on the floor and not to move, then he started going through the box. I didn't budge until an officer found me and told me it was safe to get up."

"Bart, honey!" A petite woman wearing a dark blue pantsuit ran up to them and threw her arms around him. "I just got a text from Clint, who told me what happened. Why didn't you call me?"

"I didn't want to worry you, but I'm fine. Just shaken up." He motioned toward Jonas and Madison. "Trudy, these are US Marshals. I'm giving them my statement."

"So you're really not hurt?"

"No, but they did get most of the contents of our lockbox."

"What?" She pressed her hand against her chest, then shook her head. "I don't care. All that matters is that you're okay."

"Which I am," he said. "I promise. Let me finish talking to the marshals, and then I'll let you drive me home. Why don't you go talk to Clint and tell him what's going on? I see he's just arrived."

Trudy hesitated as if she wasn't sure she could leave him, then nodded and walked away.

"Who's Clint?" Jonas asked.

"He's my campaign manager. We're in the middle of a pretty tight mayoral race."

"Do you have a list of what was inside your lockbox?" Madison asked.

"I keep one at the house and can get it to you if you'd like."

"That would help the police."

Bart blew out a sharp breath. "There were quite a few sentimental pieces that belonged to Trudy's mother. That's what I'm most upset about."

"The police will do everything they can to find them, but in the meantime, we need to know if there was anything distinguishing about the bank robber you can remember."

"I don't know." Bart shrugged. "It all happened so quickly. He had on a black jacket and a face mask that covered his nose and mouth and hair. I've heard they all did."

"Anything you can think of will help. Tattoos, birthmarks . . ." Madison prodded.

"Yes." He snapped his fingers. "There was a tattoo. When he grabbed for my box, I noticed a tattoo on his wrist when his sleeve slipped up."

"Can you describe it?"

Bart pinched the bridge of his nose. "You always think that if something like this happens, you'll remember so you can pass the details on to the authorities. And while I've always been good at remembering details, I also know how memory error can affect eyewitness testimony. All I really have are flashes of memory."

"That's okay," Madison said. "We can start with that."

"I only saw part of it, but I'm pretty sure it was a compass."

"A compass?"

Bart nodded. "I remember thinking for someone with a compass on his wrist, he sure had gotten off track with his life."

"That helps a lot. Thank you."

"I wish I could help more."

"If you think of anything else—"

"I have the officer's card who took my statement." Bart glanced across the parking lot. "Can I go see my wife? She's a strong woman, but I can tell she's pretty upset."

"Of course," Madison said.

As soon as Bart had left, Special Agent Osborne joined the marshals. "Did you find out anything from him that might help?"

"We think we're looking for a second couple," Jonas said. "But no IDs for them yet."

"We've got officers keeping an eye on Kira's houseboat," Madison said, "but she'd be foolish to return, and I'm sure she knows that. I think they were planning to ride the wave until their luck ran out, but there's a good chance the four of them are long gone by now."

"What if the two of us question her brother again?" Jonas asked. "He was living with her. Despite what he told us, even if he wasn't involved, it makes sense that he'd know something."

"I agree," Osborne said. "In the meantime, I just got word that CSU found a receipt to a storage unit in the houseboat. I sent a team in with a warrant. I'm hoping it's a storage place for the money or some kind of go bag with forged IDs."

Jonas's phone rang, and he stepped aside to answer it. Madison watched as he took the call, the frown on his face deepening.

"Jonas?" Madison walked over to him after he hung up. "What's wrong?"

"I think I might have just found two of our fugitives."

'm sorry." Jonas pulled the car keys out of his pocket. "We need to go. Now."

"Jonas, wait." Madison pressed her hand against his arm. "What's going on?"

"That was Felicia's grandmother. They're at a prosthesis clinic. A couple just walked into the back room where Felicia was seeing one of the doctors. They locked the door behind them. She believes at least one of them was armed."

"And you think our suspects are involved?" Osborne asked.

"The scenario fits. They need medical help and are desperate."

Osborne nodded. "Send me the clinic's name and address, and I'll send in local PD and tell them to wait for you."

"Where's Hazel?" Madison asked, hurrying after Jonas. "Is she safe?"

"She was calling from the restroom. I told her to stay quiet and stay put."

Madison put her hand out, palm up. "Give me the keys. I'll drive in case she calls you back."

Thirty seconds later, Madison was maneuvering as fast as

she could through the early afternoon traffic. He sat ramrod straight next to her, praying that this time God would step in and intervene. That this time, despite the panic in his gut, things would turn out differently.

"Hazel could be wrong about the level of danger they're in," Madison said, interrupting his thoughts. "We don't have all the facts."

"We know one of our fugitives needs medical help. We know that Hazel saw a couple with at least one weapon. What else do we need?"

Jonas shoved back the memories as Madison pulled into the parking lot of the clinic, parking in front of the entrance. Everything between him and Felicia had been over a long time ago, but that didn't mean he wasn't going to do everything in his power to make sure nothing happened to her today.

Madison pulled out her phone and started scrolling through something. "Officer Hartman sent a list of cars that left Pike Place Market while we were there. The license plate on that Toyota Corolla matches."

He glanced at the car she was pointing to and inhaled sharply. "How far out is backup?"

"Three to five minutes," Madison said.

"We can't wait. We need to clear the building and locate our fugitives."

Before someone gets hurt.

He wasn't going to let something happen to Felicia again.

A woman carrying a takeaway bag and an oversized purse was trying to unlock the front door.

"Ma'am." The woman spun around, and Jonas held up his badge as he ran up to her. "I'm Deputy US Marshal Jonas Quinn and this is my partner. Do you work here at the clinic?"

"Yes. I was just returning from a lunch run. The front door's locked."

"Is there another way in?" Madison asked.

She held up the large key ring. "I have a key to the side door, but I never use it."

"I'm going to need you to let us in."

"Okay." She motioned for them to follow her around the sidewalk to the other door. "Can you tell me what's going on? It's got to be something serious if the marshals are involved."

"We believe there are hostages inside," Madison said.

"Hostages?" The woman stopped short in front of the side door. "I don't understand."

"We don't have time to explain, but here's what we need," Jonas said. "Can you quickly give us an idea of the layout of the building? Then we'd like you to go next door and wait."

"Okay." Her hand shook as she tried the lock. This time the door opened. "In the front there's a reception area and waiting room. Through this door, there are four exam rooms. Two to your left and two to your right." She ran a hand down her face, looking deep in thought. "On the far side, past the nurses' station, there's a large physical therapy room along with a restroom and a storage closet."

Jonas nodded as they stepped inside, then shut the door behind them.

Where are they?

He and Madison began to clear the building. The first two exam rooms were empty. They opened the third exam room. Inside were three patients and four employees wearing scrubs, all with their hands zip-tied behind them and gags in their mouths.

"We're with the US Marshals," Madison whispered. "I need

you all to be as quiet as possible and make your way out the back exit to the building next door. There you should be able to wait for the police in safety. They'll be here in a couple minutes."

"Is everyone here?" Jonas asked.

"No." One of the nurses rubbed her wrists after Madison cut off the zip tie. "There might be someone in the restroom. They grabbed Dr. Phelps and one of our patients. I'm pretty sure they're in the rehab room."

Jonas's heart dropped. *Felicia.*

"Okay." Madison snapped the zip tie off the last person. "Go now. Quickly and quietly."

"We need to find Hazel," Jonas said. "We can get her to safety, then find Felicia."

Jonas headed down the hallway toward the other side of the clinic, his worry escalating. Felicia had always been strong. But sometimes life threw things at you that you couldn't control. And that was what scared him the most about this situation.

On the other side of the clinic, Jonas tried the handle of the restroom. It was locked. Madison watched his back as he knocked quietly. "Hazel? It's Jonas. I need you to open the door."

A second later the door clicked open.

"Jonas!" The older woman pulled him into a hug as soon as the door opened, then took a step back. "Did you find Felicia?"

He registered the fear in her eyes, sure the emotion was reflected in his.

"We know where she is, but I want you out of the building—"

"No, not without Felicia. You know how much she's been through. I can't face the possibility of losing her again." Hazel grabbed his arm. "Promise me you won't let anything happen to her, Jonas. Promise me."

Jonas sucked in a breath, meeting the older woman's eyes. "I promise. Please, now go out the side exit and wait next door with the employees. It's going to be okay."

He waited until the door had closed behind Hazel before turning to Madison. "I shouldn't have promised her that this was all going to be okay."

"She knows you'll do everything in your power to keep her safe, and that's enough for the moment."

Jonas closed his eyes. "And if it isn't?"

The question hung between them. He shouldn't have promised. He'd gotten up this morning like he did every morning, praying that there would be no issues serving the warrant. But this . . . this was the last thing he'd expected to happen.

"The rehab room has a small window," Madison said. "Why don't you figure out what's going on inside while I clear the rest of the clinic?"

He nodded. Neither of them wanted surprises.

Jonas peeked through the small window on the door of the rehab room. The space was filled with exercise equipment and stations for mobility training. Ben sat on a table in the far corner while the doctor worked on him, the injured man's finger on the trigger of a handgun. Felicia sat half a dozen feet away from the two as Kira paced behind her, holding a weapon at her side. A time bomb about to explode.

Jonas quietly stepped away from the door and called Michaels. It was a risky move, but he needed to make sure backup was ready and didn't want the hostages out of his sights for long. "Madison's clearing the clinic. I can verify that Ben and Kira are in the rehab room. Two fugitives and two hostages, including a doctor."

"Backup has just arrived."

"Keep them outside on standby for the moment," Jonas whispered as Madison headed back toward him. "Both fugitives are armed."

"Copy that."

The door to the rehab room swung open. Kira stood in the doorway, pointing a gun at him and Madison.

"Get them in here. Now." Ben's voice bellowed from inside. "Or I will put a bullet into the doctor's head."

"Hands up. Both of you," Kira said, keeping her gun aimed in their direction. "You need to do what he says. He's not messing around."

Jonas hesitated for a moment, irritated at the sudden loss of advantage, then stepped into the room with Madison. Through the windows, he could see where three local law enforcement cars had pulled up, more than likely the reason Kira had decided to check the hallway outside their room. Ben still sat on a table, blood soaking his midsection from the bullet hole in his side, while Dr. Phelps hovered over him. But his focus was on the fourth person in the room.

Felicia.

She sat perched at the edge of a workout bench, wearing her prosthetic leg. But there was no time for him to congratulate her progress.

"Are you okay?" he whispered.

She nodded. "What are you doing here, Jonas?"

"My job."

"So this is your job?" Ben asked, forcing Jonas to refocus his attention. "I'm guessing that the two of you really aren't paramedics."

"They're marshals," answered Kira, looking back and forth between the two. "They were at my house this morning."

Jonas turned away from Felicia. "Tell me what's going on, Ben."

"One of you shot me." He shook his gun toward Dr. Phelps. "And this nice man is going to fix it."

"I'm a physical therapist," the doctor said, holding up his hands. "Bullet wounds aren't exactly my specialty."

"He needs to see a surgeon," Kira said.

"I'll be fine." Ben's hand shook. "I'm still in charge, and here's how things will go. The doctor is going to sew me up, then my friend and I will walk out of here with the doctor as our hostage."

"You're in no condition to leave," Dr. Phelps said. "You've lost too much blood. You need surgery and the bullet taken out."

"He's right, Ben." Jonas caught the terror in Kira's eyes as she spoke. "Please listen to him. You need to go to a hospital. You'll die if you don't get help."

"And we'll go to prison if I do. He's not on our side, Kira."

"It doesn't matter anymore," she said. "They know who we are, and there's nowhere to run." She kept her gun aimed at the marshals, but her lip quivered a bit as she spoke.

"You're wrong." Ben's jaw tensed. "There's always a way out. That's part of the challenge."

Madison took a step forward. "Except this isn't some video game where you can get another life. If you don't get some help, you're going to die."

Ben swung his weapon at her. "Enough. I'm fine."

"We're just trying to help," Madison said. "You've lost a lot of blood and you're not thinking clearly. But we're just a couple minutes away from one of Seattle's best trauma units."

"All I need is the doctor to finish stitching me up, and then we're going."

"Where?" Kira asked. "We can't run anymore."

Jonas weighed the interaction between the two fugitives. While Ben seemed to be holding out for a miracle, Kira clearly saw the reality of the situation. They needed to find a way to convince him that this was already over.

Madison took another step toward Kira. "I know this wasn't a part of your plan, but we can make sure Ben gets the help he needs."

Ben winced in pain. "Don't listen to them."

"We can get someone in here who can help," Madison said. "Just let me make a call."

"Help? Really? Before I know it, you'll have a dozen officers breaching that door. Forget it." Ben's voice rose. "Put your weapons and cell phones on the table, and then Kira will pat you down."

Jonas didn't miss the authority in Ben's voice, but his face had paled, and he was shaking even harder now. Still, they needed to keep things from escalating any further, because he had no doubt that if pushed too hard, the man was going to snap.

"Now!" Ben said.

"Okay—"

"No, it's not okay." Ben managed to stand up.

"Ben," Madison said as they complied with the man's orders. "Think through what you're doing."

"I already have."

"I know you feel trapped," Madison continued, her voice steady, "but if this ends with someone else getting hurt—"

Ben's hands shook as he aimed his gun at Madison, his finger closing in on the trigger. "You don't get it. I have nothing else to lose."

The next few seconds played in slow motion before Jonas's eyes. Ben's gun went off at the same time that Felicia lunged off the bench, grabbed Kira's weapon, and fired back at Ben. Her shot hit its target, but Ben missed his mark.

Jonas spun toward Felicia. A red splotch started spreading across her chest. He bridged the gap between them. "Felicia . . . No." He knelt beside her. "I need you to stay with me. Madison, call 911."

Ben had managed to get up and run out the door with the doctor, but all Jonas could think about was saving Felicia. "Stay with me. Come on. I'm so, so sorry."

"No . . . you have nothing to be sorry about." Felicia's words were barely audible. "I'm the one who messed things up."

"Jonas." Madison had already wrestled Kira onto the ground and had her in handcuffs. "An ambulance is on its way."

"I've got Felicia. Go after Ben. Now."

TEN

Madison tried to shake the memory that flashed in front of her. She'd been in this situation before. Looking into the eyes of someone who was going to shoot her. Felicia had just taken the bullet that should have been for her. But Ben was running. Whatever hidden memory was trying to surface would have to wait.

She hurried out the door, where two officers stood six feet in front of Ben, who held his weapon against Dr. Phelps's head. Felicia had put a round in his leg, which meant he would only be able to go so far, but he was running on adrenaline now. Probably not even feeling the pain of the second bullet. But if they didn't stop him now, the doctor would be dead. Ben had already shot two people who got in his way.

He took another backward step toward his car. "Everyone needs to stay back, or I will shoot him."

Madison moved forward slowly, staying far enough away to not intimidate him but close enough for him to know she wasn't backing down.

The two uniformed officers moved in beside her, but she motioned for them to follow behind her.

"Ben . . ." She held up her weapon, knowing he was already spooked, and that he wouldn't hesitate to shoot again if he was pushed into a corner. "I need you to listen to me. It's over. There really is nowhere else to run, and you're only making things worse for yourself. Just put an end to this before someone else gets hurt. Let the doctor go, and we'll get you the medical help you need."

The man's hand shook. "I didn't mean to shoot her, but you weren't listening to me. No one listens to me."

She took another couple steps, following him to his car. "I've tried to listen to you, Ben."

"Have you? Because we both know it doesn't matter what I do right now. No one was ever supposed to get hurt, but now you expect me to just turn myself in? And then what? All will be forgiven? I'm not stupid. The only way out of this is for me to run."

"And then what? Are you prepared to run the rest of your life?"

"Trust me, that's sounding a whole lot better than the alternative." He was at the car now. "You don't get it. I have nothing more to lose at this point."

She looked for an opportunity to stop them from getting into the car or, if necessary, an open shot. But Ben kept the doctor between them.

As he and the doctor got into the car, Madison pulled out her phone and called Michaels.

"Where are you?" he asked.

"In the clinic's parking lot, about to follow our suspect with two uniforms," she said, running to the car. "Kira's inside and handcuffed, but Ben took a hostage and is about to leave in the car they arrived in." She gave him the license plate number.

"He shot someone inside, Michaels. It was a friend of Jonas. Felicia."

"Stay on his tail and keep me on speaker so I know what's going on, but don't take any unnecessary risks."

Madison quickly started the car, then pulled out of the parking lot. She'd seen defeat in Kira's eyes and thought they could talk them down, but she'd been wrong. She'd pushed Ben too hard, and Felicia had ended up taking the bullet for her. Anger bubbled as she gripped the steering wheel. If Felicia didn't survive, how was she ever going to face Jonas again?

Traffic flowed around her as she pressed on the accelerator, keeping her eye on the other vehicle. Ben was three cars ahead, while the patrol cars followed at a short distance behind her. The Toyota swerved to the right, then took a sharp turn.

Madison took a quick right, as they disappeared from view. *Where are they?*

She heard the crash before she saw it.

"I've got eyes on our suspect's vehicle," she said. "It looks like the car ran off the road, jumped a curb, and hit a lamppost."

"Approach carefully," Michaels said. "The guy's still armed and has the hostage."

"Roger that." She ended the call and jumped out of her car as two of the marked vehicles pulled up behind her. She signaled for the officers to follow behind her as they edged closer to the car, weapons at the ready.

"US Marshals," she shouted, approaching the vehicle. "I want you both to get out of the car now with your hands in the air."

She came closer, watching for signs of movement in the side-view mirror. The driver's side door opened. Madison steadied her stance as the doctor slipped out of the car. She hurried up to the passenger side, but it was empty.

"Where's Ben?" she asked the doctor.

"He's gone."

"What do you mean he's gone? Where is he?"

"I don't know." The man pushed his glasses up the bridge of his nose, clearly terrified. "Someone tried to cut me off. I ran off the road, and then he jumped out of the car."

"Are you hurt?"

"I don't think so. Just shaken up."

She called in for an ambulance, then signaled for the officers to follow her.

"Madison? Where are you?" Michaels said once he was on the line again.

She glanced around her and gave him the cross streets.

"Do you see him anywhere?" he asked.

"No, but he couldn't have gotten far. Make sure law enforcement has descriptions of him. We'll spread out and canvass the neighborhood."

The streets were busy with both cars and pedestrians as she started searching for Ben. The older neighborhood was primarily made up of bottom floor storefronts, everything from sushi to Subway, and either apartments or office space took up the floors above. To her left was a narrow parking garage and a small park. Ben Galvan could be anywhere.

Red drops on the sidewalk caught her attention. She bent down to examine them. They definitely looked like blood. Were definitely still wet.

She pulled her phone from her pocket. "I just found traces of fresh blood."

"Proceed carefully."

She disconnected the call, then walked slowly past a vacant storefront with a FOR LEASE sign in the window, looking for movement. She tried the door handle. Locked. She kept moving down the street. He had to be nearby. After losing that much blood, this man was quickly running out of options.

"There's an underground passageway fifty feet from here," one of the officers said.

She knew there were hundreds of miles of tunnels and pipes laid out like a maze beneath the city. Some were used as tourist attractions. Others were used for workers to be able to stay out of the rain, forming an underground city. Many were tucked under hidden doorways that most Seattleites never even knew about. For a man on the run, it would be the perfect hiding place.

She stopped in front of one of the doors. There was blood on the handle. She pulled it open, then stared down the narrow staircase, her weapon out in front of her, senses alert. Paint-chipped walls pressed in next to her. Clearing stairwells and tunnels held numerous threats because of the blind spots they created. And she had no idea where Ben was or what was on the other side. She also had no idea how much training the officers behind her had.

She kept her focus on the bottom of the stairs, alert for any movement, as she signaled her approach to the officers. Speed wasn't an issue in this situation. With little light and no cover, it was crucial to stay aware of their surroundings. Their main advantage was that Ben had been hit not once, but twice. It wouldn't be long until shock took over and he wouldn't be able to respond. Her goal was to eliminate the threat and make sure they didn't open themselves to an attack.

She paused at the bottom of the staircase, cautiously clearing the corner in sections. Careful to make sure they weren't being set up for an ambush. She signaled again at the officers, then slowly started navigating the narrow tunnel. A few lights flickered along the path.

Her stomach roiled when she noticed a body ahead of her. Ben was sitting slouched against the wall twenty feet down from the corner, his weapon beside him. She quickly approached him, kicked the gun aside, then knelt down in front of him to check his pulse. Rapid. He was alive, but his skin was clammy and there was a bluish tinge to his lips.

"He's in shock," she shouted at the officers. "Call a second ambulance. Now."

Anger flushed through her. She wasn't going to let him die. Not on her watch. He was going to live to pay for what he'd done.

She barked out orders to the other officers then called Michaels again. "We found Ben and have him in custody with an ambulance on the way."

"That's good news."

"What about Kira?" she asked.

"I had her transferred here."

"Wait for me," she said, heading toward her car. "I'm coming back to the office now and want to be there."

"That's what I planned."

She hesitated before asking her next question. "What about Felicia?"

"They are prepping her for surgery, but I don't have an update on her condition other than it's serious."

"And Jonas?"

"He's at the hospital with her grandmother. I told him he needed to stay."

✳ ✳ ✳

Forty-five minutes later, Madison pulled in front of the US Marshals building. Her hands trembled as she turned off the engine. She reached for the Americano she'd bought on the way, but caffeine wasn't the only thing she needed. She hadn't had time to process what had happened inside that clinic. And she wouldn't for quite a while. The bullet that hit Felicia had been meant for her. The reminder set off a fresh wave of guilt and frustration, but it also drove home a deep sense of determination to ensure they finished their job and brought in the other two fugitives.

Michaels was waiting for her in his office. The chief deputy, who'd gone completely gray over the past year, waved his hand at the empty chair across from him and gave her his full attention. "I want to hear this from you. What exactly happened out there, and how are you?"

Madison sat down, forcing order to her jumbled thoughts. "It all happened so fast. Jonas and I were trying to talk Ben down. Things escalated. Felicia reacted and grabbed for Kira's gun. They both fired their weapons. But that bullet . . . The shot he took." Her voice cracked. "That bullet was for me, and Jonas has every right to blame me—"

"Hold on." Michaels held up his hand. "If that's what you're worried about, I think you can give him more credit than that. We'll take an official statement, but from everything I've heard today, both of you reacted exactly the way you were trained. It's not your fault."

Guilt continued to press against her chest. "I'm not sure that matters."

"It has to matter, and if you can't put your emotions aside—"

"No. That won't be a problem." She snapped her head up and caught his gaze. It didn't matter how personal this had all become. She was going to play it out till the end.

"Good, because if it is, I'll assign someone else to the case. I need you one hundred percent focused to find the last two fugitives."

"I can do that. I'm ready to talk with Kira." She started to stand up, but Michaels motioned her to sit back down.

"Before you do that, I asked Piper to do some profiling for us." Michaels picked up his phone to call her in. "I think it will help to see what she found."

A moment later, a young woman with shoulder-length brown hair and a pair of thick black-rimmed glasses dropped a file on the desk next to Madison's coffee.

"Madison, this is Piper," Michaels said. "She's a criminal justice major and will be interning in our office the next few months."

Madison stood to shake the young girl's hand. "It's nice to meet you, Piper."

"You too, Deputy. I heard about Deputy Quinn's friend getting shot. I'm really sorry."

"We all are. It's been a crazy start back to work." She chuckled wryly. "What have you got?"

"Kira Thornton is the oldest of two children. Her father is the CEO of a tech company located here in Seattle. Her mother is a psychologist. Like her boyfriend, who clearly isn't an ex, she has no criminal record. She dropped out of college after her freshman year and has been living in the houseboat ever since, a property owned by her family. Technically, she works at her father's company, but so far I haven't been able to pin down exactly what she does." Piper coughed into her hand. "A call to the receptionist confirmed that she's over social media and marketing, but the overall description was pretty vague. I got the impression that she didn't come in regularly. On a personal level, though, she's very active on social media, which seems to be where she spends the bulk of her time. She mainly posts photos of herself. She also loves to travel, and then there are quite a lot of photos of her doing extreme sports like rock climbing, skiing, cliff diving, and skydiving."

"I'm impressed," Madison said, glancing through the file. "And Ben, he's clearly a risk-taker as well."

"Definitely, but in my book there's a huge difference between skydiving and robbing a bank." Piper smiled. "Kira doesn't seem to be short on cash. Her bank account has several thousand dollars, and she's got half a dozen credit cards. None of them are maxed out, but they are well used."

"It fits the pattern," Madison said. "The robberies seem to be as much about the thrill as the money."

Piper set down a second file. "I also have the crime scene photos you requested from the bank."

"Thank you." Madison started to flip through them.

"Whatever her motivation has been," Michaels said, "our number one priority is to find out who they're working with. Without IDs on our last two fugitives, we're moving ahead blind. Get that information from her."

"Yes, sir. I intend to."

Jonas walked into the office as Madison was standing up to leave.

"Jonas." She pulled the files against her chest. "What are you doing here?"

His hands clenched at his sides. "Have you already interviewed Kira?"

"Not yet." She glanced back at Michaels before continuing. "I was just about to go in, but you don't have to be here."

"She's right," Michaels said. "Go back to the hospital and wait with Hazel. We can handle this."

"No." Jonas waved away his boss's comment. "I need to be here doing something to find the rest of the team. They're just as responsible for what happened to Felicia as Ben is for shooting her."

A new wave of guilt washed over Madison. "I agree," she said, "and we will find them. But Hazel—and Felicia—they need you right now. And you need to be there for your own sake as well."

He shook his head. "Hazel's sister is staying with her, and she's promised to give me an update when the surgery's over. So it's either that or my wearing a hole in the waiting room carpet. Something you should be able to understand more than anyone else."

Her jaw tensed at the comment, because she understood his desire to stop whoever was behind this. She didn't want him to later regret that he hadn't been there with Felicia and her grandmother, but sometimes . . . sometimes waiting on the sidelines wasn't an option.

ELEVEN

Madison dropped her empty coffee cup into the trash outside the interrogation room, then stopped in front of the one-way mirror where she could see Kira sitting, her gaze glued to the table, hands clamped together in front of her.

Madison turned her attention over to her partner, who had filed in behind her, his expression stony. "Jonas, if there's anything I can do—"

"I really don't want to talk about it," he said. "Let's just focus on what's going on right now and get the information we need from her."

Madison opened her mouth to say something, then stopped. She knew he was torn. That there were unresolved issues between him and Felicia that might never be solved if she didn't make it through the surgery. There would be a time and place to address her concerns, but this clearly wasn't it.

"How do you want to approach this?" she asked instead.

"I'll let you take the lead, but if we're going to bring in our other fugitives, we need information from her as quickly as possible. She needs to realize she's in way over her head.

That her boyfriend just let her take the fall for a long list of felonies that very well might put her in prison the rest of her life. We also need to know what they planned to do if things went south."

She nodded at his matter-of-fact statements. "Let's go then."

Jonas opened the door to the interrogation room without further comment, letting her go inside first. She dropped the file she'd carried in with her onto the table, then took a seat across from Kira. Jonas stayed standing behind her.

"Kira, you've already been read your rights and understand them, correct?" Madison asked.

The woman raised her head. Tears welled in her eyes. "I understand."

"Good," Madison said. "We don't have a lot of time, so I'm going to make things very clear for you. You need to know two things. One, whether or not you decide to cooperate, we will find your other two friends. Two, lying to a federal marshal is a felony, and so is aiding and abetting a fugitive. So in case you were planning not to give us the information we need, I would suggest you think twice and remember just how much is at stake."

"Wait." Her eyes widened. "You found Ben?"

"He's currently undergoing surgery, though I'm surprised you sound worried about him," Madison said. "He didn't seem to have a problem leaving you to take the fall on your own."

Kira's face paled. "He . . . he didn't have a choice. He knew I would want him to try and save himself."

"Really?" Madison sat back. "He's in surgery because he made the choice to rob a bank today. He shot a security guard, who's now dead, then decided to take hostages in a clinic, including two federal marshals. Those were his choices. Now let's look at yours."

She flipped open the file, then pushed a photo across the table. "This is Vincent. He was a retired police officer who worked security at the bank. He has three kids who are now planning a funeral instead of his sixty-first birthday party. All for trying to help one of the hostages this morning."

"I didn't know. I never went inside the bank. I was just supposed to drive the car." Tears slid down her cheeks. "I never killed anyone."

Madison pressed her hands against the table. "Except that doesn't really matter. You know what it means to be an accessory to a crime? Because that's what you are. You're just as guilty as if you pulled the trigger yourself."

"No . . . No one was supposed to die."

"Because you thought you had it all planned out, didn't you? Every detail of what needed to be done even if things went wrong."

Kira reached up to wipe her cheek, smudging her makeup. "They made the plans. I just . . . I agreed to help, but I can't go to prison. I don't know what happened." Kira started picking at a broken fingernail. "The plan was just to get in, take the cash, and get out, but—"

"But people got hurt," Madison said. "The plan was to walk into a bank full of customers with loaded weapons, Kira. What did you think was going to happen if something went wrong?" Madison pushed the photo of Vincent closer to her. "I need you to tell me the names of the other two people who you have been working with and what their escape plan is."

Kira pressed her lips together. "I can't."

"Sorry," Madison said, scooting back her chair. "Wrong choice."

"Wait a minute." Jonas slipped into the seat next to Madison.

"Despite what you've already said, I don't think she realizes just how much trouble she's facing."

Kira choked on a sob. "You don't understand. I can't."

"Can't, or don't want to?" Madison caught Kira's gaze. "Because the bottom line is that *not* telling us what we want to know isn't going to lessen the charges the DA is about to formally bring against you."

"We already have a slew of evidence," Jonas said. "The ammo from your houseboat matched the ammo in a previous bank shooting, as well as a stash of cash we found in your car."

"Enough." Kira stared at the table. "There was a detailed plan we were supposed to follow if things went wrong."

They waited for the woman to continue, but when she didn't, Madison asked, "What was the plan, Kira?"

Any arrogance she'd seen from the woman earlier that morning was completely gone.

"They had a plan to get out if the cops showed up. No hostages, no one hurt, they were just going to leave. There were smoke bombs in their backpacks for a distraction, so they could slip out with the crowd. And it worked, but then . . . then one of you saw us leave and started following us and everything went wrong."

"And their names? The names of the other two who were there with you?"

Kira bit her lower lip. "I can't tell you."

Madison frowned, but she could read the fear in Kira's eyes. It was only a matter of time before her resolve failed. "They must be pretty good friends, if you're willing to go to prison for them."

"We made a pact. If things went south, we'd cover for each other."

Madison placed her hands on the table, trying to control her temper. She took a deep breath. "You're out of options. Your solid exit strategy has left you with one of your teammates in emergency surgery, and the other two on the run. If you ever want to see a blue sky outside a prison yard again, I need the names of the other two and where they're heading. Because the longer they run, the worse off they're going to be as well. And any opportunity to make a deal for a reduced sentence for you will be gone."

Kira's leg bounced under the table. "I can't."

"Do you really think if they were in your place that they would be protecting you right now?" Jonas asked.

"Yes."

"Surely you don't really believe that," Jonas said. "I've been working in law enforcement for over a decade, and it's always the same ending. No matter how close you think you are, no matter how many promises you make each other, someone always ends up caving to save themselves. It's human nature. Which means all of those good intentions to stay loyal to each other suddenly vanish."

"Not this time."

Madison slid the photo off the table and stood up. "Just know that we will find them. And the fact that you refuse to cooperate will only make the DA work even harder to ensure the long list of felonies against you sticks, especially considering that someone is dead because of your group's actions."

Kira turned away, refusing to meet Madison's gaze.

"Oh . . . and I do have one other question," Madison said. If asking Kira flat out wasn't going to work, they were going to have to come up with a different angle to narrow down their suspects. "I saw where you live. That place has to be worth at least a million dollars. Why did you feel the need to risk everything and rob banks?"

She shrugged her shoulders. "You wouldn't understand."

"You know what I think?" Madison said. "I think you and your friends were bored. You dropped out of college and were living off your parents' money, but for whatever reason that wasn't enough."

Kira just stared at the table in front of her.

"There's a saying that an idle mind is a dangerous one. You went from no criminal record—not even a parking ticket—to robbing banks. So I'm guessing it started out innocently. Illegal drugs in college and drinking for a rush. Cliff diving over spring break and—"

"There were never drugs involved, but yeah." Kira shrugged like it was no big deal. "We did a lot of risky things back then."

"So you went from cliff diving to robbing a bank?"

"I'm done talking. They're long gone by now anyway. You'll never find them."

Madison stepped outside after Jonas, then shut the door behind them. "So there's a high probability that the four of them went to college together."

There was a connection out there. All they had to do was narrow it down.

"Piper." Madison signaled to the intern. "I want you to scour Ben's and Kira's social media posts and Facebook friends and compile a list of mutual friends, and mark in particular on that list those who went to the same university together, or those they did extreme sports with."

"I can do that." Piper was already typing away on her phone. "Plus we have another lead as well."

"What did you find?" Jonas asked.

LISA HARRIS —— 109

Piper handed over a black-and-white photo. "I was able to pull a frame of the other two suspects off security footage at the parking garage. It's grainy, but it's better than nothing."

"Searching their social media accounts in combination with the photo might get us exactly what we're looking for," Michaels said, walking up to them. "I want the BOLO updated and sent out to every police department in the state as well as to news channels. Let's ask the public for their assistance. Someone is going to recognize them."

"I'd still like to talk with Kira's brother again," Madison told Michaels. "Even if he isn't involved, he has to know something."

"I can arrange it now."

Jonas turned to Madison. "We need to talk first."

"Okay."

"In private."

She followed him into an empty meeting room, then shut the door behind them.

"I need you to know that I don't blame you for what happened," he said as soon as she'd turned to face him. "I just . . . I didn't handle things well with Felicia the last time I saw her. I've always felt guilty the way I left things between us."

"You don't have to explain—"

"Yeah. I do."

She waited for him to continue, not missing the layer of anger simmering just under the surface over what had happened. She also knew how a sequence of decisions could force you toward a moment that was impossible to escape no matter how bad you wanted to go back and change things.

"Today was too close to that raid a few years ago," he said finally.

Madison didn't need any clarification as to what he was talking about. Or about the pain that resurfaced today.

She waited silently as he detailed the rest of the story she'd heard him tell once before, wanting to tell him that the guilt he felt wasn't worth it. She'd played the same "what-if" games with herself when Luke died. If he hadn't walked through the garage at that moment. If he'd taken one more patient. If he'd called in sick that day . . .

"Why don't you go back to the hospital," she said. "I'll handle Kira's brother."

"I'll go if I'm needed, but for now, I can work this case and leave the emotions out of it."

She nodded, grateful that he'd opened up to her.

His phone rang, and he pulled it out of his pocket and took the call, taking a few steps away for privacy. She watched his face and tried not to eavesdrop. His frown deepened before he hung up a few seconds later.

"Jonas?"

"That was Hazel. Felicia's out of surgery. She's stable at the moment, but not out of the woods. She asked if I would come."

"You need to go," she said.

"I will. Just keep me in the loop."

She nodded, then watched him walk out of the room. She knew firsthand how essential it was to distance themselves emotionally from their work, but today had made it impossible.

TWELVE

Jonas walked down the hospital corridor past a row of windows overlooking the parking lot. It was overcast again, as the city hunkered down under gray skies for another few days of rain. The weather fit his mood perfectly. He'd wrestled with the fact that he hadn't been able to understand what Felicia was going through after her accident all those months ago. In the end, he'd had to let go of his anger toward her for distancing herself and for leaving him. Even if they never spoke again. But this . . . how could he forgive himself for not protecting her better—again?

Hazel was sitting in the waiting room with two women on either side of her. She looked up as he stepped into the room, then hurried toward him.

She pulled him into a hug for a long moment before taking a step back. "I'm glad you're here."

He took in her tired smile, her normally perfect hair a little disheveled after a day of worry. "How is she?"

"I just saw her. She's groggy and worn-out, but she made it through surgery."

"What are the doctors saying?" he asked.

Hazel lowered herself back into a chair between the women and took a deep breath. "There are a few symptoms they are monitoring, including the infection at her amputation site. There is also some swelling in her other leg, and her oxygen levels are low. Overall, though, her vital signs are stable at the moment. She's in good hands, Jonas, and there are a lot of people praying for her."

"I know." He glanced at the hallway before turning back to her. The urgency he'd felt on the way over had morphed into a heavy anxiety over seeing Felicia again. Despite Hazel's assurances over the phone, his mind buzzed with worry. Would Felicia really want to talk to him after so much time had passed?

"Can I see her?"

Hazel nodded. "Just for a few minutes, though. They want her to rest as much as possible. Her body's been through a lot." She reached out and squeezed his hand. "This isn't the way I would have ever wanted things to play out, but the two of you need to find closure. Things have been unsettled between you for far too long."

"And I've always felt guilty about that. I'm still not sure what happened."

"My granddaughter's stubborn," she said, dropping her hand from his and leaning back, "but I have a feeling she's not the only one. And looking for closure isn't always easy, is it?"

"No. I just wish I could have understood her better."

"So you could fix her?"

Hazel's words pierced straight through him. "Did she tell you that?"

"I know it was part of why she walked away."

"I just wanted to support her."

"I know. And I think she knows that now as well. Losing a

leg was a steep learning curve for her, but she's come a long way." Hazel nodded toward the hallway. "She's in room 420 if you want to see her."

A moment later, he stood outside her room, trying to gather enough courage to step inside. He didn't have any romantic feelings for Felicia anymore, but that didn't mean he didn't still care about her.

He drew in a deep breath and stepped into the room, then stopped in the doorway. She was sleeping. Something he knew she needed. Monitors beeped behind her, and she was hooked up to an IV pole and an oxygen cannula. In the hectic confrontation at the clinic, he hadn't had much time to look at her. Her long, dark hair was shorter now, hitting right at her chin, but other than that, she'd hardly changed at all.

He started to leave, then heard her voice. "Jonas . . ."

"Hey." He took an awkward step forward. "How are you feeling?"

She shot him a weak grin. "Like I just got hit with a bullet."

He looked down. "I'm sorry."

"Me too." She shook her head. "Funny how I thought lightning couldn't strike twice in the same place, and yet here I am once again, getting a bullet dug out of me. I guess I have a bad habit of being in the wrong place at the wrong time."

"No, I should have—"

"Stop. No apologies." She patted the bed next to her, motioning for him to sit down. "Though I have to say that while a thousand things ran through my mind as I sat in the room with a gun pointed at me, I never expected you to show up."

"I went into that building with plans to save you." He forced himself to cross the tiled floor, then sat down on the edge of the bed. "Instead you took a bullet."

She shifted her position, then winced at the movement. "There are so many things I regret not saying to you, Jonas. But the first thing is that this wasn't your fault. Just like my losing my leg was never your fault."

He glanced at the beeping monitor, avoiding her gaze. "You're not the only one who wishes they'd have figured out the right thing to say. I botched up everything."

She reached out and squeezed his hand. "It doesn't matter anymore. We're both different people today."

"True, but that doesn't erase the guilt I can't seem to shake."

"What would you have said different?" she asked.

"I would have made you understand that I still wanted you. I didn't care that you'd lost your leg."

"Which was part of the problem." Her smile faded. "Because it did matter to me. I felt like I lost everything that day, and you wanted to go on like nothing happened. Like things would somehow stay the same between us. But for me, things would never be the same again. I needed you to understand that. And while it wasn't your fault, that wasn't something you could do."

"If we could have communicated better . . ."

She pushed a strand of hair behind her ear. "The problem was that I didn't know how to deal with the loss of my leg. How was I supposed to make you understand what I needed?"

"I don't know." He shook his head, wishing they'd somehow been able to face each other months ago and find resolution. "I could never understand how you felt, and I got that, but there were things that I should have done different to avoid what happened in the first place."

"What do you mean?" she asked.

"I made a bad call. I should have taken point that day. I

should have been able to take that guy down so no one died. So you didn't lose so much."

"You're wrong, Jonas, and deep down you know that." Her voice broke. "It wasn't your fault. It was never your fault. You're a hero if anything. You put your life on the line that day, just like you do every day. We all take that risk, not knowing what threat is on the other side of the door. That's what we signed up for. What happened that day was not the fault of anyone on our team. It was just a part of the job."

He shook his head, still convinced things could have had a different outcome. "That's how I'll always see it, and there's nothing heroic about what happened. And now today, I had another chance to save you, and you're lying here in a hospital bed again."

"I guess we both looked at things wrong," she said, closing her eyes for a moment before opening them again and catching his gaze. "I always felt like I failed you. Like without a leg I couldn't do my job. Couldn't be enough for you."

"You were always enough, Felicia."

A heavy pause hung between them for a few long seconds as emotions swirled inside him.

"Maybe everything that happened today will be worth it in the end for both of us to find closure," she said. "Closure we should have given ourselves a long time ago."

He wanted to believe her, but not this way. He glanced at the heart monitor she was connected to. Her blood pressure was elevated slightly, along with her pulse. Memories pounded in his head. How had they found themselves here again?

"It wasn't closure I was looking for back then," he said finally. "I just wanted things to work out between us."

"I'm not sure they would have no matter what happened.

We're both too stubborn for our own good. It never would have worked between us."

He wasn't sure he agreed. "I had planned to marry you, Felicia."

She nodded slowly, her eyelids drooping a little. "I asked you once why you didn't propose to me before the accident. Have you thought about why?"

"Yes. It just seemed like . . ." He shifted uncomfortably beside her. "The timing just never seemed right. We were both busy advancing our careers and working too many hours."

"Or maybe it was simply because on one level you knew we weren't right for each other."

He wasn't sure how to answer her. Maybe she was right. Maybe the closure he'd needed all this time was simply knowing she was okay, so they could both move on.

"I've accepted what happened, Jonas. It took me a long time, but I'm done living in the past and on what-ifs. And you need to do the same thing. Let the guilt go and start living again." Her lip quivered as she drew in a slow breath.

"Are you okay?" Jonas asked.

"Still feeling groggy and sore," she said.

"Do you want me to get one of the nurses?"

"No. I'll be fine."

He nodded. "Your grandmother told me you're working in intelligence now?"

"I am, and I started dating someone. His name is Rex. He's a veteran." She paused for a second. "I met him during rehabilitation. He lost a leg in Afghanistan. He understands me like I never thought anyone could."

"Do I need to get ahold of him?" Jonas asked.

"Grams already did. He's coming in on a red-eye." A soft

smile curled her lips. "Tell me about her. Looks to me like you have a thing for the woman you work with."

"Madison?" He shifted his attention to the floor. "It's complicated."

"Love shouldn't be complicated. We make it complicated. I saw the way you looked when you thought he was going to shoot her. You have feelings for her, don't you?"

Jonas didn't know how to respond to the turn in conversation. He was still trying to figure out what he felt about Madison. There was no way he was going to talk to Felicia about her.

She reached out and squeezed his hand again. "It's okay. I know you let go of me a long time ago, which is exactly what should have happened. But I've always wanted you to fall in love again. From the little I saw of her she seems beautiful, smart . . ." She yawned.

She needed some rest. He stood up, then glanced at the monitor. Her heart rate had dropped, and her face had paled.

"I'm going to leave now and let you get some sleep," he said.

She nodded. "I'm just so . . . tired."

"We'll talk later, okay?"

"Okay. Because someone's not after . . . not finished at the house. But I need to go . . ."

She was rambling, not making any sense. "Felicia, what's wrong? Can you hear me?"

Her eyes rolled back in her head and she started shaking.

"Nurse!" He ran to the hallway. "Help! I need someone in here now!"

A middle-aged woman in scrubs ran toward the room and pushed Jonas aside, then two more nurses joined her. He had no idea what was wrong, but he couldn't lose Felicia now. Not this way. She'd survived a bullet that took her leg. Made it through months of physical therapy. She was walking again with a prosthesis, but now all of this . . .

He glanced at the monitor. Someone yelled "Code!" The room started to spin around him. Machines beeped frantically. Someone shouted directions in the organized chaos. And Felicia . . . she wasn't moving.

"Sir, I need you to leave the room. Please."

"No . . . Tell me what's wrong with her."

He stumbled into the hallway without getting an answer. He'd been in this situation before. Moments after the raid went wrong and the ambulances arrived, he'd watched them load Felicia onto a gurney and take her away.

A voice in the chaos broke through his haze. "Time of death, 20:48."

Time of death?

His mind snapped back to the present as he tried to head back into the room. "What happened?"

Someone stopped him at the door, laying a hand on his shoulder. "Her heart stopped. I'm so sorry."

"She can't be gone." Panic washed over him as he tried to process what he'd just seen. "I was just talking to her. The surgery was successful."

The nurse nodded. "That's all I know, but I truly am sorry."

Time slowed as he walked back down the hallway. Death was something he'd been trained to deal with, but nothing could have prepared him for this.

✳ ✳ ✳

Jonas let the memories of him and Felicia flood him as he strode down the wide trail overlooking Elliott Bay. Myrtle Edwards Park and the path along the water had always been one of his favorite spots. Now it was the place he'd come to look for answers. Life had taken a shift when Felicia was shot the first time. And today, it had taken yet another unexpected turn. He'd spent the past thirty minutes praying for some kind of direction and clarity. An answer to why Felicia had died.

And yet for some reason all he could hear was silence.

The cool evening air slipped under his collar, but he barely felt the chill that settled through him. He couldn't erase the picture of Felicia surrounded by the code team trying to save her. The warning sound of machines. The shouts of the medical staff as they worked frantically to save her life. And then the deafening quiet when it was over. He'd seen Hazel's broken expression when he told her what had happened. He knew her faith would carry her through the darkness ahead, but that didn't mean the pain wouldn't engulf her. Or the questions wouldn't come as they had for him.

"This wasn't your fault. Just like my losing my leg was never your fault."

He moved out of the way for a couple runners. Felicia, it seemed, had been able to let go. But had he just found resolution with his relationship with her only for her to die? Maybe none of this had taken God by surprise, but that didn't stop the guilt from piling up.

Maybe Felicia was right. Maybe he hadn't asked her to marry him because he knew deep down that things would never work out between the two of them. And maybe he had tried too hard to fix things for her when all she really needed was for him to listen and be there.

His phone rang. He checked the caller ID, then shoved it back in his pocket. He knew Madison was worried about him, but he couldn't talk to her. Not yet. Michaels would have told her, but unwrapping how he felt and trying to put it into words wasn't possible.

Wind from the water whipped around him, sending another chill down his neck. Felicia had been right about something else as well. Madison had somehow managed to slip through the wall around his heart and made him want to consider something long-term with her. But as he'd learned with Felicia, he knew better now. Having a relationship with someone he worked with, someone who put their life on the line, was nothing more than a recipe for disaster. Just because they had their work in common didn't mean they were suited for each other. Still, if that was true, then why did being with Madison make him feel like he was ready to take a chance on falling in love again?

He sat down on one of the benches and stared out past the rocks along the shoreline. The gray water of the bay lapped up in small waves. On a clear day you could see the mountains in the distance, but tonight, darkness marred the view. Like the intense pain marring his heart. Right now, he'd shove aside whatever feelings he had for Madison to be dealt with later. Michaels might insist he take time off, but any grieving would have to wait. There were still two fugitives out there, and he wasn't going to stop looking until he found them.

THIRTEEN

Madison parked her car in the driveway of her sister's house, then shut off the engine. She'd already driven around for an hour, praying as she tried to figure out how to help Jonas. How to accept the fact he didn't want her help right now. The sun had set a few hours before, but she knew Danielle would still be up. Three kids six and under had taught her sister to grab every slice of quiet she could. Madison had heard her confess more than once how she loved late nights when she could curl up with a book or have an hour or two of uninterrupted time with her husband.

Madison shoved away any guilt from knowing she was bothering her sister and placed the call.

Danielle answered on the second ring. "Madison, hey . . . are you okay?"

"Yeah, I'm fine. Sorry. I know it's late, and you're probably exhausted, but I needed someone to talk to."

"Of course. Always. Do you want to come by?"

Madison hesitated. "I'm here, actually. In your driveway."

"I'm on my way downstairs now."

Clad in a pair of comfy pj's, Danielle was already waiting

by the open front door by the time Madison stepped onto the porch. Danielle pulled her into a hug before shutting the door behind them.

"Your timing's perfect," Danielle said, ushering Madison into the living room and picking up the toys scattered across the hardwood floor. "Ethan's still working, and the kids and Dad are asleep."

Madison stopped in the middle of the room. "Which means I'm totally interrupting your quiet time."

"Are you kidding? You're never an interruption. Are you hungry?"

The smell of spaghetti and garlic bread lingered in the air, but nothing sounded good to Madison. "Not really."

"What about some coffee or tea?"

"Do you still have some of that vanilla tea?"

Danielle grinned. "With milk?"

"Of course." Her sister knew her too well.

"Good, now go sit down on the couch and catch your breath while I get the water going."

"I can help."

Madison tried to follow her sister, but Danielle waved away the offer. "I can handle it. Go sit down, and I'll be right back."

Too tired to argue, Madison sank into the couch and pulled her legs up under her. Maybe coming had been the right decision, after all. She leaned back, closed her eyes, and took in a long, slow breath, wishing she could still the anxiety churning in her gut. She knew Jonas would be okay, but she hated knowing how much he was hurting, especially since she wasn't able to do anything.

"Aunt Maddie?"

Madison opened her eyes as her six-year-old niece plopped down on the couch next to her.

"I didn't know you were here," Lilly said.

Madison grinned and pulled her closer. "And I didn't know you were still up, you little munchkin."

Lilly gave an exaggerated sigh. "I can't sleep."

Join the club.

"I'm sorry. Are you worried about something?"

"Not really." Lilly lowered her voice. "It's Sophie. I'm six years old and still have to share a room. She's messy, stinky, and only three."

"Oh . . . I see." Madison stifled a laugh. "I had to share a room with your mother until I was twelve."

"Twelve?" Lilly looked disgusted. Apparently the thought of waiting that long to get her own room was one of the most awful things she could imagine.

"You do know that being the older sister comes with a lot of benefits."

Lilly rolled her eyes. "I'm not sure what."

"For one, Sophie looks up to you."

"How do you know that?"

"Because even though I probably never would have admitted it, I definitely looked up to your mother growing up. And there were times when I even wished I could be just like her."

Lilly still didn't look convinced. "Well . . . You didn't have Sophie."

"No, I didn't. There were also times when your mother just plain irritated me."

Lilly's blue eyes widened as she stared back at Madison. "How?"

"For example, she was the oldest and she got everything

before I did. She got her ears pierced, a new bike . . . I was the one who always had to wait."

"Sophie makes the room a mess and keeps getting into my stuff."

"But," Madison said, pretending not to hear the complaint in an effort to stay positive, "your mother also looked after me. In fact, she still does. And that, in my opinion, is the most important job of an older sister."

Lilly tilted her head, clearly processing what she was hearing. "It just seems like someone with an important job should get their own room. We have an extra room for guests."

Madison took a moment to think through her next line of reasoning. "I also remember feeling safe at night, knowing my sister was in the bed next to me. I have a feeling Sophie sleeps better knowing that as well."

Lilly's nose scrunched. "Maybe."

"Young lady." Danielle stepped into the living room, carrying two cups of steaming tea. "What are you doing out of bed?"

Madison jumped to her niece's defense. "We were just talking about the important role of an older sister."

"Really?" Danielle's gaze shifted from Madison to Lilly before she set one of the cups on the end table next to Madison. "And what role would that be?"

"Aunt Maddie says that when you shared a room, she always felt safer at night because you were there."

Danielle's eyes widened as she joined them on the couch. "She did now?"

"I might never have admitted it back then," Madison said, picking up her tea and blowing on it before taking a sip. "But it's true."

"There are definitely advantages to being the oldest." Danielle kissed Lilly on the forehead. "One of which is that you get to stay up later than your younger sister."

"I suppose."

"The downside is, you're six and still have a bedtime." Danielle smiled.

"But—"

"No buts," she said, scooting Lilly off the couch.

The little girl frowned. "Yes, ma'am."

"Give your aunt a kiss, and I will see you bright and early in the morning."

Danielle waited until Lilly had disappeared up the stairs before turning back to Madison. "I have to say, I don't remember you ever acting grateful to have me in the same room as you. In fact, I remember you getting in trouble for making a line down the middle of the room with nail polish. Bright red polish, if I remember correctly."

Madison shook her head. "You would have to go there."

"You're the one that brought up the 'I felt safer when my sister was in the same room as I was.'"

"I was trying to help, and there were nights—one or two—when I woke up from a bad dream and I was glad you were there. Honest."

Danielle picked up her tea and cupped it between her hands. "While I'm happy to see you, I get the feeling that you're not here because you were feeling social."

"Not really. I guess all these years later I still need my big sister when I'm having a rough day."

"So what's going on? I thought about you a lot today with this being your first day back on the job. You look exhausted."

"It has nothing to do with my first day back." Madison's breath caught. "There was a shooting at a clinic today."

"Wait . . ." Danielle leaned forward. "I heard about that on the news, but I didn't know you were involved. I'm so sorry."

"Me too."

"What happened?"

Madison took another sip of her drink, still trying to process everything that had happened, but the day's events just continued to swirl around her like one big nightmare. "It was connected to a bank robbery this morning. Long story short, two innocent people are dead."

"It sounds personal."

Madison's breath caught. "One of the people who died was a friend of Jonas."

Danielle blinked slowly. "Wow . . . I'm sorry."

Madison ran her finger around the rim of the mug. "Felicia was shot in the cross fire. There were complications after she got out of surgery, and she didn't make it."

"Wait a minute." Danielle set down her drink. "I remember you mentioning a woman named Felicia. Wasn't she an old girlfriend of his?"

"He was planning to propose to her, but things have been over between them for a very long time." Madison looked up at her sister. "She saved my life, Danielle. If she hadn't, I'd be the one lying in that morgue today. And now . . . I just didn't think it could shake me up so badly."

"I don't know what to say. It's why I hate your job, and yet I know how much good you do at the same time. I don't know. Sometimes I'm not sure it's worth it."

Madison sipped her drink, trying to find a way to put her feelings into words. "Most days I can handle it, but today was hard."

"And it reminds you about Luke."

"Yeah."

Her sister always had been able to express what she was feeling so clearly. Luke's death had pushed her into a place she'd never wish on anyone. One where she'd barely been able to get through each day. Not that she was fully finished grieving, but the days where the pain reared its ugly head were fewer and farther between. She'd come to the conclusion that those days would always be a part of the fabric of who she was, and that was okay. But watching someone else deal with fresh grief always managed to dig up her own reservoir of pain.

"How is Jonas?" Danielle asked, breaking Madison out of her haze.

"I'm not sure. Still in shock, I guess. Angry."

"I don't blame him."

"I know." She took another sip of tea. "Or at least my head knows. This just hit him really hard."

"Have you talked to him?"

"Not really." Madison wiped away an uninvited tear, hating how emotional she felt. She'd learned to keep her emotions separate from her job, but today, all her defenses had broken down. "He's not answering my calls, and I have no idea how to help him."

"You really care for him."

"Of course. He's my partner."

"I mean on a personal level. The two of you have spent a lot of time together over the past few months. It would be normal for feelings to develop."

Madison pushed back the familiar irritation. "Don't go there again, Danielle. Please. There's nothing between us. I respect him highly as a marshal and we're friends, but that's all."

"So you haven't noticed that he's drop-dead gorgeous with

those dreamy eyes of his, or that he happens to be single and available?"

"Danielle," Madison drew out her sister's name, rolling her eyes.

"I'm sorry. I know that now isn't the time to push that narrative, but I just want to see you happy. And from what I've seen, he makes you happy."

"We're just friends. I'm not interested in something complicated that could interfere with my job. And becoming romantically involved with Jonas would definitely interfere with my job."

And my heart.

She shook off the thought. Danielle was wrong.

"All I know is that Luke's been gone over five years," Danielle said. "I know there is no time frame for grief, but maybe it's time you let go and see what's out there. If not with Jonas, then with someone else."

Madison clenched her jaw. She should have known that coming here held the risk of her sister playing matchmaker, but there were no romantic feelings between her and Jonas. She cared about him. Respected him as a partner, but beyond that she felt nothing. Besides, she'd fortified the wall around her heart after Luke died, and letting someone else in—especially her partner—wasn't going to happen.

She sipped at her tea as a revelation swept through her. Maybe she was doing the same thing she was upset at Jonas for doing today. Pushing him away because she was terrified of losing someone again. Because if she was honest with herself, she'd seen the shift in the way he looked at her, but instead of exploring the possibility, she'd fought against opening her heart. Because she knew what it was like to love and to lose, and exposing her heart again fought against every instinct inside her.

"Sometimes I forget you studied psychology until you wow me with your insight," Madison said, grinning. But the smile quickly faded. "The bottom line is that I don't know how to help him through this."

"Actually, I think you, more than anyone I know, can understand what he's feeling. Just remember people deal with grief in different ways. Give him space when he needs it, and if he needs you, be there for him. Just like I know you will be."

Madison took the last couple sips of her tea, knowing the advice was spot-on. She just needed to be patient. "I need to go. I promised my boss I'd get some sleep. Plus, I know you're tired and have to get up early."

Danielle waved away the concern. "At this point, I'm convinced I'll never have another good night's sleep. In about an hour, the baby will wake up starving, then if I'm lucky, I won't be disturbed until morning. That is, unless he decides he needs a middle-of-the-night snack that only his mama can provide, or if Sophie has a bad dream or needs help to flush the toilet at three in the morning."

Madison laughed. "You're a great mom."

"I try, and I love every minute of it, except when I feel like I'm losing my mind from lack of sleep." Danielle yawned as if to emphasize the point.

"Perfectly normal, I'm sure."

"Listen, we don't have to solve the world's—or our—problems tonight. Why don't you stay here? The guest bedroom is ready, with an extra toothbrush and pajamas in the drawer."

"I don't want to impose."

"You're my sister. Since when are you an imposition? Plus,

Ethan's making blueberry pancakes in the morning, and I promise you don't want to miss those."

"Now that's tempting." As was the thought of company and the security of family after this hectic day.

"He goes in late tomorrow, so we might even be able to catch a run together if you don't have to go in too early."

"I might be able to handle that."

Danielle squeezed Madison's hand. "I know this is hard on so many levels, but Jonas will be okay. He'll come to you when he's ready."

Madison nodded, feeling a thin layer of peace settle over her. "Thank you."

"What are big sisters for? And on top of that, you know I'm praying for you."

"It's probably what kept me alive today."

"Just get a good night's sleep and promise me you'll try to stay out of the path of any stray bullets. I almost lost you once. I don't want to come that close again. Ever."

Madison nodded.

Danielle got up from the couch and gathered their mugs. "I'll go get you a towel. Let me know if there's anything else you need."

Madison pulled out her phone as she stood up. She sighed. There were no messages from Jonas.

FOURTEEN

L ocal law enforcement is asking the public for help in identifying two suspects—one male and one female—in connection with a recent rash of bank robberies across the state. Another bank was robbed today, leading to a string of events that left two people dead and a chase—"

Jonas hit mute on the office TV as a freeze-frame of a security footage shot appeared on the screen in the corner of the room. While the photo was grainy, it had been decided that involving the public in the search for the two suspects was worth any risks. But he didn't need to hear the news to be reminded that two people were dead.

That Felicia was dead.

He still felt numb but giving in to that numbness wouldn't help him find their other two fugitives. He'd deal with the grief later. Right now he had a job to do. Tips had already begun to come in. Most of them would come from people simply hoping for the reward money, but that didn't mean that one of their tips wouldn't pan out. With Kira still not talking, they were going to have to broaden their circle. Piper had screened the calls, so he could follow up on any that seemed promising. All they needed was one hit in the right direction.

Michaels stepped into the room, breaking his train of thought. "Did Madison go home?"

"Far as I know." Jonas shrugged. "I haven't seen her."

He frowned at the guilt that surfaced over the way he'd pushed her away. He needed to call her back, but he just wasn't in the headspace to answer the questions he knew she was going to ask him.

"She had the right idea. It's late," Michaels said. "I want you to go home, eat something, and get some sleep. We've got every officer in the state looking for them right now, which means they have nowhere to go. We will find them."

"With only a vague description pulled off a grainy photo?" Jonas arched his brows. "That isn't enough, and you know it. I'm just going through the tip list and following up on calls."

Michaels crossed his arms over his chest. "In case you missed it, that wasn't a suggestion. It's an order. It's that, or I will pull you off this case completely, which is probably what I should do anyway."

"Michaels—"

"Try me. You know I can, and I will." The older man sat down on the edge of the desk. "Listen, I know this has been a rough day for you, and I'm sorry."

"I promise I'm only going to make one more call, and then I'll be out the door."

"Good, because as I recall, you were the one who came to me worried about Madison coming back to work too soon because of emotional entanglements."

"Felicia was a friend, that is true, but anything that was between us was over a long time ago."

"Maybe, but that doesn't change the fact that someone you cared about was shot in front of you. I've scheduled you to see the grief counselor once this is wrapped up, but if I don't feel like you're able to handle things, I will pull you off this case."

"Fine."

"I'll see you tomorrow."

Jonas rubbed the back of his neck as Michaels walked away. His boss was right. He needed to get out of here and clear his head. From the back of his neck up to his temples was throbbing. But a bite to eat and a good night's sleep wouldn't change the fact that Felicia was dead.

And then there was Madison.

He never should have pushed her away, but the events of the day had reminded him just how high the stakes were. He'd lost Felicia long before she'd died. And now, he had no idea how to deal with how he felt toward Madison on top of everything that had happened today. Which was why he'd ended up bungling everything again. But whatever he was feeling didn't matter. He'd made the rule to never get involved with a coworker after Felicia broke things off between them, and after today, he was determined not to cross that line again. Feelings or not.

He grabbed a couple pain pills out of the top drawer of his desk and swallowed them dry. He would call Madison, but right now, he couldn't worry about her. He'd have time to fix things later. What mattered was finding the people behind Felicia's death. Ben Galvan might have been the one who pulled the trigger, but as far as he was concerned, all four of them were responsible. And even if this was the only thing he could do, he owed it to Felicia to put all of them behind bars.

He glanced at the clock as he picked up his phone. So far, every call he'd made from the tip line had ended up as nothing more than a wild-goose chase. People who thought they might have seen someone or something. No details. No way to really follow up. He'd make one more call like he'd promised Michaels, then leave.

"This is Deputy US Marshal Jonas Quinn," he said as soon as someone picked up the line. "I'm calling about a tip Sam Spade phoned in this evening. Is this him?"

There was a long pause on the line.

"Hello?" Jonas said. "Sam?"

"I . . . yeah . . . I called, but I don't think—"

"Sam, wait. Please . . . don't hang up." Jonas gentled his tone. "I have a note here that you believe you know the man in the photo from a bank robbery this morning. If that is true, I really need your help."

"Listen, I want to help, but the photo's a bit grainy, and the more I think about it, I just can't be sure."

"Can you at least give me a name for us to follow up on?" There was another long pause. Jonas decided to take another route. "Can you tell me how you know him?"

"If it's him, we used to go to school together. It also looked like the guy in the photo has a tattoo. The guy I'm thinking of has a tattoo of a compass and forest on his wrist and forearm."

Jonas's heart skipped a beat as he zoomed in closer on the photo. Bart Wells had mentioned something about a tattoo on one of the fugitives.

For the first time in hours, Jonas felt a thread of hope run through him. He decided to push his luck. "What about the woman?"

"It's hard to tell, but I'm pretty sure I've never seen her."

"Listen . . . Sam," Jonas said. "I'd like to meet with you. Ask a few more questions. I really need to find the man in this photo. Two people are dead because of what happened today—"

"I know, but I think this was a mistake."

"Sam, wait . . . Please . . ." He couldn't lose the most promising lead he'd had all night. "It sounds like you were friends with him, which can make it hard, but it's very important that we find the man in the photo."

"The news said he robbed some banks."

"Does that fit your friend's character?"

"I don't know." Another pause. "Maybe."

"We can meet somewhere neutral," Jonas said. "You choose."

"If I'm wrong, I don't want to drag in the wrong person."

Sam was nervous. Jonas could hear it in his voice. It wasn't the first time he'd encountered a scared witness. And yet he couldn't let the guy go without getting at least a name. It would be even better if he could help him figure out where the suspect might be.

"Listen, Sam. Here's what I can promise you. Your friend will be brought in as a person of interest. Nothing more unless we can verify it's him. But we need to talk with him."

"Fine. There's this place I hang out at sometimes. I'll text the address to the tip line."

Jonas waited for the ding that verified Sam's message, then blew out a breath of air. "I'll be there in twenty minutes."

✳ ✳ ✳

Fifteen minutes later, Jonas slipped out of the car. The glowing sign across the street marked a karaoke and sports bar. Michaels had been right about one thing—he needed to eat. Maybe he'd combine the interview with a late dinner.

The lamppost above his car was broken, leaving dark shadows from the lights across the street that seemed to swallow the empty road. His phone went off and he checked his messages. Madison. He hesitated, dropped the phone back into his pocket, and crossed the street. Someone whistled behind him, and he turned around. Four punks wearing hoodies had formed a half circle behind him.

You've got to be kidding.

"You're making a mistake," Jonas said. "I'm—"

One of them took a step forward, pulling a gun out and pointing it at him. "We don't care who you are unless you want to try and take on all four of us. Just hand over your wallet and keys, and we'll be on our way."

"You know, I have to say that it really isn't a good time to question my thoughts on humanity." Jonas didn't even try to press down the wave of anger. "I've already had a gun pointed in my face twice, and watched a friend die, so I've had enough for one day."

"Don't really care about your day, man." The stranger turned the barrel of his gun sideways while the others snickered. "Just hand over your stuff."

Jonas pulled out his own weapon and aimed it back at the speaker before any of them could react. "Either you put the weapon on the ground now, and all four of you get on your knees, or I'll blast a bullet in your kneecaps." Shock kept the men in place, so Jonas repeated himself. "All four of you! And I promise I know what I'm doing. I train cops. I can shoot four rounds faster than you can get off one."

He studied their surprised expressions. It might have been a slight exaggeration on his abilities, but he was too tired to quibble over details. He had no doubt he could take down at least three.

The guy on the far left looked at his buddy with the gun, worry crossing his face. "He's a cop, Baxter."

"No," Jonas said. "I'm a Deputy US Marshal. And I'm giving you to the count of three to do as you were told."

He started counting. At two they glanced at each other. At three the leader set the gun on the ground, and they started dropping to their knees.

"Sorry," Baxter said. "We didn't know who you were."

Jonas motioned for the tallest to hand over his bandana. He laid it on the ground in front of them. "Shouldn't matter who I am. Put your cell phones and any other weapons on the ground. Now."

"Forget it, man—" Baxter said.

"My earlier offer's still open . . ."

They exchanged glances, then started complying. "Fine."

"Now you're all going to walk away." He picked up the bandana full of weapons and phones. "You can retrieve your belongings at the district office on Eighth and Stewart."

"What?"

Jonas ignored the protests and walked into the diner. Except for the music playing too loud, inside was fairly quiet for a weeknight. It took him about five seconds to eliminate everyone in the room except a twentysomething who was nursing a cup of coffee at a table by himself.

Jonas walked to the back of the room, ignoring the feeling that everyone was staring at him. "Sam Spade?"

The young man nodded, and Jonas dumped the bandana on the seat, then slid into the booth. "I wasn't sure you were going to show up," Jonas said.

"I almost didn't, but I don't know." He shrugged. "It seemed like the right thing to do."

"It was."

Sam glanced at the rest of the tables. "The whole restaurant saw what you just did out the window."

Great.

"Just doing my job."

"No, man . . . that's not just a job. You're like . . . you're like a superhero. I grew up with those guys. They're always causing trouble. They've been plaguing this neighborhood for as long as I can remember."

Jonas shrugged off the compliment. "Superhero might be taking it a bit too far."

Felicia had called him that once. Her superhero. They'd laughed at the time. Then he'd learned that even a superhero couldn't always fix things.

"I'm going to assume that Sam Spade isn't your real name," he said.

"My mom's big on old detective movies. It was the first thing that came to my mind. My name's really Matt. I'm sorry."

"Well, I appreciate your agreeing to meet me anyway." Jonas dropped the photo from the security footage on the table in front of them. "So you recognize this man?"

Matt took a sip of his coffee, then picked the photo up. "That's definitely him. Jesse Archer."

"Okay . . . and you said you knew him from school?"

"From high school. We were both on the football team. Used to hang out some."

"What can you tell me about him?"

Matt stared down at his coffee. "He was always cocky. Loud. Popular, and surprisingly did well in school, though I know he didn't want people to know he cared. After school we went our separate ways."

"Have you seen him since then?"

"A few weeks ago, he was back here in this neighborhood for his grandmother's funeral. He hadn't changed at all. He's still loud and obnoxious."

"Do you know where he works?"

"No." Matt's gaze shifted. "I did hear a rumor or two after the funeral."

Jonas leaned forward. "What kind of rumors?"

"Rumors that he'd been bragging about something big he was involved in."

"Like a bank robbery?"

Matt moved his head from side to side for a second. "That wouldn't have been my first thought, but it's possible."

The fact that Jesse Archer was having a hard time keeping things quiet didn't surprise Jonas. Whoever was behind the robberies had gotten away with thousands of dollars of cash and, until today, hadn't gotten caught. At some point, they were going to have a hard time keeping this winning streak a secret. Especially if it was a game to them.

Jonas looked at the kid. He seemed conflicted and Jonas needed more out of him. Maybe he'd give up more info if he felt comfortable? "Why did you hesitate to talk to me?"

"I keep asking myself that same question, and honestly I don't know. Jesse always had this cocky attitude that annoyed me. Always thought he was better than anyone. Back in high school, he was a bully and got away with it. He wasn't someone you wanted to cross. At least back then."

"So this is personal?"

"I don't know if I'd call it personal." Matt rolled his shoulders forward. "I honestly haven't thought about the guy for years. But I also wouldn't mind it if he finally got what was coming to him. Especially since two people are dead. I figure I'm probably not the only one who recognized him, but what if I was the only one who actually called in?"

"And you said you didn't know who he was with?"

"I'm sure it's him, but no . . . I'm not sure."

"Do you know if he's dating anyone?"

"I met his girlfriend when he was in town for the funeral. Nadine . . . No. I think it was Nadia. Yeah, that's right." He picked up the photo again. "It could be her, but the photo's just too grainy to recognize who he's with."

"That's okay." Jonas had one last question before he left. "Can you tell me where you were this morning around nine o'clock?"

"Sure. I'm a bicycle messenger. I clocked in to work at eight and went out for my first delivery and was back at the office for a second pickup about nine. I can give you my boss's number."

"Thanks. I'll check it out."

He knew the fugitives were risk-takers, so he hadn't dismissed the thought that one of them had called in a tip in an attempt to figure out exactly what the police knew.

Jonas handed Matt his card. "If you think of anything else, or if you happen to hear from Jesse, give me a call."

FIFTEEN

Madison woke with a start from a bad dream, then rolled over onto her back and stared at the ceiling. Perspiration beaded across her forehead as details of yesterday—worse than the dream she'd just awoken from— hit her like a punch to the gut. How could so much have gone wrong in the first twenty-four hours back on the job?

She grabbed for her phone on the bedside table and glanced at the time. Four forty-five. And still no messages from Jonas or any hits on their BOLO. She drew in a deep breath, trying to push away the anxiety. Exhaustion weighed her down. She'd tossed and turned all night while her mind refused to stop racing, but she'd never get back to sleep now.

She stared at the screen of her phone, debating whether she should call Jonas. She knew he'd be okay. He was strong, and Danielle was right. When he was ready, he would call her. And if she were honest with herself, she couldn't blame him for needing to deal with things on his own first. Hadn't she spent the past five years doing just that? Letting people help her deal with the pain had always been a struggle for her. For now, she was going to have to take her own advice, pray, and let God do the rest. Which wasn't easy for someone used to diving in and finding the solution on her own.

She clicked on the bedside lamp, then sat up and pulled her computer off the nightstand. She'd ended up staying awake well past midnight, going through the Facebook friends Piper had compiled from Ben's and Kira's profiles, then systematically eliminating as many as she could. She'd whittled the list down so that it only included friends currently living in Seattle and those who'd gone to school with Ben and Kira. The grainy photo they'd pulled would help narrow the list even further.

She typed in another name. It always seemed foolish to her, but social media had become more and more crucial to their investigations over the past few years. And with Kira still refusing to divulge names, and Ben in the ICU, they were going to have to search for the answers they needed outside the box.

The About page on this woman's profile listed work and education, places she'd lived, and details about family and relationships. College education matched Ben and Kira's, but a quick look at the time line showed that she was currently in Portland visiting her sister, who'd just had a baby. The fact that Madison discovered all of that information in a span of sixty seconds was frightening. But at least she was able to cross another name off the list.

She moved on to the next person. Their window of opportunity to find the remaining fugitives was quickly closing. They were already looking at an eighteen-hour lead. Forged passports could have taken them across the border, or they could have gone into hiding. How hard would it be to disappear in a city with a population of over three million if you'd planned ahead?

She skimmed through the next Facebook page, looking for clues that might connect the woman to the robberies. The team they had put together was smart. There was no doubt about that. But there was something else that had Madison worried. All four were adrenaline junkies. They had defied the odds of getting caught and continued robbing banks across the state. In turn, it had left them feeling invincible.

But despite that belief, they'd also prepared for a worst-case scenario. A scenario they'd had to play out the day before. In case the cops showed up, they had a well-thought-out exit plan that included smoke bombs and taking hostages, and they clearly weren't afraid to use their weapons. If they'd risked everything to escape the bank, how much would they risk to ensure they didn't get caught? For Ben, it had meant taking another hostage at the clinic and shooting someone in the process. For Kira, it had meant refusing to tell them who her other teammates were. They were cocky and reckless but also determined to win at all costs. Something Jonas and she better remember as they hunted them down.

Questions continued to pile up as she continued down the list. What motivated these four to risk everything when the cost of failure was so high? Could it really be all for the shot of adrenaline that came with seeing how far they could go?

A noise coming from the main part of the house shifted her attention momentarily. More than likely, Danielle was up with the baby. Either way, Madison needed coffee if she was going to make it through another day. She slipped on a pair of house shoes sitting next to the bed, then headed for the kitchen.

Her father stood by the counter with a cup of tea steeping beside him. His look of confusion at seeing Madison in Danielle's house was quickly replaced by a warm smile.

"You spent the night?" he asked.

She nodded as she crossed the kitchen. "What are you doing up so early?"

"I couldn't sleep, but it looks like I'm not the only one."

She hugged him tightly and breathed in the familiar scent of Old Spice. Knowing he had Alzheimer's was hard for her to accept, but life moved forward with the seasons. He'd always been the one who was there for her, supportive and encouraging no matter what life threw at her. Now their roles had shifted, and she was the one sharing the role of parent with her sister.

"Danielle said you went back to work yesterday," he said, pulling the honey out of the cupboard before squeezing it into his tea. "I'm going to miss you spending time here."

"I promise I'll still come by as much as I can." She was surprised he remembered. Surprised how much it hurt her heart that he was slowly forgetting threads of his life and eventually he would be unable to remember who she was.

"How was your first day back?" he asked, stirring his tea. "I went to bed early last night. I didn't know you were coming over, or I would have stayed up."

She grabbed a coffee pod out of the drawer, then checked to make sure the water in the machine was full and a mug was centered before popping it in and pushing start. "We're in the middle of a case and things aren't going too well."

"I'm sorry," he said, patting her hand on the counter.

"Me too. My partner lost a close friend yesterday, and now he's not responding to my messages."

"That's why you spent the night here?"

She nodded. She felt guilty about dumping her problems onto her father, who didn't need to be bogged down with extra stress. At least he probably wouldn't remember it tomorrow.

"I'm sorry," he said. "It's hard to lose someone you love. I know."

"You mean Mama?"

He nodded. "My biggest fear is that I'm going to forget her. I don't want to forget her."

"I know." She squeezed her father's hand. "Remember I told you she will always be in your heart. The two of you were so close. That won't go away."

"I'm trying to hold on to that," he said. "And when I can't remember what her face looks like, I look at her picture."

He sighed, then looked at his youngest daughter. "You know what it's like to lose someone you love. It's like a piece of you is missing, isn't it?"

She leaned against the counter while the coffee maker gurgled in the background. "Yes, and I know it always will. But just like you, I'm trying to keep moving forward. It's just hard sometimes."

"Maybe moving forward isn't all it's cracked up to be," he said.

Madison scrunched her brows together. "How so?"

Her father took a moment to dump his tea bag into the trash, then took a sip from his mug. "A year or so after your mother died, everyone started telling me it was time to move forward. It was as if I was supposed to leave her and everything we had been together, and simply walk away. But I realized that grief and healing didn't mean hiding that part of my life away in a box and moving on to a place where it didn't affect me anymore."

Madison grabbed the cream out of the fridge and poured some into her coffee. "Because that part of your life can't just be packed up and stored away."

"Exactly. Your mother was an integral part of my life, and she made me who I am today. It's no different with you and

Luke. You can't just take off that part of your life, put it in a box, and move on. Life doesn't work that way. Luke will always be a part of the fabric of who you are, and that's okay." He moved slowly toward the kitchen table, mug in hand. "You will never be able to move on like it didn't happen. But it doesn't mean you can't fall in love again."

She smiled, wanting to grab on to these moments of clarity when she could almost forget the diagnosis that had changed the way she viewed her father's strength. "I think I'm beginning to see that I can move ahead without him, knowing he will always be a part of me, and that's okay."

"Exactly." Her father set his drink on the table and sat down. "And there is one other thing. You are not your sister. I want you to remember that."

Madison sat down across from him. "What do you mean?"

"I've seen you interact with your sister and her kids. Sometimes I think you look at her and wish you had what she had. A husband, children, a house full of noise." He let out a low laugh. "Maybe not the noise part, but someone to come home to at night when you get off work."

She frowned, not sure she wanted to go in the direction he was steering the conversation. "I'm not sure that will ever happen again, and I think I'm okay with that. At least most of the time I am. Moving on also doesn't mean that I have to get married again to be happy, Daddy."

"The funny thing is that I think Danielle sometimes wishes she had what you have. A career that challenges and pushes her. Instead she spends her days cleaning toilets and wiping noses. I'm not saying she doesn't love those grandbabies of mine or that what she does isn't important, because it is. I just know how easy it is to believe that the grass really is greener—and easier to manage—on the other side. Truth is, it isn't."

"Maybe. I don't know that I ever really took the time to think about it."

"The two of you have always been different. She was more of a nurturer with her dolls and stuffed animals, and you always wanted to be in on the action, no matter if it was a bike race around the block or a ski trip up to the mountains."

"We had a lot of good times, didn't we?" Madison took a sip of her coffee.

"Yes, and while I might be slowing down, I'm not done with life yet." He grinned before taking another sip of his tea. "I want you to keep believing in yourself. Run the race that the good Lord set out for you to run."

A comfortable silence settled between them for a few moments. "But if you did decide to get married again . . ."

Madison laughed. "Maybe one day, but you were right about my having a different race to run, and I'm just now finding some peace in the place I'm at right now." She pulled her mug toward her. "And maybe that's exactly where I need to be. Maybe that's all I need."

"I was married to your mother for forty-seven years. They were some of the best and some of the toughest years of my life, but we did it together."

"I just always imagined Luke and I doing life together and growing old together like you and Mama." She took another sip of her coffee. "But I have good people around me. People I love and care about. You, Danielle, her family, my church family."

"Maybe that's enough for you. I just don't want you to hold back because of fear."

The contents of her stomach soured, swirling chaotically.

Fear of losing someone again. It was a legitimate concern that had been reinforced yesterday with Felicia.

"Did you ever think of marrying again?" she asked.

"We talked about it once—your mother and I—before she died. She told me she wanted me to be happy and if that meant marrying again, that's what she wanted for me. But being thirty-something and sixtysomething is completely different. All I know is that for me, one love was enough."

"I know several widows and widowers who married in their eighties and never regretted it."

Her father's smile faded. "Were their minds failing like mine?"

Madison caught the fear in her father's eyes. Knowing where he was headed—at least for the moment—was part of what made the disease so frustrating.

"I'm sorry."

"Don't be sorry." He patted her arm gently. "I'm not. I've been blessed with a long marriage, two beautiful girls, and three grandchildren, though I have been hoping for more. And as for you, just don't close yourself off to possibilities."

Someday. First she needed to find closure with Luke. Needed to get past the wall that was blocking the memories that refused to surface. And after that? After that, she still wasn't sure.

"People always do tend to stay where they feel safe. Just don't get too comfortable. Take a risk or two. That's all I'm saying."

She took her father's hand and shook her head. "If you knew everything I had to do over the past twenty-four hours, I don't think you'd be asking me to take any risks."

"Just think about it." He squeezed her hand, then stood up. "I think I'll make myself some tea, then go watch some TV."

Madison glanced at the near-full mug of tea still sitting on the table. How long would it be before he couldn't remember how to make his own tea? How long before he couldn't remember her name?

She pushed away the thoughts, then carried the cup to the counter, where her father was standing in front of the cupboard. "Do you still want your tea, Daddy?"

He shook his head, then kissed her on the forehead. "I think I'll just go back to bed."

She watched him start down the hallway to his room and pushed back the emotions that threatened to erupt. She finished the last of her coffee, then forced her mind to shift back to their fugitives. Her best plan at the moment was to continue going through the list Piper had sent her so they could start tracking them down.

Her phone rang and she grabbed it out of her pocket.

Jonas.

Madison stepped out onto the back patio where she could see the first hints of light from the sunrise. She took a deep breath and answered the call. "Hey. Are you okay?"

"Yeah. I'm fine. I'm sorry to be calling you so early. Were you up?"

"It's fine. I'm up." She tried to interpret the tone of his voice but couldn't. "I tried to call you last night. I've been worried."

"I know, and I'm sorry I didn't pick up." He sighed. "I needed some time to clear my head."

"I understand."

There was a short pause on the line. "How long until you can get down to the office?" he asked.

"I don't know." She ran her fingers through her hair. What had he been doing all night? "Thirty . . . forty minutes, depending on traffic, I guess. What's going on?"

"I've got the ID of one of our suspects."

SIXTEEN

Jonas was sitting at his computer inside the US Marshals headquarters when Madison walked into the dimly lit space. He shifted his attention from the security footage he'd been going through on his computer and looked up at her. He could see the marked fatigue in her eyes and wondered if she'd gotten any more sleep than he had last night. Which only made him feel more guilty.

He should have called her back. Should have answered her texts. Instead he'd found himself battling to make sense of the nightmare he'd just been thrown into. But none of it was her fault, and he didn't want her to think that he blamed her for what had happened.

"Hey." She set a takeaway bag along with a drink carrier on the desk in front of him. "I wasn't sure when you ate last, so I figured it was only fair that I return the favor. At this time of the morning, though, you'll have to settle for fast food and coffee."

He forced a smile, not wanting to tell her that he'd ended up skipping dinner last night and still didn't have an appetite this morning. "I appreciate it. And thanks for coming in so early. I'm sorry if I woke you up."

"You didn't, and it's not a problem." She slid into the chair across from him. "Did you get any sleep last night? I know I didn't get much."

"Not a whole lot, though the food and coffee will help." He leaned across the desk and picked up one of the cups. "Did you get anything out of your interview with Brandon?"

"No, but I don't think he knows anything else."

She glanced across the room that held a smattering of empty desks that would be filled in a couple hours. "Honestly, I'm surprised Michaels is still allowing you to work the case. Did you update him?"

"I've spoken with him." Jonas dumped two packages of sugar into his coffee, then reached for a stirrer. "There will be more to process later, but I've given my statement and filled out a bunch of paperwork. He understands that there's no way I can sit at home. I've been digging through security footage from the Pike Place Market."

"You said you have a name?"

"A name and a face." He took a sip of the coffee, then slid the photo he'd pulled from the DMV across his desk. "I spoke with someone who identified the man in the security photo. His name is Jesse Archer."

Madison met his gaze. "A legitimate source?"

"Check it out for yourself." He motioned toward the picture. "It's definitely him."

She reached for the photo they'd pulled from the security video and laid it beside the one from the DMV. "It definitely looks like a match. Similar build, hair style—"

"And my source said Archer has a tattoo on his arm." Jonas tapped on the photo. "That matches the ID we got from the witness at the bank."

Madison leaned back, a contemplative look crossing her face. "What do you know about this guy?"

"He has a record, though just a handful of misdemeanors. He never ended up serving any time. And from the information I have, he's currently unemployed."

"Interesting." She pulled a breakfast burrito from the takeaway bag, then peeled off the wrapper and took a bite. "Do we have an address for him?"

"That's our first problem. The address on his driver's license is outdated."

"You're sure?" she asked after swallowing another bite.

"I went there myself early this morning. It was the address for his grandmother, who passed away recently. According to a neighbor who was coming back from a run, he used to live there, but it's been at least a year. I've got someone trying to track him down, and in the meantime, I've been going through traffic cams, trying to see if I can establish how they left. By car, public transportation . . ."

"And?" she asked.

"So far I haven't found anything. They seem to have simply vanished."

"We know that didn't happen." Madison picked up her coffee, then took a big sip. "What about the storage unit receipt we found at Kira's place?"

"We haven't been able to reach the unit owners to verify the unit number."

She rocked forward in her chair. "So we have no way of knowing how the storage unit and key are connected, or even if they are?"

"No, but we do have a patrol car surveying the location just in case they decide to show up."

She shook her head. "I think they're long gone. They're not going to wait around here where every law enforcement officer is looking for them."

"Maybe, but my gut tells me they're lying low. They know that both Ben and Kira are in custody. Maybe they assume that their friends threw the pact out the window and turned in their names, and that the police are looking for them. How hard would it be to disappear in a city of millions until they can get what they need together—like passports and money?"

Madison shook her head again, clearly not convinced. "They've had a plan every step of the way. Why wouldn't they have one now? A few fake passports and IDs, and they could be across the border before anyone even knows who they are."

"I might agree, except these guys were cocky. I don't think they planned where they were going, because I don't think they believed they needed an exit strategy."

"And yet, Kira said they made a pact if one of them was caught. They'd at least thought that far ahead."

He nodded, but he could still sense the doubt in her expression. Tracking down people was what they did. They would keep searching until they found them.

"We both know that speculating isn't going to get us any-where." She took a sip of her coffee, then set it back down on the table and started gathering the trash from their breakfast into a pile without mentioning that he'd barely touched his. "What about fugitive number four?" she asked. "Could your source recognize her?"

"Unfortunately, no. But if they are still in the city, they're going to need help. A place to crash for a few days until they can gather what they need."

"I agree with you on one thing. Unless we can get Kira or Ben to talk, we're going to have to figure this out on our own."

"I did call in for an update on Ben."

"And?"

"He's still in the ICU on a ventilator."

"So he's not going to be of any help."

Jonas's phone buzzed and he glanced at it. "Just a sec. It's Hazel."

He unlocked the phone, then quickly read through her text. He assumed she hadn't slept all night and was still in shock over what had happened. And yet she was checking in on him.

"Is everything all right?" Madison asked.

"She just wanted to know how I was doing. Figured I wouldn't be sleeping. Wanted me to promise to call her if I need anything." He slid his phone into his pocket. "I had to tell her Felicia was gone."

"How is she handling things?"

"She has a lot of support, but she's devastated. Felicia was everything to her. Hazel practically raised Felicia after her parents died. I'm not sure I helped at all, but at least I was there."

"Sometimes that's all that really matters."

He shrugged. "It doesn't seem like enough. I felt like there was really nothing I could even begin to say to help."

"That's because there isn't anything you could have said. You can't fix this, Jonas, just like you couldn't fix things when she lost her leg." Madison got up, took their trash to the waste basket, then sat back down next to him. "But that's not your job. You were there, and sometimes that's enough."

"She just didn't deserve to lose her granddaughter." He rubbed the back of his neck. "I'm sorry. I'm trying not to make this personal, but I think what upsets me more than anything else is the simple fact that this shouldn't have happened."

"You have no reason to be sorry, because you're right. This shouldn't have happened." She reached out and squeezed his hand. "I know this isn't easy for you, but you don't have to pretend you're okay. Not with me."

Another stab of guilt sliced through him, even though he knew she understood. "I'm sorry I never called you back. I should have—"

"Stop apologizing."

"I'm just trying to figure out how to deal with all of this. Not seeing her for so long with so many unresolved issues between us has been tough. And I'll be honest. This has hit me harder than I thought it would."

"Michaels told me you were there when she died. Did you get to talk to her at all?"

"We spoke briefly after she got out of surgery. Talked about some things we should have said to each other a long time ago."

He squeezed his eyes shut briefly, knowing he'd never be able to erase that moment from his memories. He could still hear the machines beeping and people shouting as the code team tried to save her. "I felt like there was some resolution between us, but I also can't stop thinking of all the things I wish I would have had time to say. Things she deserved to hear from me."

"It's going to take time for you to process everything," Madison said. "Time to grieve. And you have to give yourself that time."

"I know. It's just hitting all at once."

"I'm sorry, Jonas. I really am."

He sat back in his chair, the urgency of finding their fugitives forgotten for the moment. "I still cared about her. Not in the way I once did. I accepted that door was closed a long time ago, but I still wanted what was best for her. And just when I felt there was a chance for closure between us, suddenly she's gone."

His emotions had been pulled tight the past twelve hours. So tight, he felt as if they were about to snap.

"She asked me if I'd ever come up with an answer to why I never asked her to marry me," he said, not sure why he felt the need to pour salt in an open wound.

"Did you have an answer?"

"Just that I'd been waiting for the time when our careers and our lives would slow down." He took a deep breath, blowing the air out slowly. "She told me she didn't think we'd ever have made it, and I think she might have been right." He glanced up and caught Madison's gaze. "I guess no matter how hard you try, some relationships were just never meant to be."

And others are worth pursuing.

The thought struck him hard. Madison sat across from him, intently listening. She understood love and loss, and yet while his heart was screaming at him to let her in, his head wanted nothing to do with another risk.

"Jonas?"

He waved his hand in front of his face, wishing there was a way to lighten the situation. "You know what loss is. Loss much deeper than an ex-girlfriend."

"You can't quantify loss, though. You have to take the time you need to grieve and let go. It's part of life. Part of loss. I'm just . . . I'm sorry you have to go through this. I truly am."

He grabbed an egg burrito out of the bag, then pulled back the wrapper. "She implied there was something between you and me."

Madison's brow furrowed. "Why would she say that?"

"I don't know. Maybe it was her way of assuring me she'd let me go."

"Maybe that was something you needed to hear from her."

"I know I have held on to the guilt from that day for so long. I just could never get past wondering what would have happened if I would have made a different call during that raid. That guilt has always hung over me."

"But those questions don't lead to any resolution, because you can't change the past, or know how different choices would have turned out. It just adds to your guilt and frustration."

"I know." He paused for a moment before continuing. "She did tell me something that made me happy. She's seeing someone." The bite he'd just taken turned rubbery in his mouth. "*Was* seeing someone."

Since their relationship ended, he'd determined not to be bitter, but instead had only wanted the best for her. Now she was dead.

"Does her boyfriend know?"

"He took the red-eye into Seattle last night and a friend of Hazel's picked him up, so yes, he knows."

A tense silence settled between them, then Madison cleared her throat. "There's something else we need to talk about." She shifted in her chair. "Felicia saved my life. That bullet was meant for me—"

He held up his hand, wishing he could erase everything he knew she was feeling. "I already told you not to go there. Don't take hold of the guilt like I've been carrying for far too long." He paused. "Someone once told me that you can't change the past."

"Touché." She shook her head, but he didn't miss the half

smile that formed for a brief moment on her lips before disappearing. "I admit I deserved that, but I'm afraid that every time you look at me, you'll remember what happened to the woman you loved. I don't want that to become a wedge between us. I don't think I could live with it."

Her confession took him by surprise. "Is that what you actually think?"

She shrugged. "You were planning to marry her."

"Yes, but a long time ago. I didn't go into that hospital room hoping to get back together with her. I just wanted to find some closure from how we left things between us. Yes, I still cared for her. She was important to me. And I wanted to be there to support her and Hazel." He locked eyes with her. "But I don't blame you for what happened in there, Madison."

"Because you blame yourself?"

Her question hit him like an arrow straight through his heart. How did she always see right through him to the most vulnerable places? "You know I felt responsible for when Felicia was shot the first time."

"Maybe, but I know you well enough to be certain that you did everything you could to protect your team. That is who you are. Sometimes things go horribly wrong no matter how well laid the plans are."

"That's what Felicia told me."

"Let the guilt go and start living again."

He leaned back in his chair again, his mind racing. Was he using the past as an excuse to stop anything from happening between him and Madison? Fear of what might happen. Fear of what *could* happen. No. He'd been right with his decision not to date someone he worked with. The job they did was dangerous and unpredictable. And he'd gone through more than enough personal loss.

"We can talk about this later," Madison said, seeming to sense his need to move on. "Just know that I'm here. Whatever you need."

"I know that. And I appreciate it."

She nodded. "So your contact. He couldn't identify who Archer was with?"

"No." Jonas followed her lead and shifted his mind back to the case. "Though he did tell me that he met Jesse's girlfriend not too long ago. Her name was Nadia. But he wasn't sure if she was the one in the photo."

"Nadia. Wait a minute. I've got a Nadia on my list." Madison grabbed the bag she'd brought with her and pulled out a file folder.

"What list?"

She dropped a few papers onto the desk. "I took the list Piper made off of social media and started to narrow it down to people who both live in the area and went to school with Ben and Kira. Nadia's not a common name, so if we can connect the two—"

"We might be able to ID our fourth fugitive."

"Exactly." She ran her finger down the notepad she'd been working on, then stopped. "Look up Nadia Bower on Facebook and see what we can find out."

He typed the name into the search engine, then waited for a match to pop up.

"This is getting very interesting." He clicked again and started skimming through profile information. "Yep, I found one Nadia Bower living here in Seattle, and she's a friend of Kira Thornton."

"That's definitely not a coincidence."

"No, it's not. From her posts, it looks like she and her boy-friend just celebrated their six-month anniversary."

"And her boyfriend is?"

"Bingo." Jonas enlarged the photo he found on her profile, then turned the computer around so Madison could see it. "Jesse Archer."

"Despite the graininess of this photo, that's got to be her." She held up the security footage photo again. "I'd say we now have a match to our fourth fugitive."

"I agree, though this gives a new meaning to high-octane dating. Grabbing takeout once a week seems a bit underrated suddenly."

She glanced up from the photos. "So our weekly dinners were dates?"

Heat rose to his face. "No, I . . ." He tried to find a way to backpedal from what he'd just said. "I just meant if we were to call them dates—"

"Forget it, Jonas." A smile spread on her face. "Now that we've ID'd the other two fugitives, we need to update our BOLO. If they are still in the city, we'll find them."

He hoped she was right. His phone rang, and he snatched it up. "It's the kid I met with last night."

Jonas set the phone on the desk in front of them, then switched it to speaker. "Matt, is everything okay?"

"Yeah. I'm sorry to be calling so early."

"That's fine. I'm already here in the office with my partner. I have you on speakerphone."

"That's fine. I might have found something."

Jonas and Madison shared a look. "Great. What have you got?" he asked.

"Jesse's not big on social media, but we have some of the same friends, so it wasn't hard to poke around a bit. I found his girlfriend—"

"Nadia Bower?"

"Yes. She posted something last night on Snapchat."

"Okay." Jonas glanced up at Madison, surprised. These guys didn't exactly seem like the type who were going to end up being hauled in because of a photo on social media. "What was it?"

"It was a photo of Seattle, at night, overlooking Elliott Bay."

He deflated. "There's got to be thousands of shots of that scene."

"I agree. But here's the interesting thing. I told you that I was a bicycle messenger."

"Yes?"

"So I know the city pretty well. I've made hundreds of deliveries, and I recognized exactly where that photo came from."

"Where?" Madison asked.

"A high-rise apartment building, not far from Pike Place Market."

"You're sure?"

"Positive."

"That's great information," Jonas said, "but there could be hundreds of people living in those apartments."

"I agree," Matt said, "which is why I didn't stop there. I did a bit more digging. Like I said, Jesse doesn't have much of a presence on social media, but his girlfriend does. *And* she has a friend who lives in the building where the photo was taken. Zac Cannon. He moved in about a year ago."

"Now we might actually have something," Jonas said, writing down the name and address Matt gave him.

"I just . . ." Matt hesitated. "I'd appreciate your keeping my name off of anything official."

"I will, and thanks, Matt."

"You still think they left the city?" Jonas asked Madison after he hung up the call.

"It's certainly possible they're still here," she said, "or the photo could be nothing more than a red herring."

"While I agree that they're smart, I still don't think they planned this far ahead. They're desperate, and desperate people usually stick to what's familiar."

"We need to talk to Zac Cannon."

SEVENTEEN

M adison ducked out of the light rain beneath an over-
hang a block away from the downtown high-rise
apartment building. While she wasn't completely
convinced that Jonas's contact was right in his assumptions
about the photo, she did agree that it was worth following
up on. Plus, she hadn't missed the fact that Jonas's mood had
lightened with the lead. Finding their fugitives might not bring
back Felicia, but it would go a long way in serving justice in
a horrible situation.

"I have two confessions," she said as they walked toward the
lobby doors. "When I was looking for a house a few months
ago, I took a tour of one of the apartments on the twenty-
second floor here. What I didn't tell them was that the only
thing I could afford was a studio on the first floor."

Jonas let out a low laugh. "And your second confession?"

"I might be slightly jealous of those who can afford the
penthouses. Okay, more than slightly jealous."

"If it gives you any consolation, I think your place is beautiful. Especially with all the changes you've made. And it fits
you far better than a ritzy apartment building."

"You're probably right, but do you know what these places offer?"

"I've never had the official tour, but I bet I could make a pretty educated guess."

She stopped in front of the glass doors to the lobby. "There's a rooftop space with an outdoor lounge, a fitness center, a yoga studio, and if that isn't enough, there's a 24/7 concierge in case you need, I don't know"—she waved her hand in the air—"an ice cream delivery at 2:00 a.m."

"How often do you need ice cream delivered at 2:00 a.m.?"

She shrugged. "That's not the point. I'm just saying that you could, if you wanted to. And on top of that, the views are incredible."

"I get it, but you chose the wrong career path if you expected to be able to afford that. Or you're going to have to marry up in the world. Way up."

"Maybe that's not a bad idea." She shot him a smile as he opened the door. "The view might be worth it."

She stepped inside the well-lit lobby with its tiled floors, rich wood accents, and long reception desk. To the right were two elevators, available only to those with a key card. Madison flashed her badge at the concierge, who looked half-asleep.

"Dylan," she said, reading his name tag. "I'm Deputy US Marshal Madison James and this is my partner, Deputy US Marshal Jonas Quinn."

"Okay . . . Is there a problem?"

Jonas showed him a photo of Nadia and Jesse on his phone. "We need to know if you've seen this couple come through the lobby."

"Even during a night shift you'd be surprised at how many

people come and go." He leaned closer, then shook his head. "But I don't recognize them. Sorry."

"What about Zac Cannon? He lives on the seventeenth floor."

"I know who he is. Is he in trouble or something?"

"We just need to ask him some questions."

The man hesitated as if he wasn't quite sure what he was supposed to do. "I guess I could give you access to the elevators."

"Thank you."

He opened a drawer in his desk, then handed Madison a plastic card with the apartment logo on it. They stepped into the elevator a moment later, and she punched the button for the seventeenth floor.

"Personally, I would never live in a place like this," Jonas said, leaning against the mirrored back wall as the doors slid shut.

"Why's that?" she asked.

"What happens if the place catches on fire, and you're twenty, twenty-five stories up?"

"I don't know." She shrugged. "Unless I find myself some rich husband, I guess I won't have to worry about it."

He laughed, but she didn't miss the hollowness in his expression. Humor might be a way to cope with the stress in their line of work, but everything that had happened yesterday was still simmering beneath the surface.

"How are you doing?" she asked, as the elevator began to climb.

He blew out a breath. "I'm worried that we're wasting our time. We're here because of a photo some bike messenger saw on Facebook and is convinced was taken from this building."

"You're worried he might be wrong." It was a statement. Not a question.

"I'm convinced he probably is wrong. You don't think it's a bit far-fetched?"

"I agree he could be wrong, but this is what we do. Follow leads and talk to witnesses until we track our fugitives down. Which we will. I think you're worrying about something you can't control."

"Like a fire in a high-rise building."

"Exactly."

The elevator dinged, and they stepped out into a small landing accessing the five apartments on the seventeenth story.

Madison paused in the middle of the tiled floor as the doors shut behind her. "Are you having second thoughts on the legitimacy of your witness?"

"Our witness," Jonas countered. "I did a background check on him and he seems legit. Volunteers at a food bank, is involved in a bicycle club, and is really into fantasy sports."

"Looks like you've learned to use social media pretty well."

"Funny. But what keeps nagging at me is that our fugitives all seem like average people who normally stay out of trouble."

She studied his face, trying to read between the lines. "Jonas." She touched his arm lightly. "What's really bothering you?"

He rubbed the back of his neck as if he wanted to avoid her question. "Felicia's dead, and I'm worried that I'm grasping at anything no matter how unlikely it is."

"This is personal. You can't avoid that."

"Yes, and I know you understand."

She nodded, wishing he wasn't having to grapple with so much. "It's hard when you're mentally and emotionally drained. Hard when you feel like you're losing perspective."

Because she did understand.

After Luke died, it was all she could do to get up in the

morning, go to work, then crash when she got home. Anything beyond that was too much. She kept her personal life to herself, but realized in the end, if she didn't take care of her emotions, she was going to burn out. She was going to have to ensure Jonas didn't do the same thing.

"I can't lose my focus," he said.

Madison caught his gaze. "The first time we worked together in Nashville at the shoot house, I saw you function in some very difficult situations during that murder investigation. And do you know what impressed me?"

"What?"

"You never let emotions get in the way of what you were there to do. And I have no doubt that you will do that exact same thing again with this case. Let's find out what this guy knows."

He nodded as she crossed the small foyer in front of him, knocked on the door, then took a step back.

A few seconds later, Zac Cannon, a man Madison recognized from a DMV photo they'd pulled earlier, opened the door, wearing a T-shirt and sweats and holding a mug of coffee. She held up her badge and quickly introduced herself and Jonas.

"US Marshals?" Zac asked as he stared at the badge. "Is something wrong?"

"We need to speak with you for a few minutes. May we come in?" Madison asked.

Zac's eyes widened. "I need to get ready for work—"

A neighbor stepped out of his apartment, glancing at them as he headed to the elevator.

"Fine." Zac motioned them through the small entryway and into the kitchen, obviously trying to avoid a confrontation.

"But like I said, I'm about to get ready for work and don't have a lot of time."

"Where would that be?" Jonas asked.

"My work? I'm . . . uh . . . I'm a computer analyst for a tech company. I'm sorry." He shut the door behind them. "What's going on? Am I in some kind of trouble?"

Jonas held up the photo on his phone. "We are looking for Jesse Archer and Nadia Bower. We understand they're friends of yours."

"Yeah . . . I know them." He set his mug down on the kitchen counter. "Why?"

"When's the last time you saw them?" Jonas asked.

Zac combed his fingers through his thick brown hair. "I don't know. We're not super close. I guess it was Jesse's grandmother's funeral a few weeks ago."

Madison leveled her gaze at him. "So you haven't seen them or spoken to them recently?"

"No. Sorry."

Without invitation, Madison walked toward the floor-to-ceiling windows of the living room that overlooked the city and a section of Elliott Bay. "This is quite a view."

"Yeah, it is, but—"

"I've always wanted to see the view from one of these high-rise apartments." She paused in front of the window for another couple seconds, then turned back to him, taking in the details of the open living room and kitchen at the same time. There was no sign anyone else had been there. The photo posted on social media very well could have been a red herring.

"I just bought a house," she said, "and while I love the neighborhood, it can't compare to this."

"The view's what sold me on this place but listen"—he shoved his hands into his pockets—"I wish I could help you, but I really need to get ready."

"Of course," Jonas said. "We're sorry to have bothered you."

Madison headed to the door with Jonas, trying to figure out what they were missing. She'd noticed how Zac couldn't stop fidgeting his hands. How his jaw had tensed at the mention of their fugitives. The irritation in his voice. He was hiding something. The question was, what?

She stopped at the end of the kitchen counter. There was a box of hair dye in the garbage can. She reached down and picked it up. "What's this?"

"I'd like to hear the answer to that question as well," Jonas said.

"So I colored my hair." Zac shrugged.

"Golden Copper? I don't think so." She looked at him, but he avoided her scrutiny. "There are clippings in here that are definitely not yours. I'm thinking Nadia and Jesse were here, and one of them decided to change their appearance. Is that true?"

Zac pressed his lips together.

"My partner asked you a question." Jonas crossed his arms. "And next time you try to cover for a couple fugitives, you might want to do a better job."

"Fugitives?" Zac looked at the gun on Jonas's hip, then shifted his gaze up to his face. "So you really are US Marshals?"

Madison furrowed her brows. "Yes, and your friends are persons of interest in a string of bank robberies."

"Bank robberies? You're kidding, right?" Zac laughed. "That's a little hard to believe. I know Jesse's had a few run-ins with the law, but Nadia . . . She works at a hair salon. She's not exactly the type to rob a bank."

"Then they lied to you," Jonas said.

He held up his hands. "Sorry, but I'm lost. I'd believe their story way before I would believe they'd been out robbing banks."

"Then you don't know your friends very well," Madison said. "The charges against them range from bank robbing to murder—"

"Wait a minute. Murder? This has to be a mistake." Zac's face paled as he sat down on his leather couch, pressing his palms against his thighs. He seemed to be thinking over her words. He blew out a long puff of air before looking up at them. "About a year ago, Nadia filed a restraining order on her ex after he beat her up. I knew that was true. Knew he was a cop. Jesse called me yesterday while I was at work and asked if they could stay here a couple days off the radar because the ex was acting crazy again. I owed Jesse a favor, so I said yes. When Dylan called up from the front desk and told us the cops were here, we assumed it was him."

"Who's her ex?"

He shook his head. "I don't know his name."

Irritation wound tighter inside Madison. "Zac—"

He looked up at her. "Do you really think I would have covered for them if I knew they were fugitives?"

"I don't know. Would you have?"

"Of course not."

"So you never thought something might be off with their story?" Jonas asked.

"Why would I? They were clearly in a panic and needed time and a place to figure out what to do. I just apparently didn't know the real reason."

"Why not just tell us that to begin with?" Madison asked, ignoring his question.

"Sorry if I was thrown off by having marshals show up on my doorstep and start drilling me for information. Nadia warned me that her ex might use his badge and connections to find them. But I swear, as far as I knew, they were here because of him. That's it."

"When did they leave?" Madison asked.

Zac glanced at his watch. "Not long before you showed up."

"I'm calling for backup." Jonas headed for the door. "They can't be far."

"Where were they headed?" Madison asked, turning back to Zac.

"I don't know."

"We don't have time for games. We need to know where they were going. And just so you know how serious this is, they're already connected to two murders. If you have any idea where they might have gone—"

He held up his hands. "I swear, I don't know."

"You didn't overhear any conversations or phone calls?"

"They didn't say anything to me directly, but I did hear them talking about passports over the phone."

✳ ✳ ✳

Jonas was on his cell, still waiting for the elevator, when Madison stepped back into the small foyer. "I've requested backup outside the building and the surrounding blocks," he said, "but the elevator's not moving fast enough. We'll have to take the stairs."

She stifled a groan. "Why do we always have to do things the hard way?"

"It's only seventeen flights."

Seventeen flights.

She frowned, then followed him into the stairwell. Their

steps echoed as they made their way down. She hadn't gotten enough sleep last night, but for the moment, that didn't matter. Knowing their fugitives had been in this building was enough to keep her adrenaline flowing and her energy up. She'd make up for the lack of sleep later.

A door to the stairwell opened above them, then a couple seconds later, slammed. She stopped and looked up.

"Do you think they're still in the building?" he asked.

"It's possible but seems unlikely."

"Agreed." Jonas motioned for them to keep heading toward the lobby. "Local backup should be here any minute. If they are in the building, we'll know it."

She kept running down the stairs. Whoever had opened the door had decided—for whatever reason—to avoid the stairwell. She knew they had to reach the lobby, but she wasn't convinced their fugitives had left the building.

Her heart rate was rising and her breathing heavier, but she kept up her pace until they finally reached the bottom. Jonas shoved the door open. Getting in required a key pass. Thankfully, getting out didn't.

Two officers stood just outside the lobby entrance.

"We're with the US Marshals," Jonas said, holding up his badge.

"We were told you were here," one of the officers said. "No one matching the description of your fugitives has left the building since we arrived. Additional officers are on their way and will begin searching the neighborhood, including public transportation and ferries. We will find them."

Madison turned to Jonas. "And if they are still in the building?"

"Then we need to look at the building's security cameras."

EIGHTEEN

Jonas strode back into the lobby toward the reception desk, working hard to keep his anger in check.

He held up his badge. "You remember us?"

Dylan frowned.

"The warning you gave wasn't very helpful."

"I don't know what you're talking about," he said.

Jonas braced his hands against the desk. "You're seriously going to play that card?"

"Look, all I know is that whoever you're trying to find, I never saw them. That's the truth."

"Then what did happen?"

Dylan let out a sharp puff of air. "Zac came down right after I got here at midnight and told me his friend was in trouble. Something about an ex-boyfriend. I didn't want any problems here, but he slipped me a little something and told me to let him know if anyone came asking for him."

Jonas held up the photos of Jesse and Nadia again. "Did they come through here before the officers outside arrived?"

"No." Dylan held up his hands in front of him. "I promise. I haven't seen them."

"Is there a back way out?" Madison asked.

"There's a back service entrance, but it's not directly accessible to residents or visitors."

"But they could have left that way?"

He bobbed his head. "I suppose."

"We need to look at your security footage."

Dylan tugged on his tie. "I can't just let you access our footage without a warrant."

"Your help could mean a lot—otherwise, you'd be responsible for aiding and abetting two fugitives—"

Dylan held up his hands at Jonas's words and motioned them behind the desk. "I can access the footage from here. What do you want to see?"

Jonas and Madison moved behind the desk to examine the large security screen that was split into half a dozen squares of views from cameras monitoring the building. "Can you pull up the footage on the seventeenth floor outside the elevators? Start at six a.m. and speed it up."

Jonas stared at the grayscale footage of the landing. A man got off the elevator at six fifteen and headed into the apartment next to Zac's. Other than that, the floor was quiet. Dylan skipped ahead.

"Wait. Pause it now." Madison tapped on the counter. "That's them."

A couple exited Zac's apartment. Jesse and Nadia. A moment later they stepped onto the elevator.

"So they definitely got on the elevator." Jonas glanced at the time stamp. "That was just after we arrived in the building."

"But we didn't meet them on the elevator, and you didn't see them leave, Dylan," Madison said. "Which means they went where?"

"They had to have gotten off on another floor to avoid running into us." Jonas shook his head, trying to anticipate where they would've gone. "Let us see the main entrance and the back footage between this time stamp and now."

Dylan clicked a few buttons, and the two exits popped up on the screen.

Jonas leaned forward and studied the footage as it played. A dozen people came and went through the lobby, but not their fugitives. His irritation was growing. Every minute they spent trying to figure out where Jesse and Nadia went was another minute they had to get away. Before they even considered searching the entire building, they were going to have to verify they were actually still here.

Dylan took a step back once the tape cut off. "Sorry, but that's it."

"So if they didn't leave the building," Madison said, "then where are they?"

"They could have gotten off on another floor and taken the stairs." Jonas tapped his fingers on the counter.

"Are there cameras in the stairwell?" Madison asked.

Dylan nodded. "A few."

"Can you give us the view from the stairwell this time? We need to see exactly where they got off."

Dylan searched the monitors for a few seconds then stopped. "There they are. It looks like they went up instead of down."

"Why would they do that?" Madison asked, turning to her partner.

"I don't know, but we need to find out what floor they got off on." Jonas frowned. They'd heard a door slam shut above them. Had that been their fugitives?

"There they are," Madison said, motioning for Dylan to pause the video again.

"What floor is that?" Jonas asked.

"The twenty-fifth."

"What's there?"

"It's one of the penthouses." Dylan folded his arms across his chest. "The owner's in the middle of renovating one of the apartments, but there hasn't been anything going on for several weeks. There's some kind of dispute with the city and the paperwork."

"Is that the only apartment on that floor?" Madison asked.

Dylan shook his head. "No. There are two, but the other's currently vacant as well."

"Do you have a floor plan?"

"Yeah. Give me a sec."

Jonas waited while Dylan pulled up the schematics of the suite, then he studied the layout beside Madison. Past the entryway was an open living room, dining room, and kitchen, then four bedrooms laid out in an L-shape, allowing maximized views of the city. "We need access to that floor."

"I'm not allowed to just let anyone into—"

Madison glared at the young man. "I'm pretty sure your management isn't going to be happy when they find out you didn't cooperate with the authorities who were tracking down two fugitives involved in a double homicide."

"Murder?" Dylan held up his hands. "Do whatever you need to do."

Jonas called in an update as he hurried to the elevator with Madison, with backup on standby. He didn't want another hostage situation. He might not know what the fugitives' plan was, but they were clearly desperate. The problem was that shedding one's identity and disappearing was never as easy as it seemed on TV. In today's world, it was almost impossible to avoid leaving behind breadcrumbs. Databases, corporate files, IP addresses, and GPS-enabled phones meant that one false move could end everything.

They stepped off the elevator into darkness. Jonas flipped the light switch. Nothing.

"Dylan failed to mention that the power's apparently been shut off." He flipped on his flashlight, then opened the door to one of the penthouses.

"I have to say this is a bit creepy."

The apartment was dark, with the only light coming from a long line of windows. Dark storm clouds loomed over the city as thunder rumbled across the bay. Lightning flashed, revealing appliances and cupboards covered with plastic. The view had to be stunning on a clear day. Maybe Madison had been right. Living a couple hundred feet above the ground might not be so bad.

He crossed the wood floors, checking every square inch of the apartment as they headed toward the hallway and the four bedrooms. Shadows flickered against the walls, but the space was eerily quiet. If they weren't here, where were they?

According to the schematics they'd looked at, half of the floor belonged to one owner who was in the middle of renovating the entire apartment, but there were only so many places to hide in the unfurnished space that was littered with building supplies.

He opened the door to the first bedroom. A noise to his right caught his attention. He shifted his flashlight and caught movement.

"It's a mouse."

Madison took a step back. "I hate mice."

"Think of him as another wanted fugitive on the run."

She chuckled. "Very funny."

Jonas headed into the hallway, then froze. "Did you hear that?"

"Yeah, and this time it was definitely not a mouse."

Someone was in the apartment.

Jonas started back toward the living room, carefully calculating each step. Both Jesse and Nadia had been armed at the bank, and he wasn't going to take any chances of stepping into an ambush. He pulled his weapon out in front of him and cautiously made his way around the corner, searching for their target with each step.

The sound of crinkling plastic permeated the silence. Lightning flashed and he spotted a silhouette walking toward him.

Jonas shouted at the figure. "Put your hands in the air and lean against the wall."

"Wait. It's just me. Zac."

"Do it now!"

Jonas moved in quickly with Madison just a step behind him. He quickly patted Zac down. When he was done, he clasped the man's arm and turned him around. "We told you to stay in your apartment."

"I know, but Dylan said you came up this way and I think I know why they came here," Zac said, his breathing labored. "I started thinking after you left my apartment. Realized you were right and they'd just used me, but then I had to start asking myself why they would come here in the first place."

"And?"

Zac glanced toward the row of windows. "I had to come up here and see if I was right. Can I show you something?"

Jonas glanced at Madison, then nodded, releasing his grip on Zac.

"In college, we used to rappel off buildings at night," Zac said as they followed him toward the last bedroom on the west side of the apartment. "The previous owners of this place left behind some of those rescue backpacks with a control descent device used for emergencies."

"Or for escaping US Marshals," Jonas mumbled.

"Jesse and Nadia came by a few months ago," Zac said, clearly not hearing the comment. "We got to talking about rappelling. I showed them this apartment. The construction people don't always lock it, and it's been empty for months. I'd been curious to see the place and figured no one would notice. We planned to try it out, but we never did."

Jonas and Madison followed him into the last bedroom, where something was flapping along the far wall.

"You were right." Madison tugged on a cord that had been clipped to an anchor on the wall.

"They must have remembered this place and figured if the cops showed up, they'd have an alternative route out of the building that would in turn buy them time," Jonas said. "Though I have a feeling they weren't expecting us to find them so soon."

"I don't think so either," Zac said.

Madison pulled out her phone. "I'll update Michaels. How much of a head start do you think they have?"

Jonas glanced at his watch. "I'd say ten to fifteen minutes."

Her phone rang before she had a chance to place the call. She hung up a few seconds later. "We can arrange for SPD to take official statements from Zac and the concierge, but Michaels wants us back at the office ASAP."

*** * ***

"You're going to like this," Michaels said as soon as they walked into his office forty-five minutes later. "We found out what was in that storage unit."

"The key fit?" Madison asked. She picked up the plastic bag sitting on their boss's desk. "Passports, driver's licenses, social security cards, cash . . . So they definitely had an exit strategy."

"Someone dropped the key in the chaos of getting away and now they're stuck," Jonas said. "Without all of this, they can't leave the country."

"Not easily, no," Michaels said.

Jonas couldn't help but smile at the discovery. "Which means they're going to need new passports and IDs."

Michaels nodded. "And a new place to hide out until they get them."

"Is there any way to know who forged these passports?" Madison asked, setting the bag back down on the desk. "It would make sense for them to go back to the same forger and ask for another set."

"It's possible but would take time. I'll hand these over to someone I know who might be able to figure it out. But for now," Michaels said, "I want the two of you to keep combing through everything we have, including all of this. We need another lead."

*** * ***

Madison leaned back in her chair, trying to work the kinks out of her stiff joints after sitting in one position for so long. The past few hours of going through every piece of evidence and multiple social media accounts had netted zero clues to where Jesse and Nadia might have gone after escaping the high rise.

"They have to still be in the city," she said to Jonas, who was seated at the desk beside her. She stood up and walked to the window. The morning rain had cleared off, leaving behind blue skies and a trail of wispy clouds. They were out there. Somewhere.

Piper stepped into the room with a piece of paper in her hand.

"Piper? What have you got?" Madison asked, turning around.

"I'm sorry to bother you, but I've been screening the calls coming through our tip line and Michaels asked me to give you this one. It's from a security guard that works at St. James Cathedral. He says he thinks he saw our suspects inside the church about fifteen minutes ago."

Madison glanced at Jonas. "Sounds like the perfect place for a clandestine meeting with a forger."

"Yes, it does." Jonas pulled his keys out of his pocket and turned to Piper. "Tell Michaels we're on our way."

NINETEEN

Jonas pulled into an open parking space along the tree-lined street near the cathedral while Madison surveyed the surrounding area. The cathedral with its twin spires was located in the First Hill neighborhood of Seattle, but the quiet street revealed no signs of their fugitives. Just the continual wave of passing traffic along with a handful of pedestrians walking by.

"I remember coming here once with my grandmother," Madison said, stepping out of the car and onto the sidewalk. "She loved history and brought me here one summer to show me the remarkable collection of stained glass windows. If you haven't seen them, they're definitely worth a visit."

"I've never been inside, but I've driven by a number of times. I can see why she loved it." He followed her onto the sidewalk, locking the car behind them. "It is beautiful."

"She loved living in the United States, but always wanted to take me to France so I could see some *real* history, as she used to say."

Jonas chuckled. "I suppose most of the cathedrals there make this seem like new construction. So she was French?"

"She was. She was a war bride." Madison smiled at the memory as they hurried toward the front steps of the church's entrance. "She was eighteen years old when she met my grandfather. He was a staff sergeant with the air force, and her family had worked with the French Resistance. Whenever he had some free time, they would go for walks around Paris to visit the museums and different cathedrals. They ended up getting married and settled here after the war. My father was born nine months after they married."

"My grandfather fought in World War Two as well," Jonas said, pausing at the entrance of the church, "but ended up in England. When the war was over, he came straight back and married his sweetheart in rural Kansas. Spent the rest of his life being a farmer. They'd been married over sixty years when he died."

"So how did your mom end up in the Northwest?"

"She followed my father here for work. They lived here their entire married life."

Madison felt the unexpected tug of emotion as she stepped through the doors and into the cathedral foyer. Stained glass windows filtered the light overhead beneath vaulted ceilings. Ornate furnishings and shimmering candles lined the walls. A few people sat scattered in rows of wooden chairs. But it was the sense of peace that had always drawn her to places like this, especially in the world she dealt with that was so often void of peace. A peace her grandmother had reminded her she could find no matter where she was, because God's Spirit lived inside his people. At the time, Madison had no idea just how important those words of encouragement were going to be. They were words Madison had clung to among the uncertainties that had crept in over the past few years. No matter what her emotions said, God's presence would never leave her.

She scanned the inside of the cathedral, looking for the guard they'd been told to meet. He must have been watching for them, because a moment later, a uniformed security officer headed toward them.

"Officer Thompson?" Jonas asked.

"Yes." The man rested his hands against his hips. "You're with the US Marshals?"

Jonas and Madison held up their badges.

"We appreciate your calling in the lead," Madison said.

"Of course." Thompson rubbed his jaw. "I'm pretty sure I saw the fugitives you're after, though they look a little different than they did in the news footage."

"Can you tell us what you saw?"

"Of course." He motioned them toward a small alcove where they'd have more privacy. "I probably wouldn't have even noticed them normally, but I'd received the BOLO on them this morning and was keeping an eye out. About an hour ago, a couple walked in. They seemed quiet and respectful, and honestly, I didn't think anything about it at first. They went and sat down. Again, there wasn't anything odd about their presence."

"But you saw some kind of exchange?" Madison asked, pulling out her notebook.

Thompson nodded. "I can't tell you what was exchanged, but yes. They sat there about ten minutes, then a man walked in and sat down next to them. They gave him something—a small envelope—then he left. The couple sat there another few minutes before getting up, lighting a candle, and leaving."

"Did you see him give them anything?"

"No, but I could have missed it."

"You said that they didn't match exactly to the photos and descriptions," Jonas said.

"Height and build, yes, but her hair was reddish and shoulder length. And he didn't have any facial hair like he did in the photo."

Madison jotted down some notes. "Anything else?"

The officer paused for a moment. "I decided to get a closer look at them."

"And did you?"

He nodded. "There are always things in the lost and found, so I grabbed a woman's scarf. As they were leaving, I went up to them and asked her if she'd dropped it. She said no, but I could tell she was nervous."

"What about him?" Jonas asked.

"He looked"—Thompson cocked his head—"I guess irritated is the best word to describe him. Let's just say I'm pretty sure he didn't come here to pray."

"Any tattoos?" Madison asked.

"Yes. That was the other thing I noticed. He had one on his forearm and wrist that I was able to get a good look at. It was a compass surrounded by a forest."

Madison glanced at Jonas. "Then that was definitely them."

"Would you like to look at the security footage we have?" the officer asked.

"Definitely."

They followed him toward the church offices. "What about the person they met with? Did you get a good look at him?" Madison asked.

"Yeah. He was around six foot tall and thin. Brown, curly hair. I've never seen him before, but I'm hoping there's some footage of him on the security cameras, because I want to ask one of our volunteers who works here full time if she knows who he is. Kim's one of those people who knows everyone."

Madison nodded, hoping he was right, but it was possible none of them had a connection to the cathedral, and they'd only chosen this place as a safe drop.

"I'll get you started on the footage, then I'll go and find Kim," Thompson said, as he motioned them inside a small office where video equipment and screens were set up along the back wall.

As soon as he had the footage cued up and had showed them how to use the equipment, Madison rolled a chair in front of the screen and started slowly going through the recording while Jonas leaned over her shoulder.

The situation played out exactly like the security guard had told them. Cameras had caught the couple walking in the entrance of the church, then sitting down. Madison glanced at the time stamp and continued to scroll forward.

"There"—she pointed at the screen—"here's where their contact walks in."

"I'm convinced this has to do with getting new passports," Jonas said, "but he doesn't seem to be carrying anything."

She slowed down the footage, watching it frame by frame to ensure they didn't miss anything. The contact slid an envelope from Jesse into his jacket pocket, then slipped away without a word, but Jonas was right. From this angle, it appeared that the contact never gave the couple anything.

"Maybe they were simply making a payment in advance," she said. "Which would make sense. It could easily take a few days to get new passports made."

For a price, you could get anything you wanted. Either a brand-new, forged passport, or a doctored stolen one. The right person could slip in a new photo and make a few subtle changes, giving the buyer the ability to invisibly slip through airports or across the border. And if the public didn't catch on to their new aliases, Jesse and Nadia would become virtually invisible.

Jesse and Nadia had just walked out of the line of sight in the camera footage when Thompson came back into the room.

Madison paused the video. "Could you get a copy of this for us?"

"Of course. I can put it on a thumb drive," Thompson said. "And I just spoke with Kim, the woman I told you about. She'll be here in a few minutes. Maybe she'll recognize the second man."

Madison stood up so Thompson could have the computer back. She wanted to believe he was right, but she wasn't going to count on it. They'd update the BOLO with Jesse and Nadia's new appearances and get the footage to one of their techs to see if facial recognition software got them what they needed.

"We'll wait outside," Jonas said, stepping out of the way.

She followed Jonas into the hallway, then paused in front of a stained glass window for a moment before sitting down on a wooden bench next to Jonas.

"How are you doing?" she asked. "I know you didn't get much if any sleep last night. You have to be exhausted."

"I'll be fine, though if I'm being honest, it feels a bit ironic being here. The last twenty-four hours have found me wrestling some with God. Maybe I'm still in shock. Maybe it's because I still feel there are unresolved things between Felicia and me, and now it's too late to settle them." He laughed. "It sounds selfish when I say it out loud."

"Not at all." She leaned forward and rested her forearms against her thighs. "I know I questioned God a lot when Luke died. Wondering why he didn't intervene that day. I tried to convince God of all the reasons why he should have saved him, including the miraculous testimony I would have told the world. I understand. Death is hard."

"And it's even harder when it's senseless," Jonas said.

Over the years she'd learned how to better control her emotions when they were triggered, but talking about death and loss always revealed just how close to the surface they actually stayed. That same loss had taken her down a path she never would have volunteered to take, but it had also given her a strength she hadn't expected.

"I remember having a long conversation with my father a few weeks after Luke's death about everything I was questioning," she said. "I told him I didn't know what God wanted from me."

"What was his response?" Jonas asked.

"That I already knew what God wanted. It was more of a question of if I was willing to surrender and trust him."

"Your father clearly isn't one to pull any punches."

"He was always good at making me look at an issue from a completely different angle. The bigger picture. Though I feel like it's still something I'm just beginning to unravel and understand."

"It's hard when it doesn't make sense."

"I agree, but he also reminded me that God is okay with us struggling for answers. And in the end, he simply wants us to trust him through the journey, even when it doesn't make sense."

Jonas put his arm around her shoulder. "I know you feel like you're slowly losing your dad too. I've always enjoyed being around him. Wish I would have known him before he got sick."

"Me too." She stared at the stained glass until it blurred,

letting the ripples of emotion seep through the cracks of her heart. "He was and always will be a special man."

Footsteps on the tile pulled her back to the present. Officer Thompson stepped out of the security office just as a middle-aged woman with gray hair pulled back into a ponytail stopped in front of them.

"Great timing, Kim," Officer Thompson said. "Thank you for coming by." He turned to the marshals. "Kim arranges tours of the church and has volunteered here longer than probably anyone."

"It's nice to meet you," she said, as Madison and Jonas both stood up. "Officer Thompson said you would like me to try and identify someone who visited the church today."

"Yes," Madison said. "We appreciate your willingness to help."

"I printed off a couple freeze-frames while I was copying the security footage," Thompson said, handing them both to Kim.

"The couple definitely doesn't look familiar," she said, holding up the black-and-white photo.

"What about the third person?" Jonas asked. "The man."

Kim flipped to the second photo. "I've seen him, though I don't know his name." She tapped a finger against the image. "I remember him because we had to call and have his car towed away a few weeks ago when he parked in the staff parking lot. If you'll give me just a minute, I'm sure we have a record of the incident on file."

"That would be great," Madison said. "Thank you."

Thompson's hand shook as he handed her the flash drive. "Here's a copy of the footage. If there's anything else you need, just let me know."

"Are you okay?" she asked.

"Yes, I just . . . I hate the thought of having fugitives in the sanctuary." He paused for a moment. "I heard they're wanted for a bank robbery and the shooting of a bank security guard."

"That's right," Jonas said.

"All of this hits a little too close to home," he said, shoving his hands inside his pockets. "I know enough about US Marshals to know they go after people with pretty serious raps. Except for a few incidences of vandalism, it normally stays pretty quiet here. I think having a uniformed officer helps people feel like this is a safe place, but knowing those two fugitives were here made me realize that something like a robbery and shooting can happen anywhere." The officer was visibly shaken. "I've got a wife and two little girls at home."

Madison glanced at Jonas's guarded expression but knew what he was thinking. Anywhere. Anytime. The unexpected was often harder than the anticipated.

Kim emerged from an office with a paper in her hand. "All I can find is the complaint we filled out for the police. I still don't know his name, but I do have the license plate number of the car we towed." She handed them the paper. "Hopefully that will be enough."

Jonas and Madison thanked them both, then headed for the car. Madison texted the plate number to Michaels. By the time they got to the car, her phone was ringing.

"His name is Ryan Kent," Michaels said. "I'm sending you his last known address now."

TWENTY

*A*ll of this hits a little too close to home."

The security guard's words echoed in Jonas's head as he drove toward Ryan Kent's address. Thompson had reaffirmed what had been nagging at Jonas. This case had become far too personal.

"What do we have on Kent?" he asked.

Madison was scrolling through the information Michaels had sent them on her phone. "He's been arrested a couple times, but all for petty crimes. Nothing violent. He does have an outstanding warrant for a class C misdemeanor for criminal trespassing."

"We might be able to use that as leverage to get him to talk," Jonas said. "What about a job?"

"Looks like he picks up day jobs at a local dock."

"And obviously delivers packages," Jonas added.

The address they'd been given for Kent was in a run-down housing complex. Half a dozen cars sat in the parking lot, several Jonas was certain would never run again. According to the information they had, the man had been living here for the past six months.

"This guy certainly isn't bringing in the cash," Madison said as she looked around.

"Maybe he's a middleman. Some kind of courier," Jonas said.

They made their way to apartment seven on the ground floor of the two-story building. Music blasted from one of the apartments above them, while a couple argued in the doorway three doors down. Jonas stepped over a beer bottle and frowned. The entire outside of the building could use a coat of paint, and several of the windows were cracked. He couldn't imagine what kind of work was needed on the inside.

They stopped in front of Ryan Kent's apartment, and Jonas pounded on the door. "Ryan Kent? Open the door. This is the police."

Madison moved in front of the window and looked through a gap in the curtains. "I see movement. Someone's in there, and the TV's on."

"We know you're in there," Jonas said, knocking again. "We can hear you."

The TV clicked off.

"Ryan?" Jonas said.

"Who is it?"

"US Marshals. Open the door now."

A man in his early thirties, wearing a white T-shirt and jeans, opened the door six inches, leaving the chain in place. "What do you want?"

"I'm Deputy US Marshal Jonas Quinn and this is my partner, Deputy US Marshal Madison James. We're here to ask you a few questions."

"About what?"

"We have video footage of you at the St. James Cathedral late this morning."

His brow furrowed. "Since when is going to church a crime?"

"It's not," Madison said. "But it is when you're delivering illegal goods to fugitives—"

Ryan slammed the door shut, then opened it again, this time without the chain. "Get in here. Quickly."

They stepped inside, while he rushed to lock and chain the door behind them. Jonas glanced around the room that smelled like takeout, cigarettes, and beer. He guessed it hadn't been cleaned for weeks. Dishes were piled up in the small sink, a can of pork and beans sat open next to a hot plate, and clothes lay strewn across the carpeted floor.

"I wasn't delivering *illegal* goods," he said, keeping his voice low, though Jonas had no idea who he didn't want to overhear their conversation.

"Then why were you at St. James this morning?" Madison asked.

"I'm a courier and was hired to pick something up from them."

"So you admit to being there this morning?" Madison asked.

"I was, but . . ." He hesitated, clearly unsure of what he could say that might keep him out of trouble. "But I swear, it's nothing illegal. Sometimes I deliver or pick up things for a friend. That's it."

"What was in the envelope they gave you?"

Ryan shrugged. "I have no idea. I got a hundred bucks to pick it up and deliver it to an address. No questions asked. No courier in the city knows the contents of what they are delivering. Or at least they're not supposed to. Not even UPS or the post office."

Madison folded her arms across her chest and frowned. "You looked inside the package, didn't you?"

He glanced at the floor.

"Ryan . . ."

"Fine. It was cash."

Jonas kicked aside an empty box from Chinese takeout on the floor in front of him. "So who gave you the job?"

"I can't answer that." He glanced at the door, clearly nervous at the direction of the conversation.

"Oh, I'm pretty sure you can," Madison said.

"Don't I have the right to remain silent?"

"We're not arresting you," Jonas said. "Just making conversation."

Ryan looked back and forth between the two marshals. "Maybe I need a lawyer."

"What do you think?" Madison turned to Jonas. "If he's not going to cooperate, we should just go ahead and arrest him for the outstanding warrant for trespassing—"

"Wait a minute." Ryan's jaw tensed as he pressed his lips together, clearly debating his options and not liking either of them.

Jonas took a step forward. "We can take you in if you don't cooperate."

"You can't do that."

"Yes, we can."

"You don't understand." Ryan rubbed the back of his neck. "If I tell you who I work for, you'll have to give me some kind of police protection. There's no telling what he'll do to me. My boss is not exactly a nice guy. And trust me, if I end up crossing him, forget the warrant out on me. You'll be peeling my dead body off the street."

"You have quite an imagination," Jonas said.

"I'm not kidding. You don't mess with the people I work for. You do your job. Do it right, and then still worry that they'll come after you because they didn't like the way you combed your hair."

"Tell us who he is, and we'll get him off the streets," Madison said. "Then you won't have to worry."

"And if he finds out who turned him in? Then what? It won't matter if he's off the streets. He'll still find me. He has people everywhere."

Jonas scowled. They didn't have time to play games. They needed the name of the forger. Clearly Ryan was scared, and from the way he was living, it wasn't as if he had a lot to lose.

Tires squealed in the parking lot. Jonas crossed the floor, then shifted the curtain slightly. A car pulled up in front of the building, windows rolled down and weapons pulled out.

"Get down. Now!"

Jonas threw himself onto the carpet, forcing Ryan down with him, as Madison followed his order. Rapid gunfire pelted the front of the apartment, shattering the window and pinning them down. A lamp exploded. He held his ears as dozens of slugs embedded into the wall behind them.

The attack seemed to be over as quickly as it started.

Jonas got up onto his knees, still staying low, his ears ringing. "Madison?"

"I'm okay."

"Ryan?"

"I told you they'd come after me," he said, pressing himself closer to the floor.

"Well, for the moment, let's just be glad that we're all alive." Jonas crept across the shards of glass to peer out the shattered window, lifting his head just enough to see what was going on outside. Car doors slammed shut. Apparently shooting up the apartment wasn't enough. Four armed men were coming to make sure they finished the job.

Jonas rose to his feet. "We need to get out of here."

Madison nodded and turned to the door, but Ryan let out a low groan.

Jonas noticed the red stain that had already begun to spread across Ryan's sleeve and down his bare arm.

"You're going to have to hang in there for the moment," he said. "We've got four armed men headed our way."

"Is there another exit?" Madison asked.

Ryan inhaled sharply. "There's a window in the bathroom that's big enough to squeeze through."

Jonas pulled Ryan off the floor, then helped him toward the bathroom. "Do you know that from experience?"

Ryan winced at the movement. "I might have had to make a quick exit once or twice."

"What's behind the apartment?" Jonas asked.

"Just an alley with a couple dumpsters and a maintenance shed."

Jonas jumped on top of the toilet, then forced open the window above it, while Madison held on to Ryan, who was leaning against the wall, groaning. The crack of splintering wood came from the front of the apartment as Jonas shoved out the screen. This was no simple drive-by shooting. These men were going to make sure their targets were taken out.

He motioned at Madison to go through first. As soon as she was on the ground on the other side, he hoisted Ryan up to the window. The front door in the living room slammed against the wall as the men filed inside.

"Hurry, hurry!"

They had seconds to get out. He wasn't sure if any information they got out of the man was worth this, but if they left Ryan now, it would be a death sentence.

As soon as the opening was clear, he squeezed through the

window, feet first, emerging on the other side just in time. Madison had already pulled Ryan behind a dumpster, but it wasn't going to be long until the men figured out where they'd gone.

Ryan leaned against the side of the dumpster, blood dripping down his arm. "I'm not feeling too good. I don't know if I can go any further."

"It's just a graze," Madison said.

"No . . . you need to get me to a hospital. I could bleed out before we leave the parking lot. Please. I don't want to die. I have a kid."

Jonas bit back his irritation. "You'll survive the gunshot, but if they catch up to us, you will die. Where does this alley lead?"

Ryan paused, still staring at his arm. "To the main street where there are a couple strip malls."

"Okay. We should be able to lose them if we move quickly."

"But my arm—"

"You're just going to have to move, Ryan."

A shot rang out of the bathroom window, hitting a cement slab nearby. Jonas shot back, giving cover to Madison and Ryan as they ran down the alley. He fired off a couple more rounds, then took off after them.

They reached the end of the alley, and Jonas quickly assessed the strip malls on either side of the busy road. A storefront three doors down caught his attention. He called out to Madison to follow him. The door buzzed as they walked in. Inside was a mismatched selection of food, beauty products, and car parts. It would have to work for the moment.

Jonas held up his badge at the man standing behind the counter. "Do you have any customers in here?"

The employee shook his head. "No. It's just me."

"Good. I want you to lock the door, then go hide in the back until I tell you otherwise."

"What's going on?" he asked, eyes widening.

Jonas ignored his question. "We're going to do everything we can to keep you safe."

The man froze.

"Go. Now."

The man nodded finally and hurried to lock the front door, then scurried to the back of the store.

"Find something to patch him up and keep him quiet. I'll call for backup," Jonas said to Madison, then turned to Ryan. "Stay away from the front window."

"This is the last thing I ever imagined," Ryan said, walking through the rows of the store. "Running like a fugitive in the middle of the city."

"And don't talk," Madison said, as she grabbed a few items off a shelf.

Jonas put in a call to his boss.

"What's your status?" Michaels asked.

"We need backup. We've got a wounded Ryan Kent with us and someone doesn't want him talking. Our car's currently cut off by four armed men who are after us."

"Where are you?"

"Holed up in a strip mall a block from the apartments."

Michaels started shouting orders in the background. "We're tracking your phone now. Stay where you are."

"What happens if they start checking the stores and they find us?" Ryan asked, while Madison bandaged his arm in order to stop the bleeding.

"Then we fight them off."

Ryan's face managed to pale a shade whiter than it already was. "Two against four? Are you kidding?"

Jonas frowned. "This is why you don't get involved in couriering packages for criminals."

Ryan squeezed his eyes shut. "Ouch."

"Stop fighting me," Madison said. "If you stop moving, it won't smart so much."

"Sorry, but it hurts. Have you ever been shot?"

"She has, actually." Jonas crossed his arms over his chest, a steely look covering his face.

Ryan turned away, his mouth finally shut. But no doubt it wouldn't stay that way for long.

Sirens whirled in the distance.

"Do I have to come with you?" he asked, wincing again as Madison finished up.

"The way I look at it, you have two choices," she said. "You can go back home and take your chances with whoever's after you. Alone. Or you can come with us."

"And if word gets out that I'm holed up in a US Marshals' office?"

Jonas shot him another irritated look. "I won't tell, if you don't."

＊＊＊

They made it out the back door of the strip mall and all the way to the marshals' offices without more than a dozen words from Ryan. Michaels sent someone to retrieve their car before they made it back.

As they entered the interrogation room, Jonas motioned for Ryan to sit down at the table, then he took a seat across from him, with Madison standing behind him.

"Can I at least have something to eat?" Ryan asked, breaking his self-imposed silence.

"I was hoping we were done with the whining," Madison said.

"I've been shot, chased, and pretty much had the most terrifying day of my life. So yeah, it kind of makes me want to keep whining."

Jonas tapped the table. "Then let's put an end to all of this. Are you ready to tell us who ordered that hit? Because it's been a long day, and I'm ready to go home. But unless I get some answers from you, it's going to be a very long night."

Ryan stared down at his hands. "I meant it when I said he'll kill me."

"Yes—we experienced that just now," Jonas said. "Which means getting him off the streets is your only way out."

Ryan didn't look convinced. "He doesn't do his own dirty work."

"He also clearly doesn't trust you." Madison leaned forward, resting her palms on the table. "He probably knows you looked inside the package. You actually should be thankful we were there to save you. Because this isn't going to just disappear."

"Fine." Ryan scratched at a spot on the table. "His name is Adam Cain."

Jonas glanced back at the one-way mirror, knowing Michaels was listening to every word being said.

"Tell me about him," Jonas said, turning back to face Ryan.

"He's been super paranoid lately. Apparently, there are a couple Feds who have been poking around, trying to find him. So he's been lying low. Using couriers like me."

"He's a forger?" Madison asked.

"Yeah."

"And how does someone find out about his services?"

He shrugged, then winced and reached for the bandage on his arm. "You have to know the right people and do a bit of asking around. He usually only works on recommendations from people he trusts in order to make sure he's not being set up, but honestly, I don't get involved in what he's doing. I drop off packages or pick things up for him. That's it."

"Where can we find him?" Jonas asked.

"Like I said, he's lying low and hiding out. Even I don't know."

"Then how do you communicate with him?"

"We use a burner phone."

Jonas signaled for Madison to step out of the room with him. Michaels was waiting on the other side of the glass.

"The guy's telling the truth," Michaels said. "Adam Cain popped up on a wanted database."

"Do you have any idea how to find him?" Jonas asked.

"Apparently, the Feds have been after him for months in connection with several different cases, but so far they haven't been able to track him down. He seems to be pretty good at staying invisible."

Jonas rolled his eyes. "So we're looking at another dead end?"

"Maybe," Madison said. "But if Jesse and Nadia found a way to get ahold of him, that means we can too."

Madison's phone rang and she excused herself to take the call. When she turned back to them, she had a dazed look on her face.

"Who was that?" Jonas asked.

"My neighbor." She stared at the phone.

"Madison, what's wrong?"

"She just called 911. Someone broke into my house."

TWENTY-ONE

Madison grabbed her bag off the desk. "I need to go—"
"Of course." He followed her to the door. "But
I'm going with you."

She thought about telling him he didn't need to come with
her. That she could handle the situation. But she stopped herself. She'd gotten used to doing everything on her own for so
long, it was nice having someone have her back.

They headed out of the building, toward the parking lot.
"And I'll drive," he said.

It was early evening, and the sun was peeking out from
behind the clouds, creating a soft, golden glow over the city.

"I'm fine, Jonas. A bit shook up, I'll admit, but I don't even
know for certain if anyone actually got in."

Jonas clicked on the key fob and unlocked his vehicle. "I
just don't want you to have to worry about traffic on top of
everything else."

But she knew what he was really thinking. The last time
someone had broken into her house, she was home alone,
and they shot her.

A car backfired on the main road, making Madison jump.

"Are you okay?" Jonas asked.

"Yeah. I'm sorry." She shook her head to clear her thoughts. "I guess I'm more on edge than I thought I was."

She slid into the passenger seat, then closed her eyes, willing herself to relax. Her counselor had given her tips on how to recover repressed memories. She'd watched her diet, tried hypnosis, and done cognitive therapy, but none of that had managed to surface the truth about what had happened that day three months ago.

Memories from the past forced their way to the forefront of her mind. She'd just arrived home after a stressful week of chasing a fugitive halfway across the country. She was exhausted and glad to be home with a couple days off ahead. Then she'd heard something in the house.

She squeezed her eyes tighter as Jonas headed toward the freeway, willing herself to relive the experience. The house she and Luke had bought together had been old and always made strange noises. But something had been different. She'd pulled out her weapon and started walking through the first floor, making sure she was alone. She'd cleared the rooms, finally deciding she'd imagined something. Once her guard was off, she set her service weapon on the counter and started making a protein shake.

And then someone . . . someone had been standing there, in her kitchen, pointing a gun at her.

"What is going to happen?" she'd asked the intruder, trying to plan out her next move.

"We'll talk a few more minutes, then I'm going to shoot you."

A piece of the puzzle had clicked into place.

"Like you did to my husband?" she'd asked.

Panic engulfed her. Madison opened her eyes, but as hard as she tried to hold on to the memory, it was gone. No different than a lost dream after you wake up. There in vivid detail one moment, and then gone forever. She let out a sharp breath of air, trying to picture whoever had been holding the gun. If she could just see their face . . .

"Madison? What's wrong?" Jonas's gentle voice brought her back to the present.

She rubbed her temples in an attempt to alleviate some of the tension in her head. Her hands felt clammy. "I don't know, I heard that noise, and then for a moment, it was like I was there again. Standing in my house in front of the shooter."

"That's good, isn't it?"

"I don't know. I still can't see their face." *Who pulled the trigger?*

"You will . . . you just have to give it time."

She pulled at the seat belt strapped across her chest. Suddenly it felt like a noose. "It's been three months. I can't see them, but I can still feel the panic."

"Has that happened before?" he asked. "Something triggering a memory?"

She paused for a second before answering. "Once."

He flipped on his blinker, then took the exit toward her house. "The psychologist told you this was a normal part of the healing process."

"Maybe you're right. Maybe the pieces are starting to slowly come back."

"Just give it some time."

She nodded but couldn't help but feel that time was running out.

***

The police had already arrived at the house by the time they pulled into the driveway. Madison jumped out of the car and hurried to the porch, where one of the officers stood, talking into his radio. Her next-door neighbor Venessa was talking to a second officer in front of her house, holding her six-month-old daughter, Charlotte.

Madison introduced herself as the homeowner. "My neighbor called and said someone was breaking into my house."

"Officer Acosta," the police officer said, shaking her hand. "My partner is talking with your neighbor right now. There doesn't seem to be anyone on the property, but we haven't searched the house yet. Your neighbor actually got video of the suspect, though from what I've seen, it's not enough to ID our suspect." The balding man rubbed his chin. "That said, there has actually been a string of break-ins in this area over the past couple months, so there's a good chance it's connected. The suspect breaks into the back of the house while another stands guard. The first grabs what he can and is in and out within a matter of minutes."

Madison frowned at the information. "So more than likely, someone has been watching my house."

"It is possible," Acosta said.

So much for moving to a safer neighborhood.

"We need to make sure the house is clear," Jonas said.

Acosta held up his hand. "Don't worry, folks. My partner and I are about to handle that ourselves."

Madison grabbed her badge and showed it to the officer and his partner, who had just returned from Venessa's house. "We're US Marshals," she told them.

"I see, then," Acosta's partner said, shrugging. "It can't hurt to have more hands on deck. We can clear the house together."

Madison pulled out her service weapon, then unlocked the front door. The alarm pad was off. Had she forgotten to set it when she left the house yesterday morning? Setting the alarm had become a habit, but she had been distracted.

She began systematically going through the ground level of the house with Jonas while the two officers headed to the unfinished basement. There were a number of boxes in the three-bedroom house she still hadn't unpacked, but for now, they were neatly stacked up between what would one day be a guest room and her office. The second floor held the master bedroom and bath she'd repainted, but there was no sign of a burglar. The house was clear.

"Does it look like anything was taken?" Jonas asked as the officers headed outside.

She opened a couple dresser drawers, her irritation growing. "I had some cash here that's gone. Less than a hundred dollars. A few pieces of jewelry."

She checked out the bathroom, then returned to the main floor, taking a mental inventory as she went back through, more slowly this time. "The only other thing I'm noticing right off the bat is a missing bottle of prescription pain medicine I had left over from my surgery."

Jonas holstered his Glock. "Then, like the officer said, it's likely this is connected to the string of robberies."

Maybe, but she still wasn't convinced. The uneasiness she'd been feeling since Venessa's call settled inside of her. What if this wasn't connected to the burglaries, but had something to do with whoever had broken into her house the last time? What if she had been here when they broke in?

"Madison?"

A shiver slid through her as she turned back to Jonas. "Sorry. I'm just trying to process all of this."

"I know what you're thinking." He reached out and squeezed

her hand. "But there's no reason to assume this is connected to the last break-in."

"But it could be." She pulled her hand out of his. "We both know that."

She stepped back outside onto the front porch and let the words hang between them. She had no idea why someone had shot her. Or what they might want by breaking into her house a second time. But she couldn't simply dismiss the idea that they were connected.

Officer Acosta finished searching the outside perimeter and headed up the sidewalk toward them. "Is anything missing?"

"Some jewelry, cash, and a bottle of prescription painkillers," Madison said.

"How much cash?"

"Less than a hundred dollars. And the jewelry wasn't necessarily valuable. More sentimental. Other than that, I don't keep a lot of valuables in the house." Madison glanced over at her neighbor Venessa. She turned to the officer. "I'd like to talk to her."

"Of course, though she's pretty upset. Worried about the break-in being so close to her."

Jonas and Acosta followed Madison across the grass to where Venessa stood with a wide-awake Charlotte on her hip.

"Venessa," Madison said, squeezing the baby's bare toes. "You remember my partner, Jonas."

Venessa nodded. "Yeah. It's good to see you again."

He smiled at her. "Are you okay?"

"Not really." Venessa's voice cracked. She turned to Madison. "I told Jimmy when you moved in how much safer I felt knowing we had a US Marshal for a neighbor, but I was alone when it happened, and it really freaked me out."

"Can you tell us what you saw?" Madison asked.

"I was trying to put Charlotte down for a nap. I thought I heard something. Jimmy said I'm always paranoid, but you know how it is. When he's out I always feel uneasy."

"I understand," Madison said. "Go on."

Venessa pulled a strand of her hair out of her daughter's fingers. "You know how Charlotte's room overlooks your backyard. I heard something, so I put her down and went to check out the noise. There was a figure moving across your backyard, and then they broke into the back door. And I have video to prove it."

"You recorded it?" Jonas asked.

"I'd left my phone downstairs. My husband is always reminding me to keep it with me so he can get ahold of me, but instead I grabbed the security camera we keep in the nursery so we can watch her."

"Can I look at it?" Madison asked.

"Of course." Venessa handed over her phone. "I pulled up the footage on our monitor app."

Madison held it up so Jonas could watch as well.

"Right there," he said. "Freeze the footage."

"The picture's actually fairly clear," Madison said, staring at the paused recording. "But he's wearing a hoodie. You can't see his face."

Madison turned to Venessa. "Can I keep the SD card?"

"I can go get it if you'll hold Charlotte for a moment."

"Of course. I'll have our IT guy go through the footage. It's very possible he'll be able to pick up something we missed."

Venessa handed Madison the baby, who immediately grabbed for Madison's hair. "I'm sorry I couldn't help more."

"You did great," Madison said, carefully disentangling Charlotte's fingers. "Especially thinking to record it."

"I looked over the footage as well," Officer Acosta said. "He was in there six minutes. And like I said earlier, it's the same pattern we've seen in the area where one goes in the house, while the other one keeps guard from the street in a getaway car."

"They must have heard sirens," Madison said, automatically rocking the baby against her chest.

"More than likely." Officer Acosta's phone went off. "Please excuse me."

"You're good with kids," Jonas said as the officer walked away.

Charlotte had nestled into her shoulder and was starting to fall asleep.

"I can't tell you how many nights I went over to Danielle's and rocked her babies to sleep to give her a break," Madison said, resting her chin against Charlotte's head. "Her two oldest were super colicky, and her youngest just doesn't like to sleep. I think he's afraid of missing something."

"My mom said I was like that." Jonas shoved his hands into his back pockets. "You'd make a great mom."

She felt herself flush and hid her reddening cheeks by burying her face in Charlotte's hair. "What about you? Do you see yourself with kids someday?"

"I don't know. Felicia brought it up a few times, but the idea of fitting family into a career isn't easy. I think she was convinced that I wasn't willing to put her and family above a career."

His confession surprised her.

"And now you feel like you'll never know?" she asked.

He nodded.

"Or maybe she just wasn't the right one for you. I don't

know. Life and love get complicated. But love and the right relationship is worth it."

She looked down at Charlotte, who was fast asleep, and felt her own body relax. As much as his confession surprised her, her own response had taken her off guard. Talking about love and relationships wasn't something she was used to doing. Neither was opening up her heart.

Venessa hurried out of her house toward them. "Here's the SD card. I have another one, so you can keep this one."

"Thank you," Madison said, handing Charlotte back to her. "Are you going to be okay?"

"I think so. Jimmy's on his way home now, and you can be sure that I'll lock up the house once I'm inside."

"If you need anything, you can just call."

"I will. Thank you."

✳ ✳ ✳

The wind was starting to pick up as Madison headed back to her house with Jonas. She'd forgotten that a warm front was predicted to come in later tonight, bringing with it the possibility of storms and more wet weather.

Once she'd given her statement to Acosta and his partner and sent them on their way, her thoughts shifted back to the break-in. She'd never been one to live in fear or worry, but somehow the thought of sleeping here alone left her uneasy. Maybe it was because memories of the last home invasion still hovered too close to the surface. Her physical therapy and doctor appointments had been the constant reminder that the past was still very much a part of her present. And now with a second break-in . . .

She thought about calling Danielle as she and Jonas walked

back inside the house. She could always spend the night there but knew her sister would only worry more. Besides, there was nothing anyone could really do at the moment. Days like this she missed her mom. Missed the comfort and protection her dad used to be able to offer. When he'd wrap his arms around her in a big hug and make her feel like she was a kid again. Safe and loved. There were days when she could almost forget he was sick. But there was nothing he could do either.

She turned to Jonas as she flipped on a couple lights. "You can go home. I'll be fine. I'll meet you back at the office in the morning."

Jonas shook his head. "You're not staying here tonight. Not alone, at least."

"I'll be fine, Jonas. I'll make sure the alarm is set tonight. And before you suggest I go to Danielle's, I have thought about it, but I'm not dragging her into this again. The last time I was on a case that turned personal, her family ended up in a safe house."

"We have no reason to believe they are at risk this time," Jonas said.

"I know. I just . . . I can't forget that whoever shot Luke— whoever shot me—is still out there. And if this was somehow connected—"

"But why?" Jonas stepped in front of her. "When they broke into your house before, they didn't try to hide the fact that they'd been there. They didn't make it look like a robbery by stealing a handful of cash. There were no games. They even left a black rose like the ones you find on Luke's grave every year so you knew who was behind it. So if this was them again, why make this look like a random burglary?"

She crossed her arms, hugging herself. "I don't know."

"You can come stay at my place."

"I'm not leaving, Jonas." She headed into the kitchen, grabbed a couple water bottles, then tossed him one. "I can't let whoever's behind this scare me."

"Then I'll sleep on the couch here."

She twisted off the lid and chugged half the bottle. "You know you're impossible."

He smirked. "But I also come with a loaded Glock and the ability to defend beautiful ladies."

She ran her hand unconsciously across the scar on her stomach. "I don't need a bodyguard—"

"I was thinking more along the lines of a superhero, though my cape is at the dry cleaners."

"Very funny." She glanced up at him. "You can stay. But just so you know, I can take care of myself."

"I know you can." He smiled. "I just don't want anything to happen to you. I just lost one friend. I can't lose you too." He grabbed his keys out of his pocket. "I keep a gym bag in the car with a change of clothes. I'll go get it, then make sure all the doors and windows are locked."

"Make yourself at home. I've got leftover Chinese takeout in the fridge if you're hungry."

She started for the living room, then turned back toward the hallway. Something Jonas had said stuck with her. Why make this look like a random burglary? She walked into the extra room she planned to make into an office and stopped in the doorway. On the surface, it didn't look as if anything had been touched. Against one wall was a rolltop desk that had been a gift from her father and held two file folder racks where she'd organized evidence from Luke's case. On a second wall, she'd piled up two dozen boxes she still needed to unpack.

A third wall held the eight-by-four-foot bulletin board she'd mounted to the wall.

She stood in front of the board that held evidence she'd arranged from Luke's murder: time lines, photos, police interviews of witnesses, including the woman who called 911 that day, plus a list of patients with possible grudges against Luke. But nothing had gotten them closer to the truth.

Jonas leaned against the doorway and cleared his throat. "Everything okay?"

She stared at the board, dread sweeping over her as she turned around. "What if this wasn't a random break-in?"

TWENTY-TWO

Jonas sat on the edge of the desk while Madison stared at the bulletin board covered with dozens of crime scene photos and notes. From what he knew about her late husband's case, he could tell the board outlined Luke's crime scene. But the one obvious omission was any photos of Luke. Something that he couldn't blame her for. Though he also couldn't help but wonder if her husband's murder, the home invasion, and the shooting three months ago hadn't affected her more than she'd chosen to let on. She'd clearly spent a lot of hours organizing all the evidence from the case and meticulously labeling everything.

She turned around. "What if the real target was this room? The robberies have been on the news. It's the perfect cover."

"Is anything missing?" Jonas asked.

"I'm not sure, and it will take some time to go through everything. But after spending five years going through every scrap of evidence from Luke's case, I know what was on this board and in my files. I just . . . I can't put my finger on it, but someone has been in here."

"We could have CSU check for fingerprints. See if they can get a match."

Madison nodded, distracted by her theory.

"I'm assuming you have copies of everything?" Jonas asked.

"Everything's digitally backed up, yes. And besides, anything I have was copied from the official evidence report."

"I know you're still searching for answers," Jonas said, hoping he wasn't overstepping his welcome. "Have you been following any new leads in Luke's case? It's possible your questioning has someone nervous."

"Maybe." She pointed to the photo of a thick black ring etched in silver. "I made some more phone calls last week. Called a couple new sellers who stock these kinds of rings on Etsy. It's always a long shot, and I don't really expect to get any new information, but that's how cold cases are solved. New witness testimony, going through all the evidence again and again. We all know how easy it is to zero in on a theory then miss what's right in front of you."

Jonas studied the photo she'd pointed out. "It's a unique ring."

She rested against the desk beside him. "It's a gaming ring they found at Luke's murder scene, but I was never able to find the owner."

"A gaming ring?"

She turned to him. "I'd never heard of them either, but you can get custom-made rings for your favorite video games."

"I'll admit, that theory makes sense. You started asking questions and are getting close to the answer. Maybe whoever is behind all of this wanted to see what you know."

Her shoulder brushed against his as she moved away from the desk. She was dressed in gray sweatpants and a T-shirt.

His gaze drifted to her lips. They were off the clock, and his compartmentalizing wasn't working. Maybe he shouldn't have offered to stay. His instinct was always to try and fix things, but he knew she was able to take care of herself.

Leave your heart out of this, Jonas.

If he'd learned anything with Felicia, it was that his job and relationships couldn't mix. And in the end, if he didn't rein in his feelings, it could ruin everything between him and the best partner he'd ever worked with. But then why was his mind screaming to take a chance, forget about logic, and simply tell her how he felt?

"Jonas?" She touched his arm, her expression full of questions.

"Sorry, I'm listening."

"You look tired. We both are. We can take this up again tomorrow."

"It's not that. Really. And I am listening. You're the one I'm worried about. With everything that's going on, this is just another layer of stress."

"There is nothing to worry about. The house is locked, and I have you as my bodyguard. What else do I need?"

He looked around the room. "You spend a lot of time in here."

"Sometimes, when I can't sleep."

"How often?"

"Some nights." She shrugged. "Maybe most nights."

"And your dreams?"

This time she didn't answer.

"You're still having nightmares, aren't you?"

She nodded. "I didn't want to bother you."

He shot her a smile. "Since when have you worried about bothering me?"

"You're such a comedian."

"Seriously." He nudged her with his shoulder. "I thought by now that you knew I'm here for you. For anything. Day or night. But you have to let me know what you need."

"You're here, aren't you? Right now."

"Yes, but sometimes I'm not sure how best to help."

"If you ask me, you're doing a pretty good job."

They locked eyes for a second, and Jonas had to look away to keep himself from making a rash decision . . . like kissing her.

"Good," he said, clearing his throat, "then here's what we're going to do. We'll have CSU come tomorrow and take finger-prints. There's a good chance they can find something. In the meantime, you need to get some rest."

She yawned, proving his point. "You might be spot-on, but I'm worried I'm not going to be able to sleep."

"I happen to have a couple ideas that might help."

She smirked. "Still trying to fix things?"

"Just let me have free rein of your kitchen for a few minutes," he said as they headed out of the office. "I'll meet you on the couch in the living room."

"I'm not sure what I think about your taking over my kitchen."

Jonas laughed. "Trust me."

Her lips parted. "You know I do."

Five minutes later, he handed her a mug and sat down on the other end of the couch.

"What is this?"

"My grandmother's remedy for sleepless nights. She used to make this for me. It's warm milk, with vanilla, nutmeg, and sugar, and it's guaranteed to make you sleep like a baby."

Madison took a sip and smiled. "Wow. This is delicious, and after a day like today, I can definitely use all the help I can get."

"There is one other thing she always used to do that is guaranteed to help you relax."

Her smile widened. "Considering I've loved all your ideas, I'm game."

"Okay then. Take off your shoes and scoot your feet over here."

"Seriously?" Her brows rose. "A foot rub?"

"Yep." He waited till she situated herself, lifting her feet into his lap, then he started the massage.

"How are you not taken?" She leaned her head against the couch and let out a soft sigh. "I mean, really. Warm milk and foot massages would melt any girl's heart."

Including yours?

He shoved away the thought, but he was getting too close and forgetting to safeguard his heart. "I hope you don't think I just go around massaging women's feet. They might get the wrong idea."

She looked up and caught his gaze. "If I didn't know you better, I might think you were flirting with me, Jonas Quinn."

"I just want you to know that you don't have to do this alone."

"I know, it's just hard sometimes." She took another sip of her milk while he kept rubbing her socked feet. The light-hearted mood between them had vanished. "Danielle's got her family plus my father to worry about, and as much as I try to help, I feel like it's never enough."

"You've both got your hands full."

He searched for what he wanted to say to her as he watched her begin to relax on the other side of the couch, sipping his grandmother's recipe. He wanted to tell her what had started to transpire in his heart the past few weeks, but he'd promised himself he wouldn't go there. Especially now. No. If he were smart, he'd accept that there could never be more than friendship between them.

"How are you?" she asked, setting her cup on the end table next to her. "I know I'm not the only one this case has thrown off."

He rested his hands on her feet. "I've called Hazel several times, but I'll try to follow up and see what I can do to help soon. I can't imagine what she's going through, and now she's having to plan a funeral." He closed his eyes for a second, taking a deep breath. "I know she'll have a lot of support from her church, but this still isn't going to be easy."

"No, it's not." Madison leaned back against the pillows. "Thank you."

"For what?"

"For being here for me. Not just for right now, but for everything you've done over the last few months to help get me back on my feet. You're a good friend, Jonas."

And if I told you I wanted to kiss you right now, what would you say?

He swallowed hard. No. Why did his mind keep going there? They were friends. Good friends. But that was all. "I am always here for you. You know that."

"I do, and I appreciate that."

They fell into comfortable conversation. Jonas always found himself losing track of time when he was with Madison. She was just so easy to talk to.

A knocking noise pulled his attention away from the story she was telling him.

"Jonas? What's wrong?"

"I'm probably imagining things, but I thought I heard something."

He pushed her feet off his lap, then stood up, not sure what he'd just heard. More than likely, he was simply being paranoid. The house was old, and it wasn't unusual for the pipes to creak and the floors to shift, but tonight . . .

Thump. Thump.

He definitely heard something. "I think someone's in the house, Madison."

He grabbed his Glock off the coffee table while she pulled hers out of the end table drawer. He wanted to tell her to stay put, but he knew her well enough to know that wasn't going to work.

"We'll do this together," he said, taking the lead.

Clearing a house with Madison felt like second nature. They read each other's moves automatically as they started through the first floor. She moved silently behind him as he headed toward the kitchen. A few hours ago, he'd gone through the house and rechecked all the doors and windows, including the basement. He checked the back door for the second time tonight. It was locked.

They started down the hallway, checking bedroom doors as they cleared the house.

Nothing.

All that was left was the basement.

He signaled for her to follow him, opened the door, then started down the narrow wooden staircase. The wood groaned beneath his weight. This was the one part of the house she hadn't done anything to. For now, the unfinished space was filled with dark shadows.

Something banged, louder this time.

A window at the far end blew open. Wind and rain pelted the small opening.

"You came down here, didn't you?" she asked.

He grabbed a ladder from the corner so he could shut the window. "It was locked. I checked it myself."

"Maybe the wind managed to blow it open."

Maybe, but that didn't make sense. He quickly climbed the ladder, then pushed the window shut, but not before noticing something new.

"The space is too narrow for someone to go through," he said, wedging it shut with a small piece of wood from the windowsill. "But it looks like someone tried to open it. The latch has been broken."

She shivered. "So they came back?"

He climbed down the ladder, wishing he had answers, but he didn't.

"They know where I live, Jonas. No matter where I go, they can find me. They know where my sister lives, and her family and my father . . . I can't go through this again."

He pulled her into his arms, brushing off the feelings that came with her nearness. All that mattered was that he wasn't going to let anything happen to her.

"I'm sorry. I shouldn't let myself fall apart like this," she said. "We don't know it was the same person who shot me."

He tilted up her chin and stared into her eyes. "Hey. You don't have to apologize. At all."

While he wasn't willing to jump to the conclusion that this was nothing more than a random burglary, he knew they couldn't take any chances.

"I'm going to arrange for a squad car to keep watch outside tonight. Just in case. Do you think you can sleep?"

She shrugged. "Probably not, but I need to."

He climbed the stairs behind her. "And I'll be right here if you need me."

A minute later he watched her walk down the hall, then grabbed the pillow and blanket she'd left for him on the couch earlier and tried to settle in. But as tired as he felt, he wasn't sure he was going to be able to sleep. No matter how hard he tried to fight it, from the very first time they met, Madison James had captivated him.

When he'd trained her at the shoot house, he'd been amazed at her focus and determination no matter what scenario they played out. And he hadn't missed the unexpected connection he felt toward her back then. Now he knew she'd been grieving her husband's death, but then he'd just assumed she was not interested. Still, he'd always wondered what would have happened if circumstances had been different. What he couldn't have guessed was that now, all these years later, he would manage to see the wall around her heart begin to crumble.

He pulled the blanket up around him and turned on his side. No matter what his heart felt, the priority at the moment wasn't analyzing his feelings toward the woman down the hall. It was keeping her safe.

TWENTY-THREE

Jonas's phone rang, jerking him out of a chain of incoherent dreams. He sat up, quickly oriented himself, then grabbed his cell off the coffee table. He checked the caller ID. It was Michaels.

"Morning," Jonas said, blinking the sleep out of his eyes and stretching. He was surprised he'd slept past six. "What's going on?"

"Are you still at Madison's?"

"Yeah. I . . ." He stumbled off the couch and headed to the kitchen, trying to work out the kinks in his back. "I slept on her couch last night and can feel every muscle."

"That's what you get for playing hero." Michaels chuckled.

"Funny."

"Any more surprises last night?"

"None." Jonas pulled open cupboards until he found a canister of ground coffee.

"Good. Looks like it was quiet all around then. Listen, I'm sorry to call so early, but I've got a possible lead I want the two of you to check out for me personally."

"Of course. What have you got?"

224 — THE CHASE

"You spoke to Barton Wells at the bank after the robbery."

Jonas grabbed the coffeepot and started filling it with water. "We did."

"I just got off the phone with his wife. She's actually an old friend of Glenda's. She said their house was broken into last night, and she's convinced it's connected to the bank heist."

"Really?" Jonas poured the water into the coffee maker. "Why would she think that?"

"She was pretty upset, and I didn't get much out of her. I told her that the two of you were in the process of tracking down our fugitives and would come by personally to talk with her husband. I'd go see them myself, but I'm heading out soon to an early morning meeting and will be tied up for most of the day. The police already did their initial investigation last night, so I'll make sure that they pass on whatever they found."

"Great. We'll go by and see what we can find out."

"I appreciate it."

Jonas set his phone on the counter, added coffee grounds to the filter, then flipped the machine on. Except for the gurgling of the machine, the house was quiet. Maybe last night's break-in had been nothing more than a coincidence. Madison was under a lot of pressure to find out not only who'd shot her husband but who had shot her as well. Was it possible she'd made a mistake, thinking something was missing in trying to find an answer? Or was that what he wanted to believe? That the break-in had simply been a random robbery and not something personal aimed at her.

"Please tell me you're making it extra strong."

He looked up as Madison walked into the kitchen in her stocking feet and caught her sleepy smile. Her hair was mussed, and there was a crease from her pillow across her cheek.

"Good morning to you as well." Jonas laughed. "I am making it extra strong, and you're just in time. It should be ready in a couple minutes."

"Perfect."

"Should I ask how you slept?"

She leaned against the counter. "Pretty good once I actually fell asleep, though I had a hard time slowing my mind down. What about you? I know that couch isn't very comfortable."

"Trust me. I've slept on far worse."

She rolled her eyes. "That didn't exactly answer my question."

"I slept fine." He opened a couple more cupboards looking for mugs, then pulled out two. "Really."

"At least everything was quiet last night."

"Thankfully, yes." He set the mugs next to the coffee maker, momentarily at a loss for what he wanted to say next. "I've been thinking over everything last night. I can't help but wonder if we jumped to conclusions and it really was just a random break-in."

He caught her sullen expression and knew he'd upset her.

"I'm not doubting your instincts," he rushed on, "but we don't have enough evidence to solidly link it to Luke's murder, or to whoever shot you."

"No, you're right." She squeezed her eyes shut for a moment. "I'm just looking so hard for closure that sometimes my vision gets cloudy."

The coffee machine beeped as he moved in front of her. "I don't believe that. You're the most focused person I know."

She smiled. "I wish that were true, but I'm struggling to push aside my emotions and just see this as a break-in. Someone was in my house, and that leaves me feeling out of control."

"What you're feeling makes sense." He shook his head.

"I don't want us to jump to any conclusions. The last time someone broke in, they left a black rose. Just like they've done every year at Luke's grave. Why not this time? Not only that, the lock on the basement window was broken. Why?"

"I don't know."

He knew what she was thinking. Someone had wanted her to know who was behind the previous break-in. So if they'd found her new house and broken in—if they wanted to unnerve her—why not make it clear who was behind the incident?

"We're going to have to look for answers later," he said, pouring some coffee into a mug and sliding it in front of her. "Michaels just called. He wants us to go talk to Bart Wells again."

"The guy running for mayor?"

"One and the same. Apparently you weren't the only one robbed yesterday, and Wells's wife believes it's connected somehow to the bank heist."

Madison pulled open the fridge and grabbed the creamer, taking a second to pour a bit into her mug. "It seems odd she would think that, right?"

"That's what we need to go and find out. How much time do you need?"

Madison glanced down at the T-shirt and cotton pants she'd slept in and pushed back a strand of hair. "If you'll put my coffee in a to-go cup, fifteen minutes?"

"It's a deal."

✳ ✳ ✳

Jonas let out a low whistle forty-five minutes later as he drove through Upper Queen Anne neighborhood, known for its expensive residential homes, historic businesses, and cafés.

He couldn't help but notice the gorgeous views of downtown, the Space Needle, and Elliott Bay these houses afforded their occupants.

"I read recently that Bart's net worth is close to thirty-five million," Jonas said, following the GPS through the neighborhood.

"I've just been scanning a profile of him, and you're right," Madison said, looking up from her phone. "It says that most of his money came from his wife, but he has his own business as well. Something in real estate."

"I'm still trying to work out how this case is connected to the robbery. You have to admit, it would be a pretty strange coincidence."

She shrugged. "Here's something else that's interesting," Madison said as Jonas took another turn. "The mayoral election is coming up in two months, and it's pretty much a race between Bart and the incumbent mayor."

"Do you have a theory?" he asked.

"Maybe our fugitives saw the contents of Bart's safe-deposit box and thought they could get more out of him. It's not a secret he lives in a multimillion-dollar house and has a bank account to match."

"It still doesn't add up to me." Jonas parked along the curb in front of the house, then turned off the engine. "I can't imagine robbing a bank, then taking the time to pay a house call on one of the hostages just because he's rich. That's way too big of a risk."

"Except here's what changed," she said, after they'd both stepped out of the car. "We know we thwarted their exit plan because we found their go bag. Now their options are limited. We have their names and every law enforcement has seen their photo. They're desperate to get out of the city without getting caught, but unless they can find a way to disguise themselves or come up with new passports, they're trapped."

Jonas locked the car behind them. So maybe robbing the house of a high-profile figure did fit into that equation somehow. "I guess you're right."

"By the way, I've decided to forget the high-rise," Madison said, changing the subject as they started up the stone sidewalk. "I think this is where I would live if I had a few million dollars lying around. Not only do you have the incredible views but a large yard as well."

"Which requires upkeep and money."

Madison shrugged. "I figure if I can afford the house, I can afford a gardener. And for that matter, a maid."

"For the price of this house, I'd buy myself a few hundred acres in the foothills with views of the mountains, then I'd retire and spend my days fishing, horseback riding, and maybe some cross-country skiing in the winter."

"You're definitely not a city boy at heart, huh?"

Jonas chuckled. "No, I'm not."

"What about the bait and tackle shop idea you told me about?"

He noticed the teasing sparkle in her eyes. Her memory was good. "Maybe I'll run one a few months a year and relax the rest," he said, knocking on the large wooden door of the Wellses' home.

Trudy opened it a moment later.

"Morning, Mrs. Wells," Jonas said, holding up his badge. "We spoke briefly with you at the bank the other day. Our boss, Chief Deputy Carl Michaels, asked us to stop by and follow up about a robbery last night."

"Thank you so much for coming." Mrs. Wells ushered them into the large entryway. "Bart isn't happy I called you. He just wants to put all of this behind him, but I insisted we talk to Carl." She pressed her hand against her heart. "This has been such a nightmare. My husband has a possible concussion, but he refuses to go to the hospital."

"I'm sorry to hear that, Mrs. Wells," Madison said.

Trudy took in a shuddering breath. "I don't care about the money they took, but that doesn't make it less upsetting."

"So you believe that whoever's responsible for robbing the bank also robbed you last night?" Madison asked.

"Bart told me that the man who confronted him in the bank had a tattoo on his arm and wrist. One of the intruders here had a tattoo in the same place. I couldn't tell you what it was, but I saw it as he ran out. And if you think about it, it makes sense. If they knew who Bart was, they could have easily looked him up, believing they could get more money than just the contents of our lockbox."

"We aren't ruling out any possibilities," Jonas said, "which is why we would like to speak to your husband."

As if on cue, Bart strode into the room. He'd shed the suit he had on at the bank and now wore khakis and a loose, button-down shirt. "I'm sorry my wife bothered you, folks." He put his arm around Trudy's shoulders as he spoke. "The police are sending out their crime scene unit today, but the people who attacked me wore gloves, so I'm pretty sure they aren't going to find anything here."

"What about security footage?" Madison asked. "Do you have a system in place?"

He nodded. "Unfortunately, they managed to take it out before the robbery, so that's a dead end too."

Jonas frowned at the similarities in the heists. If their fugitives were involved, they would have had far less time to plan the break-in, but they had already proven they had the skills required to take out a security system and get in and out of a place without leaving any traces of evidence behind.

"Being involved in two robberies so close together is unfortunate," Madison said. "Why don't you tell us what happened before we jump to any conclusions either way."

Bart tugged on the bottom of his shirt and removed his other arm from around his wife. "I was working in my office when someone knocked on the front door. I went to answer it, expecting a friend of mine who was supposed to stop by last night. Instead, it was a couple thugs dressed in black, wearing masks and carrying weapons. They told me to get my wallet, along with any cash I might have. They followed me back to my office and asked if there was a safe, but before I answered, Trudy walked in. They got spooked and ended up fleeing through the back door."

Jonas processed the information in his head. Why would they get spooked if they were armed? Bart's wife was about five four and couldn't weigh more than a hundred and ten pounds.

He turned back to Trudy. "Do you have any idea why they ran?"

"I'm assuming they'd already gotten what they wanted. They brushed past me and were gone. I hardly had a chance to get a good look at them."

"Trudy said some money was taken," Madison said to Bart.

He rubbed the back of his neck. "My wallet, which had a couple hundred dollars in it. A handful of credit cards that I've already turned off. Hardly worth all the effort."

"And the cut on your head?" Jonas asked. "Where did that come from?"

Bart lifted his hand to the wound. "I tried to shut the door when I realized it wasn't my friend. But they forced their way in and pistol-whipped me when I tried to stop them."

Madison glanced at Jonas. "So no matter who it was, we can add assault charges as well."

Bart glanced at his wife. "I'm certain that it wasn't the same people. I tried to tell Trudy that, but she's convinced they saw an opportunity and jumped at it." He took his wife's hand in his.

"Why don't you think it could be them?" Jonas asked.

Bart shook his head. "I saw the suspects' photos on the news. Granted, I didn't see faces either time, but the two who broke in last night definitely seemed shorter and heavier."

"What about the tattoo?" Jonas asked. "You said the man in the bank had one on his arm. A compass."

Bart nodded. "Trudy was right about that. One of the guys last night did have an arm tattoo, but it was different. More of a pattern than a picture of something. And definitely not a compass."

Jonas looked at Madison. They'd both hoped that whatever had happened in this house last night would move them one step closer to finding their fugitives. But if Bart Wells was right, this had been nothing more than a random burglary.

TWENTY-FOUR

Madison sat quietly as Jonas drove them back to the US Marshals building, frustrated that they were no further ahead than they had been yesterday, with no idea if their suspects were still here in the city. And that wasn't all that had her mind racing. Something seemed off with Bart's testimony, but she hadn't been able to put her finger on it.

"You've been pretty quiet since we left. Is everything okay?" Jonas said, pulling into a parking space near their offices.

"Maybe it's just a gut feeling, but something isn't adding up for me," she said, making no move to get out of the car.

"So you're not buying the idea that Bart was in the wrong place at the wrong time twice in two days?"

"It wouldn't be impossible, but it's more than that." She shifted toward him, trying to put her thoughts into words. "I admit there isn't anything significant, but there are too many similarities in both robberies. A couple dressed in black, wearing face masks, and one with a tattoo on his wrist. Security systems were taken down in both, and we have little to no hard evidence pointing us to our suspects."

Jonas tapped his hands on the steering wheel. "I agree, but

what's his motivation for lying to us? And even more important, why would our fugitives, who have already stolen several hundred thousand dollars, decide to rob him for a couple hundred dollars in cash?"

"They have money, but there's something we know they don't have," Madison said.

He paused for a minute. She could see the inner workings of his mind spinning through the expression that crossed his face. A second later his eyes lit up. "Passports. A way out."

"Exactly. They're trapped in the city. And they are going to have to do something out of the box to escape."

"Any ideas?" Jonas asked.

"Let's play what-if."

"Okay."

"We talked about whoever broke into my house probably using the recent rise in burglaries as a cover-up. What if the one at Bart's home was staged?"

"Explain," Jonas said.

"Did anything about his story seem off?"

"That's easy. The fact that his petite wife scared off the would-be robbers?"

"I thought the same thing."

"So the robbery was simply a cover-up for . . . I don't know . . . blackmail? Extortion?"

"What if they weren't after money, but something he could give them? I need to look at something from the bank." Madison got out of the car, then pulled out her phone and called Piper.

"Deputy James, is there anything I can do for you?"

"Yes, Deputy Quinn and I are heading up to the office now. Is there any chance you got any footage from the safe-deposit room at the bank robbery?"

"Actually, yes, we did. I'm assuming that because they hadn't planned to be in there, they didn't take out those cameras."

"Great. We're on our way in. Please have the footage cued up for us."

"I'm on it."

She headed toward the building with Jonas, unable to shake what had been nagging at her ever since they'd spoken with Bart and his wife. There were too many similarities between their fugitives and whoever had broken into the Wells home. And the only thing suggesting they dismiss the connection was Bart's insistence that they weren't the same people. While she had no reason to believe the man was lying, neither was she simply going to take what he said as truth.

Piper was sitting in front of a computer and had just pulled up the time stamp Madison had asked for when they arrived.

"Can you tell me what you're looking for?" Piper asked, looking up at them.

"Honestly, I'm not sure. Let's just run through everything."

Madison pulled out the notes she'd taken during their interview with Bart to use as a reference. The angle didn't allow them to see what was in the Wellses' lockbox, but they could see Bart's back.

She watched the silent video as Bart pulled an item—an envelope, maybe—out of his pocket, then noticed that something was going on in the other room. Seconds later, he turned toward the camera. She could see the indecision on his face as he tried to figure out what was going on. He spun back around, knocking his phone off the table, then went to grab it. One of the robbers—Jesse—moved into the room and started shouting at him. Bart lay down on the floor while Jesse rummaged through the box, grabbing a few things in the process.

Madison leaned over Piper and stopped the video. The entire onscreen interaction took less than thirty seconds.

"Overall, the time line seems to fit," Jonas said.

"I agree. Except for one thing. The envelope. Let it run a few more seconds, Piper."

They watched as Jesse looked inside the envelope he'd picked up, said something to Bart, then shoved it into his pocket.

"Why take the envelope?" Piper said.

"That's what I want to know. Can you go back to the beginning? Just a few seconds before what we just saw."

Piper ran the video back to when Bart first walked in.

"Stop there," Madison said. "Bart told us he went to the bank because he was taking something out. An anniversary ring he'd bought for his wife. And yet when he walks in, he pulls something out of his pocket."

"It's hard to see because of the camera angle," Jonas said, "but I think you're right. It definitely looks like an envelope."

"And then Jesse takes the envelope with him."

"It seems like a stretch to think Bart's hiding something just because he brought an envelope to the bank," Jonas said. "The guy was rattled and could have forgotten. Or didn't think it worth mentioning."

"I agree, but I still find it significant that Jesse took that envelope with him after peeking inside it. Which makes me believe that Bart had a reason not to tell us." Madison turned to Piper. "Can you zoom in on the envelope?"

"I can try, but it will lose some of the resolution."

"Just do your best."

"Okay," she said, before enlarging the frame. "What do you think? That's as good as I can do and all I can see is a stamp that looks like it's part of a logo. Something . . . *gations*."

Jonas leaned against the edge of the desk. "Litigations. In-terrogations—"

"Investigations?" Piper asked.

"That fits," Madison said. "What if Bart hired a private in-vestigator?"

"He might have," Jonas said. "But why?"

"There are dozens of reasons, but maybe the question to ask is why someone would think that whatever is in an envelope is worth keeping." Madison paced back and forth, working to put the pieces together. They were still dealing with unsub-stantiated what-ifs, but their theory made sense. Now they had to test it.

"I think our next step should be having another talk with him," Jonas said.

"Agreed. We need to know what's in that envelope, why he didn't tell us about it, and why our fugitives believed it was worth taking."

"What can I do?" Piper asked.

"Do a deeper search into Bart Wells. If our fugitives are using him somehow, we need to know what's going on."

✳ ✳ ✳

Twenty-five minutes later, they were back in front of the home on Queen Anne Hill. Jonas knocked on the door, then stepped back while they waited for someone to answer. This time Mrs. Wells didn't seem as anxious to see them.

"Hello again, Mrs. Wells. We need to speak to your husband again," Madison said. "It will only take a few minutes."

The woman made no move to invite them in. "I'm sorry, but Bart really isn't feeling well. He went to lie down."

"This is very important."

She hesitated in the doorway. "You found who broke in?"

"Not yet, but—"

Bart walked up behind his wife. "It's fine, Trudy. I'll talk to them." He motioned them inside. "We can use my office."

"You are supposed to be resting," his wife countered.

"I promise to go back and lie down as soon as we're finished, but if you could make some tea in the meantime, I'd appreciate it. I was just coming down for some." He turned toward Madison and Jonas. "I'm still trying to knock out this headache."

"Okay . . ." Trudy ran her hand up and down her husband's arm. "Finish up quickly, and I'll bring it to the room."

"She worries too much," Bart said once they'd stepped into his office. "But maybe she has a point. The last few days have been rough."

"She has every reason to be upset," Madison said.

Bart reached up and touched the place where he'd been hit the night before, his frown deepening. "Please tell me you found something."

Jonas glanced at Madison. "We're not sure, to be honest. We do, however, need to clear up a discrepancy in your statement."

Bart sank into his leather chair and rested his elbows on the desk. "Of course. Anything you need."

He motioned to two chairs across from him, and the marshals sat as well.

"We were able to watch a video from the safe-deposit room on the day of the robbery," Madison said. "You told us that you were at the bank to pick up your wife's anniversary ring."

"I was. Did you find it?"

"Unfortunately we didn't, but we did discover something else," Madison said. "We noticed you dropped an envelope during the encounter with one of the fugitives. An envelope you'd pulled out of your pocket."

"An envelope?" Bart fidgeted in his chair. "Of course. I'm sorry, I completely forgot. I've had a splitting headache since the incident and am having trouble focusing."

"I understand," Madison said, trying to keep her voice steady. "We're just trying to track down every possible lead. Can you tell us what was in the envelope?"

"It was just some legal documents connected to my business that I recently had drawn up with my lawyer. I decided to drop it by the bank at the same time."

"It must have been important paperwork, considering you planned to put it in your box." She noticed the way Bart's shoulders had tensed. "You never mentioned what the security footage shows—that our suspects took that envelope after looking inside, which infers that whatever it held was potentially valuable to them."

Bart shook his head. "I don't know what they were thinking. There's no intrinsic value to the paperwork."

"Is that why you never mentioned it?" Jonas asked.

"It was simply an oversight on my part."

Madison's phone rang. "If you'll excuse me for a moment, I need to take this call."

She slipped out of the office and back into the entryway, where she could answer in private. "Piper. What have you got?"

"I hope it's okay I called, but I found out something that might be important. Mr. Wells owns a private plane and booked an unscheduled flight late last night that left around seven this morning."

"That's interesting." Madison glanced back toward the office. "Do you have the flight manifest?"

"No. I wasn't able to get that."

Madison bit her lip. "I want you to try to get ahold of the pilot and see if he can identify them," she told Piper.

"I've already left a message."

"Good. Where were they headed?"

"The flight was scheduled to land on Orcas Island at eight thirty this morning."

The San Juan Islands.

Madison paced the tiled floor, trying to process the information. West of the mainland were dozens of islands and reefs. Access to most of them was limited to boat or plane, or to ferry routes that connected the islands to Canada. And it made sense that the fugitives were looking for a way out of Seattle. Not money.

"Do the Wellses own any property up there?" Madison asked. "There are dozens of islands off the coast, which would make it easy to simply vanish. We need to narrow it down."

"I don't know, but I'll find out."

Madison ended her call with Piper and headed back into the office. There was no way anyone could convince her that Bart's booking a flight out of Seattle after a home invasion was a coincidence. Jesse and Nadia had been in this house.

She nodded at Jonas before sitting back down. She'd already decided to cut right to the chase. "Bart, let's stop wasting each other's time. We know the people who broke in here didn't need money, but there is something else they needed. A way out of the country. And you're the perfect person to arrange that for them."

Bart shifted in his chair. "I don't know what you're talking about."

"Oh, but I think you do," she countered. "All they needed

was a way to motivate you, and that's exactly what they found in that envelope."

"I told you, it was just some papers I had drawn up about a property I own."

He picked up his phone and started texting frantically.

"Hold on," Jonas said. "Please put your phone on the desk."

Bart hesitated. He took a look at both marshals, then complied.

She picked it up. "*They know,*" she read. "I'm guessing this is for the friends you made last night?"

"You don't understand. If this gets out, they can end my career. And if my wife finds out—"

"It's too late," Jonas said. "We've already put most of the puzzle together."

"I was telling the truth about the ring. I went to the bank to get it." He blew out a breath. "But I was also there to stow the envelope."

"And what was really in that envelope?" Madison asked. "I'm guessing photos of some sort."

"I don't have to answer that."

"No, you don't," Jonas said, standing up and placing his hands on the desk. "But you can either cooperate and help us catch our fugitives, or we'll charge you as an accessory to felony bank robbery, murder, attempted murder—"

"You can't do that."

Madison leaned forward. "On top of the evidence we already have, the pilot of that flight you scheduled for this morning will be able to identify our fugitives."

Bart let out a sharp huff of air. "I had heard rumors about my opponent in the mayoral race, so I hired a PI to see if he could get anything on him. And he did. I found out that he's a family man who's had more than one mistress on the side."

"And you thought if you blackmailed him, you could force him to step down," Jonas said. "Leaving you with the advantage to win the election."

"It was a way for me to move forward in the race, yes."

"Well, I think it's safe to say that your plans for the White House might be out of the question now," Madison said, "but that's a discussion for another day, because they clearly weren't here to rob you last night."

"No. They . . . they took the photos, realized who I was, and decided that they could blackmail me."

"Blackmailing the blackmailer." Jonas looked at Madison. "Not a bad plan, I suppose."

"And the pistol-whipping?" Madison asked.

"I . . . I thought it would make the robbery look more authentic. But Trudy heard the commotion and came downstairs, and then she had to call Glenda . . . Everything just quickly spiraled out of control."

"So why don't you tell us what really happened last night."

Bart's shoulders slumped. Madison almost felt bad for the man, but then she remembered the chaos of the last forty-eight hours. The man had successfully dug his own grave.

"I . . . I opened the door, thinking it was my friend, like I said." Bart stared at his hands as he spoke. "They forced their way in and told me that they weren't here to rob me but needed something else. I knew right away who they were, knew they had the contents of that envelope. It didn't take me long to realize what they wanted."

Bart paused for a long moment before continuing. "They said they wanted to make a deal with me—but it's not like I had a choice. They'd figured out what I was doing with the photos and said they wouldn't leak them or what I'd done to the media if I would help them leave Seattle. They were waiting on new passports, but with all the checkpoints in place, they were worried about getting to the border without getting caught. I arranged to fly them out of the city. They're planning to hole up on one of the islands until their passports are ready, then they'll cross into Canada."

"Where are they staying?" Madison asked.

"I don't know."

"It's a little late to be lying to us," Jonas said.

"I'm not lying." His voice cracked as it rose in pitch. "I figured the less I knew, the better. I said I'd get them to the islands, then they were on their own." He tapped his fingers against the desk. "So what happens now?"

"To you or your campaign?" Madison asked.

"I could tell the mayor we'll go ahead with the race, and he doesn't have to drop out. No more blackmail. Whoever wins, wins fair and square."

"It isn't really our role to decide that," Jonas said, "but it's a little too late to keep your involvement quiet."

"Can't we make some kind of deal? I'll cooperate."

Madison stood up with Jonas. "We don't make those decisions, but you still broke the law. Washington State has some pretty tough penalties when it comes to blackmail and extortion. You could easily get five, even ten, years in prison."

"Even if I cooperate with you?"

Madison nodded. She stepped around the desk, then read Bart his rights before handcuffing him. "You decided to blackmail someone and were okay with it until you got caught. But that's no different than the bank robbers that are blackmailing you."

Her phone rang as they headed toward the car with Bart. She paused for a moment on the sidewalk.

"I just received information that Bart has been blackmailing the mayor," Michaels said as soon as she'd answered.

"Yes," Madison said. She waved Jonas forward so he could help Bart into the back seat. "Our bank robbers found out and decided to use it as leverage."

"Does his wife know?"

Madison turned back toward the large house. "I don't think so, but she will soon."

"I'll be honest," Michaels said. "I never really liked the man, but made allowances because of Glenda's friendship with Trudy. But it always seemed like he married her for her money and as a way to follow his political aspirations. I've heard him joke more than once that he had his eyes on the White House."

"Let's just say, I don't think he was joking," Madison said. "We've got bigger problems than that though. We know Jesse and Nadia flew to Orcas Island this morning, but beyond that we have no way to track them."

"Bring Bart here for further questioning, and we'll plan our next move."

Madison didn't even attempt to hide her irritation. "Unless he talks, narrowing down their location's going to be almost impossible."

"Maybe not," a female voice added.

"Piper?" Madison asked at the sound of the intern's voice.

"Chief Deputy Michaels asked me to listen in on the call," Piper said. "I think I might be able to find them."

TWENTY-FIVE

Madison strode into Michaels's office with Jonas. She was anxious to hear Piper's theory.

"You're just in time," Piper said, walking into the office behind them, carrying a laptop. "I found what I was looking for."

"I think you'll both like this," Michaels said.

Jonas grabbed a chair across from Michaels's desk and sat down. "Our interest is definitely piqued."

"Actually," Piper said as she turned to Madison, "this came from your idea to go through the fugitives' social media accounts. Now I'm hoping that digging into their backgrounds is about to pay off."

"So what have you got?" Madison asked.

Piper turned back to her laptop and started typing. "First of all, I couldn't find any connection between the Wellses and the Islands, so I kept asking myself, with over a hundred border crossings between the US and Canada, why would these two choose to go to Orcas Island when they could have gone anywhere?"

"Good question," Madison said.

"When I was going through their friends' profiles, I remembered seeing photos on Nadia's site from a trip a couple years ago where they drove to Anacortes, then took a ferry to one of the islands." Piper turned the laptop around so they could all see the website she'd pulled up. "This is Reisner Island. Fifteen acres with water frontage and views of Mount Baker and other islands. There's a four thousand-square-foot main house, a caretaker's cottage, a deep-water dock."

"Wow," Madison said, as the website showcased an aerial photo of the island. "That's stunning."

"What's even more stunning," Michaels said from behind his desk, "is the fact that Nadia's father's company owns the island."

Jonas folded his arms across his chest. "That's interesting, but wouldn't they assume we'd figure out the connection? It seems like it would be the last place they'd go."

"Maybe, but as far as they know, we think they're still in the city," Piper said, setting her laptop on Michaels's desk.

"She's right." Madison stared at the photo on the website. "All they need is a few days at most until their passports are ready and they can disappear for real. It's a logical place for us to look."

"I agree." Michaels stood up and moved around his desk. "Which is why I've already reached out to the San Juans's sheriff's department. They've distributed photos of our fugitives, but I want the two of you there, in person. Check out that island first. If they're not there, we'll expand the search, but it will be harder to find them once they cross the border."

"When do we leave?" Jonas asked.

"I've already got you both booked on a private plane out of here."

* * *

Madison stared out the window of the small plane as she and Jonas left Seattle behind. Scores of waterways with miniature boats dotted the earth beneath them, while the Olympic Mountains loomed in the background. If she stared out long enough, she could almost convince herself she was returning to the chain of tree-covered islands for vacation like she'd done with her father growing up. But letting down her guard today wasn't an option.

"You do remember the first time we flew together?" Jonas said.

Madison caught his amused expression. "The thought might have crossed my mind."

"Can we agree to no repeats?"

Madison laughed. "It's a deal."

Three months ago, the two of them had been called on to transport two prisoners across the country on a private plane. Engine trouble en route had caused their plane to crash into the forest. Not a situation she wanted repeated today.

"Have you ever been up to the Islands?" she asked, switching her thoughts away from memories of that assignment.

"I've always wanted to, but for some reason I never have."

"You need to take some time to explore here one day," she said. "San Juan holds one of my favorite spots. Lime Kiln Point is this rocky bluff with views of the water where you can catch pods of humpback and minke whales and incredible sunsets."

"Sounds amazing."

"It is. My dad and I used to come up here back when my uncle owned land on one of the islands. We'd go camping every year, though this is my first time to fly in."

She studied the blue water sparkling beneath them. Four of the islands nestled between Washington State and British Columbia were accessible by ferry for both cars and pedestrians, making it fairly easy to get there from the mainland, though flying was definitely the quickest option. And the view from the sky was a definite bonus.

"I can see why you loved it here. It's stunning. I think I'd like to book a house one summer and stay a couple weeks and do nothing. Especially after this week."

"The only drawback is little or no cell reception or Wi-Fi in a lot of places. You could be pretty much completely cut off from the rest of the world."

"And that's a problem?" He leaned back in his seat, a smile spreading over his face. "Trust me, I could handle no internet. A couple weeks just reading, sitting in a hammock, and grilling out over a campfire. I'm all in."

The pilot's voice came over the cabin speaker as the plane started its descent over the heavily forested island. "We've just been cleared to land, so please check to ensure your seat belt is securely fastened. We'll be on the ground in just a few minutes."

As arranged, once they'd disembarked, one of the local sheriff's deputies met the marshals at the small airport on the north side of the island.

Madison shook the older man's hand as they made introductions. "We appreciate you picking us up, Deputy McBride."

"I'm assuming you received the information on our fugitives?" Jonas asked.

Deputy McBride nodded. "I've been in contact with the sheriff and will be your liaison. We've made sure every law enforcement officer in the area, as well as every ferry and boat rental place, has been notified. If your guys are out there, we'll find them."

"That's what we want to hear," Jonas said.

The three started walking toward the parking area. "I understand you need to get to Reisner Island," the deputy said.

"We do," Madison answered, following him to his car.

"You've got two choices. I can have one of our men take you out in a patrol boat, or I can drive you to a nearby marina and you can take a boat out yourself."

"That's not a problem," Madison said. "I spent my summers on the water. I can get us there and not tie up one of your men."

"Good. I've got a boat you're welcome to use."

"We appreciate the help."

Madison paused on the tarmac for a moment while a turbo-prop plane made a smooth landing on the airstrip. Mount Constitution and its forested peaks rose in the distance almost half a mile above the island. "Do you ever get tired of these views?"

McBride chuckled. "Never, and I was born and raised here."

She spent another moment taking in the exhilarating view before getting into the car. "What can you tell us about the property?" she asked after he slipped into the driver's seat.

"I haven't seen anyone matching the description of the couple you're after, but we'll keep looking. As for Reisner Island, there shouldn't be anyone on it right now. Ray Harper is the caretaker, but his mother's sick so he's back in Ohio for a few weeks. We've been keeping an eye on the property for him, but so far it's been quiet."

"Sounds like you stay busy," Jonas said from the back seat.

"Our county has more shoreline than any other county in the state, so between land and water, we definitely do." Deputy

McBride turned the key in the ignition. "As for the island you're wanting to go to, there's no electricity or internet, but there is a wood stove and limited solar power in the main house. Phone service is also very sketchy, but you can use the radio on the boat if you need to contact us."

Madison turned her gaze back to the mountain. So far the island sounded like the perfect hideout.

"And just in case you need it, Ray always leaves a key under one of the pots on the front porch," McBride said, putting the car into drive. "Are the two of you planning on heading back to Seattle today?"

"It's probably going to be too late," she said, "though it will depend on what we find here. We'll keep you in the loop."

***

An hour later, Madison was breathing in a lungful of fresh air as the fifteen-foot rigid hull of the inflatable boat they'd borrowed skimmed across the water in the direction of Reisner Island. The temperature was perfect, with blue skies, a few wispy clouds, and low winds out of the north. But even the amazing views weren't enough to break her focus. Two people were dead. That was something she couldn't forget.

She glanced at Jonas, who stood next to her at the helm. "It's beautiful, isn't it?"

"I could get used to perks like this, until I remember why I'm here."

"I was just thinking the same thing."

She navigated their approach toward the rocky bank of the island and its forty-foot dock. There was an old fishing vessel tied up and a couple canoes, but no other watercrafts in sight.

She secured the boat, then followed Jonas away from the

trail that led to the house, keeping cover just inside the tree line. Despite the calm setting surrounding them, they couldn't forget that the fugitives they were after were both armed and desperate.

The house stood quiet as they slipped through the shadows, making the silence surrounding them seem almost deafening in comparison to the city. Except for the occasional chirping of birds and the ruffling of tree limbs in the wind, the only thing she could hear was the sound of their footsteps.

"I say we head to the house," Jonas said. "We need to know if they're here."

Madison watched for movement as they made their way toward the front porch of the two-story, wood-framed house looming in front of them. But only an eerie stillness greeted them as they walked up the steps. She glanced around the small porch, then picked up one of the pots next to the front door, looking for the key.

"We won't be needing that," Jonas said, after turning the handle. "It's unlocked."

Madison frowned, then held up her weapon as they stepped into the spacious living room that opened to the dining area and kitchen. The floor-to-ceiling windows allowed beautiful views of the property and water while the interior walls were covered with knotty pine panels. The cozy space was filled with plenty of seating, throw pillows, and bookshelves.

Jonas signaled that he was headed toward the staircase and the second floor, while she started clearing the downstairs. She crossed the kitchen, then paused to touch the kettle on the stove.

It was warm.

The hair on the back of her neck prickled as she moved

through the rest of the downstairs, room by room, but there were no other signs that someone had been here.

By the time she'd circled back to the living room, Jonas was coming down the stairs. "Anything?" he asked, holstering his gun.

"The kettle on the stove is still warm."

"And it looks as if someone's been in one of the bedrooms. We must have spooked them."

It was possible. If Jesse and Nadia had been here, they would have heard a boat approaching. She turned to the back door that led out to a deck. "We need to keep searching."

The large wooden deck had a few outside tables and chairs, along with a barbecue grill, but that wasn't what caught her attention. Several chairs had been knocked over, and a large potted plant had been smashed. While they couldn't dismiss the idea that this had simply been a wild animal, she doubted there was anything on the island that could do this much damage.

Something else caught her attention at the top of the stairs that led down to the backyard. She crouched next to a trail of blood leading down the stairs. She studied the open yard below. Beyond it was fifteen acres of forested land.

Jonas stepped up behind her as she stood and faced him. "I think our fugitives are still on the island."

TWENTY-SIX

Madison walked beside Jonas through the spindly evergreen trees as the sun edged closer to the horizon along the water. Searching the heavily forested terrain of the island would be difficult in the daytime, but come nightfall, it would be impossible, especially when the trees blocked out most of the sunlight and the ground was full of brush. But something had happened on the back deck of the house, and they needed to find out what.

Brush crunched beneath her feet as they systematically searched the area extending out from the main house. She wished they could call the sheriff to send several deputies over to help them search, but she'd already checked her phone several times and there was no signal. If Nadia and Jesse *were* on this island, they had the advantage, and there was no time to run back to the boat. Madison had studied the aerial photo of the land during their flight. There were dozens of places their fugitives could hide across the acres of forested land, leaving her and Jonas on the defensive.

But so far, any signs of their presence on the island were

inscrutable. Jonas held up his hand, motioning for her to stop. She froze at his side, then shifted slightly to follow his gaze.

"Did you see something?" she asked.

He aimed his flashlight into the darkness. A black-tailed deer scurried off into the forest. Madison let out a sharp sigh, her nerves still strung tight. Her foot snapped a branch as they started walking again. An owl hooted in the distance. Shadows shifted around them in the wind.

"Okay, I'm not normally one to get paranoid," she said, keeping her voice low, "but this place is a bit creepy, especially now with darkness settling in."

"And I'm guessing that the probability of two armed fugitives running around out here somewhere doesn't help?"

"Definitely not," she said. "Besides, we're too vulnerable. If they're here, they would have heard us arriving on the boat. It would be easy to set up an ambush." She swept her flashlight to the side, surveying the woods. "Or maybe I read too many Agatha Christie novels growing up."

"I have noticed the stack of classic detective novels in your living room."

They continued along the perimeter of the island in the direction of the caretaker's cottage and a couple other small outbuildings. "In one of my favorites, eight people arrive on an isolated island off the English coast and are met by a butler and a housekeeper." She kept talking to stop the fear from settling in. "Then one by one the guests are found murdered because there was a killer among them."

Jonas let out a low chuckle. "And then there were none."

"My mother always used to tell me I had too vivid an imagination. I told her I loved getting scared reading those books, just as much as I loved justice being served."

She held her weapon out in front of her, unwilling to let her guard down or let the situation play with her nerves. The wind blew up around them, sending a shiver up her spine. She was letting her imagination get away with her, something she normally never did. But the last couple days had thrown her off. Felicia's death. The break-in at her house. No wonder she felt paranoid.

She zipped up the top of her jacket so it covered her neck, wishing she'd brought something heavier. Even in summer, the temperature could easily drop into the fifties at night. She just hadn't expected to be searching the grounds of a private island while the sun set in the distance.

The caretaker's cottage was a two-bedroom house on a small rise of land above the shoreline. This time, they found the key to the front door under a potted plant. They made a quick sweep of Ray Harper's quarters, but there was no sign that anyone had been inside recently.

Fifty feet from the cottage was a shed. The door was open a few inches and creaked in the wind. Madison opened it cautiously, then flashed her light inside. Lawn and garden tools hung on the wall above bags of fertilizer. Paint cans and other odds and ends were stacked on shelves, but nothing to indicate their fugitives had been there.

"Unless they're out somewhere in the woods, something tells me they're long gone," she said. "They could have had a boat tied up on the other side of the island, and when they heard us approach, they ran."

"But that doesn't explain the blood on the deck. It didn't look like someone just tripped and fell."

She nodded. "There was a fight."

Madison pulled out her phone and held it up to him, her frustration mounting. "Still no signal."

"Me neither." He shoved his phone back into his pocket. "Let's walk a little further along the ridge, but then I think we need to head back to Orcas Island. There is no way we can search the rest of the island in the dark, and more than likely they've already left."

He was right. They needed to focus their efforts on ensuring their fugitives didn't make it across the border.

They continued along the trail that followed a rocky ridge a dozen feet above the shoreline to their right and a long row of madrone trees, with their distinctive peeling red bark, on the left.

The sound of a motorboat in the distance pulled her attention to the water, where the tide sprayed against the rocks below, but there was no way to see who was on the boat in the semidarkness. She turned back to the trail. Jonas must not have noticed she stopped, because he'd disappeared over the next small hill.

She hurried to catch up, then started running when she heard a shout. But when she reached the top of the rise there was still no sign of him.

"Jonas?"

She stared down the steep decline. She could hear him, but it was too dark to make out his form.

"Jonas?" she called again.

There was no response.

Ten . . . nine . . . eight . . . And then there were none.

She reined in her mind from where it wanted to go, but how had Jonas slipped off the trail? She shook her head. It didn't matter how. She had to concentrate on getting to him, but the slope to the shore was too steep where she was, and she was afraid she wouldn't be able to get down without slipping.

Which brought up another problem. What if he was injured? Getting him help wasn't going to be easy.

She started praying as she scurried around to where the terrain was less steep, then made her way down the rocky slope to the shore, careful to watch her steps. At the bottom, she was able to double back and use her flashlight to search for Jonas.

"Jonas?"

Where was he?

A moan a few feet in front of her answered her question.

"Jonas?"

He was on his side, trying to get up, when she finally reached him.

"Wait, don't move." She crouched down beside him on the sandy shoreline, the tide lapping inches from her feet. "I need to make sure nothing's broken. Does anything hurt?"

"I'm just banged up a bit. I think I'm okay."

He groaned again while attempting to stand.

"Wait a minute. You're more than banged up. You just fell a good fifteen feet off that rocky slope." She shined her flashlight at him, trying to assess the damage. "Jonas, you're wet and your head's bleeding."

He touched his forehead that was sticky with blood. "I think it's just a cut."

She pulled her sleeve down, then wiped it across his forehead gently.

He winced.

"Sorry, but I need to see where the blood is coming from."

She frowned. It looked like he was right. It was just a small cut, but she needed to get him both cleaned up and dry.

"Do you think you can walk?"

He nodded then pushed himself up, using her partially for support.

"Let's get you back to the house," she said.

"Uh-uh. We need to go straight to the sheriff's office."

"Trust me, I'm ready to get off this island, but I saw a first aid kit back at the main house—"

He grabbed her arm and pulled her toward him. His eyes widened in the moonlight. "You don't understand, Madison. I didn't stumble off that incline. Someone pushed me."

She stared at him. She heard what he said, but the words didn't compute. Someone had pushed him? No. He had to have imagined it. She'd only been a few yards away from him and hadn't seen anyone. And besides—what was the point of pushing one of them off the ridge? It didn't make sense.

Still, another chill swept through her.

"Why would someone push you?" she asked as they began shuffling along the beach. "If it was Jesse and Nadia, as far as we know, they still have weapons. Why not just set up an ambush and get rid of both of us?"

"I don't know." Jonas kept up with her despite his slight limp. "Kira kept telling us that no one was supposed to get hurt."

"And we know that Ben's the one who shot Felicia and the guard."

She searched for an explanation but came up blank. With their faces posted all over the news and every law enforcement agency looking for them, Jesse and Nadia seemed to be getting more desperate. And dangerous.

Madison held her weapon out beside her, peering into the darkness as they made their way back down the rocky shoreline. The best option at the moment was to return to the main island and bring back reinforcements.

"Why not just leave the island?" Jonas's question broke into her thoughts. "They could have slipped away and gone somewhere else without confronting us. We're missing something."

The sun had completely dropped beneath the horizon. Out of the city, the sky no longer had so many lights to compete with, creating a swath of stars hanging above them, but there was no sign of whoever had just attacked Jonas.

He stopped midstride and turned to her. "What if there was something they didn't want us to see?"

"Like what?"

"I don't know," he said, a new determination hardening his expression. "But we need to go back and look."

"No, you were right before." She gripped his arm. "We need to get back to our boat and not do this on our own. Next time things might not end with just a few bumps and bruises."

"I'm fine, Madison, and if we wait, it could be too late."

She frowned, still not convinced.

"Just humor me." He met her gaze in the light of the moon. "Let's search down the trail a bit further. If we don't find anything, we'll return to Orcas Island."

They had just enough light to follow the trail that wound its way above the shoreline.

"Are you sure you're okay?" she asked.

"I'm sure I'll be sore tomorrow, but I'm fine."

She walked next to him, senses on high alert, still not sure what they were looking for. But something had motivated Jesse and Nadia to attack Jonas. They just needed to figure out what. And make sure it didn't happen again.

Moonlight reflected against something to her left.

"Jonas . . . It looks like there's another small shed out here."

She aimed her flashlight at a shadowy structure, struggling

between not wanting to call attention to themselves and needing to see what was out here. She surveyed the ground in front
of her. Fresh footprints in a patch of mud led toward the small
wooden building.

"They were here."

She headed toward the outbuilding, keeping the flashlight's
beam low, then paused. Half a dozen feet ahead of her, the
earth had been dug up.

"Jonas."

A shovel leaned against the side of the shed, next to what
looked like a grave. She knelt down, then brushed away a layer
of the dirt.

"What did you find?" Jonas asked.

A sick feeling spread through her. "A body."

TWENTY-SEVEN

Jonas shined his flashlight at the blank expression of the face staring up at them and felt his stomach roil. "This isn't one of our suspects."

"Yeah, but who is it then?" Madison stood up and brushed off her pants. "The caretaker isn't supposed to be here."

He glanced back toward the main house, trying to replay in his mind what might have happened. Their fugitives took someone by surprise. A fight ensued. Then someone ended up dead.

He blew out a sharp huff of air, took out his phone, and started taking a series of photos for evidence. At the moment, there was no way to ID the body, and they didn't want to touch anything else until they could get a forensics team here. They'd have to go back to Orcas for that. And in the meantime?

"I'm hesitant to leave the body here unguarded," he said.

"Except separating isn't the answer either at this point. We can go back to the boat and radio for help."

She was right. Especially with the high probability of an ambush in the equation. They'd wait together for backup to

LISA HARRIS ——— 261

arrive and search the island. And if Jesse and Nadia had fled, they'd just have to ensure they didn't go far.

They headed back to the dock in silence, save for the water lapping against the shore and an occasional owl hooting in the distance. While there was a chance that their fugitives were still on the island, his gut told him that they were long gone. Attacking him had given them time to escape. Even so, he kept his eyes on the tree line in case they were still here and had any intentions of ambushing them.

Moonlight hit the water as they stepped onto the boat, and Madison went to start the motor.

He waited for the purr of the engine coming to life, but the silence of the night continued to press in on them.

"What's wrong?" he asked, stepping toward Madison.

"Looks like they've sabotaged the boat," she said. He watched her try a few different things, a determined look on her face.

Water lapped against the side of the boat with the tide, pulling his attention to the other side of the dock. His heart sank. "They also untied that old fishing vessel and the canoes." He turned back to Madison. "Can you fix what's wrong with our boat?"

She leaned against the side of it. "I don't know. It looks like both the motor and the radio are shot."

A shiver ran up his spine. He glanced back toward the house. This left them no way off this island. No phone service, no way to contact anyone.

"This may not be ideal," she said, "but I suggest we move on to plan B."

"Which is?"

"Once I'm done patching you up, we can search the house for a radio or some way to communicate. I know McBride said there's no service here, but there has to be another way to get ahold of the sheriff." She stepped back onto the dock. "Unless you want to try and swim across the sound."

"Funny." He stepped up onto the dock after her, well aware of their surroundings. "On the positive side, I can't think of anyone I'd rather be stuck on a deserted island with."

She let out a low chuckle. "That's definitely the right thing to say, but it's not like no one knows where we are. When McBride doesn't hear from us tonight, he'll send someone to check on us."

"Unless he thinks we're waiting until morning to give him an update."

* * *

Inside the house, they made another quick search of the premises, but it was quiet, with no indication that Jesse and Nadia had been back. Which only confirmed his belief that the two were long gone. He made sure all of the doors were locked, and he turned only one small lamp on. If they had to spend the night here, he didn't want to be taken by surprise if he was wrong about his assumption. A second ambush could end very differently.

"I'll make a deal with you," he said, checking his weapon.

"What's that?"

"I'll make dinner while you search the house for a way to communicate with the sheriff's office."

"Deal, but first I need to clean the cut on your head."

He started to protest, but the look on her face and the no-nonsense way she placed her hands on her hips stopped him short. "Fine," he said, pulling up a stool and sitting down.

"Thank you."

Madison crossed the kitchen to wash her hands, then pulled a first aid kit from under the sink. "You'll probably end up with a scar above your eyebrow," she said, moving closer to clean the wound, "but at least the bleeding's stopped."

He shifted on the stool, unsettled by her nearness. He'd been joking about being stuck on an island with her, but there was also a grain of truth in his words. And ignoring that truth was getting harder and harder. He tried to focus on what he might find in this house that would constitute a good meal as she worked on the cut.

"That should do it," she said a little while later, putting a layer of antibiotics on it.

"Thanks." He ran a hand through his hair, careful to avoid the tender flesh of his forehead.

"Of course." She dug something out of the kit and handed it to him. "Pain medicine. You'll thank me in the morning."

He shot her a smile. "Whatever you say, doc."

He escaped into the kitchen as soon as she was done and started rummaging through the cupboards for something to eat. Felicia's death should only have reinforced the fact that he was playing with fire when it came to Madison and his emotions. So much for compartmentalizing his personal life from his career. But was there a way to do both? He wasn't even sure anymore.

He pulled out a large pot, set it on the stove, then grabbed a few canned goods he'd found in the pantry. While there wasn't much, he'd found a few odds and ends. His mother used to make a dump soup with whatever was in the cupboard. He figured he could do the same thing here.

The soup was just starting to simmer when Madison came back into the kitchen, her hands empty.

"No radio?" he asked.

"Nothing. You'd think they'd have some kind of backup plan here." Her brow furrowed. "Something actually smells good."

"Don't act so surprised."

"I'm not." She joined him at the stove. "Trust me, I already know you can cook. I'm just trying to figure out what exactly you're making us."

"I might have to come up with a name, I suppose, but taste it first."

She hesitated, then pulled a spoon out of the drawer and sampled the soup. Her lips turned up slightly. "It's not bad, actually."

"I told you to trust me."

"And I did, didn't I? Now, won't you tell me what I just ate?"

"A bit of everything I found in the cupboard." He divvied out their dinner and set two bowls down on the table, then sat down. "Pasta, beans, hominy, diced tomatoes, corn—"

"Never mind." Madison waved her hand, joining him at the table. "It tastes far better than it sounds. I don't think I want to know. It'll ruin it."

"You're impossible."

"Are you forgetting you said there's no one you'd rather be stuck on a deserted island with?" she said, stirring her hot soup.

"Fine. How about"—he paused to take a spoonful and think of the right descriptor—"slightly challenging."

She rolled her eyes, then her expression darkened. "We can try to laugh our way through this, but how are you doing?"

He hesitated before answering. "I'll probably be processing things for a long time. On a selfish note, some of the things Felicia told me before she died gave me some closure." He stirred his soup idly, looking down to avoid Madison's eyes. "I'm thankful for that. I had always hoped that she and I could at least be friends. I just never expected things to end this way. And I'm sad that her life was wasted when she had so much to offer."

"Me too."

He took another spoonful. "I spoke with her boyfriend before we came up here."

"He must be devastated."

"He is. Though he told me he wasn't surprised that she died the way she lived. Always wanting to make things right."

"I think the two of us would have gotten along."

Jonas paused, trying to process what he thought about the comment. "I think you would have too."

He focused on his hodgepodge soup, avoiding her gaze. Madison had been the first woman in a long time that he could imagine taking home to meet his mother. The person he could actually imagine spending the rest of his life with. And yet he knew what was stopping him. He'd planned on marrying Felicia, and then in an instant everything changed when she got shot.

Feelings he didn't want to acknowledge warred against his need to guard his heart and the boundaries he'd set. Was he making a mistake keeping Madison at arm's length?

"I think one of us needs to stay awake," she said, breaking into his thoughts.

He scooped the last of his soup into his mouth. "I can take the first watch then."

"You sure?" she asked.

"Mmhmm. Not sure I could sleep now anyway."

"I'm pretty sure I can." She took the empty dishes to the sink and rinsed them.

Jonas tried to settle his thoughts while she worked, but they were in the middle of a case. Figuring out these feelings would have to wait.

Madison finished up and dried her hands on a dish towel. "Good night, then," she said through a yawn.

"Good night, Madison."

He watched her head toward the stairs, then walked around the first floor, double-checking that everything was locked. There was no movement outside. No indication that anyone was nearby. For the moment, anyway, all was quiet.

✳ ✳ ✳

The smell of something cooking jolted him awake. He sat up on the couch where he'd managed to get a few hours of sleep. In the dim morning light, he could see Madison standing at the stove, flipping pancakes.

"You're just in time. I was about to wake you up. This isn't my brother-in-law's famous recipe for homemade pancakes, but I found a box in the pantry, along with some syrup."

She set a bottle of syrup and a plate stacked high with pancakes on the table.

"Wow," he said, heading to the dining area. "Best case scenario, I was expecting a bad coffee."

"You might be a genius in the kitchen, but I have a few tricks up my sleeve as well."

"I'm impressed."

She waved off the compliment. "Don't be too impressed. Anyone can add water and stir."

"I'm not complaining." He laughed. "And you made coffee?"

"It's hot if you'd like some."

"I would."

She finished the rest of the pancakes and turned off the burner. "Once we're done here, I think we need to search the rest of the island. There's got to be a way off this place. Maybe another boat?"

"Either that or Michaels will eventually send out the cavalry to find us."

He poured himself a fresh cup of coffee, then sat down at the table while she piled the dishes in the sink. "So nothing on your watch, I'm guessing?"

"All was quiet. I'm afraid our bad guys are long gone."

Jonas nodded, adding a spoonful of sugar to his drink. Then he heard a boat motor.

He grabbed his Glock off the kitchen bar. "Then let's hope that's the good guys."

TWENTY-EIGHT

The odds that Jesse and Nadia had returned to the island were slim to none as far as Madison was concerned. She bet the motor they heard was just the sheriff, who'd finally decided to swing by to make sure everything was okay. Sure enough, as they approached the dock, one of the sheriff's boats had just pulled up to the shoreline with two uniformed deputies, including McBride.

Madison slipped her weapon back into its holster as she made her way down to the dock with Jonas. "Boy are we glad to see you."

Deputy McBride stepped off his boat, taking a second to gain his balance before introducing them to Deputy Abrams. "I guess I was wrong to assume you headed back to Seattle without telling me. When I couldn't get ahold of the two of you, I finally got through to Chief Deputy Michaels. He told us you hadn't checked in, so I promised to come out here."

Jonas nodded toward the boat they'd borrowed. "We never saw them, but it looks like our fugitives sabotaged both the boat we borrowed and its radio. We'll need a team to search the island."

Abrams nodded. "We can organize that."

Jonas glanced at Madison. "It also looks like they left a body behind."

"A body?" Deputy McBride frowned. "You're sure it's not one of your fugitives?"

Jonas shook his head. "No, it's not."

"We'll call in marine patrol along with a few more deputies and get a search team together," McBride said, motioning to the other deputy, who headed back onto their boat. "While he does that, I'd like to see if I recognize the body."

They left the dock and, with flashlights in hand, walked along the trail toward the small outbuilding they'd stumbled across last night. The sun had already begun to peek above the horizon, making the water shimmer below them, but except for the sound of it lapping against the rocks below, the island was still eerily quiet.

Nothing had been disturbed since last night. The shovel lay against the side of the shed. And the body still lay beneath the dirt in the shallow grave.

Jonas turned to McBride. "Do you know him?"

Deputy McBride shook his head at the partially exposed face of the corpse. "I do, actually. People call him Old Whitaker. He's lived on these islands his whole life, but he tends to be a bit of a nuisance. The marine patrol usually stops him at least once a month for disorderly conduct, which usually just means he makes his way onto one of the private islands and tries to help himself to food and liquor and whatever else he can find."

"Apparently, this time he ended up at the wrong place," Jonas said. "I'm not sure exactly what happened, but it looked as if there'd been a fight up on the back deck of the house."

"And Old Whitaker lost," Madison said.

Deputy McBride moved back from the body. "I'll send in

my team and take care of this, but in the meantime, I've got someone back in town you need to talk to."

"Who's that?" Jonas asked.

"Your boss said that your fugitives were waiting on passports and asked me to look into any deliveries that stood out, so I contacted the guy who flies between Seattle and the Islands daily with mail and packages."

"And?" Madison asked.

"I just got a call from him on our way over. I've already sent one of our deputies there, but he said a package was sent to Grace's Café in town and arrived this morning addressed to a Ted Barker."

"Has the package been picked up?" she asked.

"I'm still waiting to hear from the deputy I sent out there, but if you'd like to, we can head that way now. I can take you while Deputy Abrams runs the search here."

Madison nodded. "Let's go then."

The urgency of the moment pressed tightly against Madison's chest as they sailed. No matter what they did, they always seemed to be a step behind, but without new passports, their fugitives were limited on where they could go. The sun rose high above the horizon as they crossed the water back toward town. She closed her eyes for a moment and breathed in the scent of saltwater tinging the air.

Once back on Orcas Island, Madison followed the men to Grace's Café. The quiet morning was a huge contrast to the bustle of Seattle. Shops lined the street, with jaw-dropping views of the water in the distance.

Inside, the restaurant was just as laid-back. There was a rustic fireplace, and fresh flowers decorated the tables while waiters served up breakfast plates to both locals and tourists.

"These are the marshals I said wanted to talk to you," Deputy McBride said, approaching the woman behind the counter. "This is Grace."

The young woman smiled wide. "What can I do for you, folks?"

"What can you tell us about the package that was delivered here? Did someone pick it up?" Jonas asked.

"Yes, but I don't know much." Grace ran her hands down the front of her red apron. "The guy who came for it told me he was from out of town and was here on vacation. He'd left some medicine he needed in Seattle and had a courier overnight it. He said he'd talked to one of the waitresses about it yesterday, to see if it was okay. I checked out his story, and at least that part was true, so I gave him the package."

"How long ago?"

Grace glanced at the clock on the café's wall. "I'm not sure. It was right before the other deputy showed up."

"Did he say where he was going?" Madison asked.

"No, but he acted like he was ready to get off the island."

Jonas turned to Deputy McBride. "What time is the next ferry?"

The officer glanced at his watch. "It leaves in about fifteen minutes for Canada, with a stop at Friday Harbor. I can have you there in time if we go now."

Madison nodded in agreement as they hurried toward the deputy's vehicle. If passports had been in that package, their fugitives had just received their golden ticket.

✳ ✳ ✳

Madison studied the passengers from the outside deck while she waited for Jonas to finish his sweep of the inside seating area and join her. They'd made the ferry's security team and captain aware of the situation. Their first objective had to be to keep the locals and tourists on board safe.

She zipped up the front of the fleece another female deputy lent her, trying to block the wind that had picked up over the past hour. So far there had been no sign of either of their fugitives, but if Jesse and Nadia were here, they would find them. There were only so many possible hiding places on the ship, and eventually they'd have to get off.

"They're here," Jonas said, stepping up to her. "They just took seats inside. I've got a security officer keeping an eye on them while we arrange things."

He nodded toward the door of the main section of the ferry that was filled with families and tourists.

She glanced at her watch. "We arrive at Friday Harbor in fifteen minutes. I think we need to coordinate with the local authorities and arrest them when they disembark."

"Agreed. Coast Guard is already on standby. I'll let them and the sheriff's office know that suspects are on board and have them waiting for us. We'll just keep our eye on them in the meantime."

He pulled out the two-way radio they'd been given on boarding and gave a quick update to the captain. Then both marshals headed back inside and out of the wind. Madison scanned the inside level of the ferry. They didn't want to call attention to themselves—that could spook their fugitives—but neither did they want to lose sight of them.

"Where are they?" she asked.

"I don't know." Jonas hurried toward one of the security officers they'd met earlier. "Where are they, Garrett?"

"I don't know. I lost them."

"What do you mean, you lost them?"

"I'm sorry." The man's face flushed. "Someone came up asking for my help. I looked away for just a second."

Madison tried to tamp down her anger. "Which means not only did they probably arrange the distraction, they know we're onto them. We need to find them."

She looked around at the passengers sitting inside on benches, worried about another hostage situation. Had their fugitives figured out they were under surveillance? Or was it just a coincidence they'd decided to move again?

No. Her gut told her this was no coincidence.

"Check the security footage," Jonas instructed Garrett, "and see if you can find where they went. We'll make a sweep of the deck, then head below. Keep me updated on the radio."

She stepped into the restroom a moment later, quickly clearing the stalls one at a time. The only other place to hide was in one of the cars below the seating area. They took the narrow staircase leading to the vehicle deck. Beyond the opening in the cement hull, she could see the choppy gray-blue waters as the ferry passed by green forested islands and, in the distance, snowcapped mountains.

"I'll take the starboard side," Jonas said. "You take port."

Madison nodded, then headed down the row of cars on her side, searching each one. Their fugitives had come to the ferry on foot, but that didn't mean they weren't going to try to get off another way. They couldn't assume anything at this point.

A car door slammed, echoing behind her. Madison shifted her torso, bringing her weapon up. A father and son had grabbed something out of their car and were heading back toward the stairwell. She kept walking, checking vehicles for any passengers as she went.

"Anything?" she asked Jonas through her radio.

"Not yet."

She passed another empty car. "Me neither, but they have to be here."

"I know, but where?"

She kept walking. "I'm almost down to the end of my row."

"So am I."

In front of her, the ramp led down to the churning waters behind the ferry. Movement caught her attention.

"Jonas, we might have a problem. Another boat is headed toward us."

A speedboat was still a distance out, but it was heading straight toward the ferry.

"Are you sure?" he asked.

"That has to be their plan. They've arranged for someone to pick them up and take them across the border."

"I'll inform the captain," Jonas said.

Madison let out a huff of air as she approached the last car. Where were they? Security was tight enough that if they decided to jump overboard, they would be seen. And there was nowhere else to hide.

"Jonas . . . wait . . ." Madison spotted a woman sitting in the front seat, leaning back against the headrest. "I might have something. Give me a second."

She tapped on the window. "Ma'am? Please roll down this window."

When the woman didn't move, Madison tapped again. Still nothing. "Jonas . . . head over here now."

"I'm on my way."

Madison tried the door handle of the vehicle, but it was locked. "Ma'am . . ."

The woman turned toward her. Madison recognized her immediately.

Nadia.

"It's over, Nadia. I want you to step out of the vehicle with your hands where I can see them. Now."

"I'm coming." Jonas's voice called out through the radio. "What's going on?"

"I've got her, Jonas, but I don't have eyes on Jesse. I repeat, I don't have eyes on him. I need you—"

Nadia moved to open the car door, but something had grabbed Madison from underneath the vehicle. She felt her body slam against the pavement. Pain shot through her, disorienting her, as her radio and weapon tumbled to the ground. She reached for her gun, but Jesse pushed it away. Her phone was in her pocket. She needed to get away and let Jonas know what was happening. The car door swung open, and Nadia stepped out, carrying a bag and shouting something at Jesse. He pulled Madison up, wrenching her arm, then shoved her inside the car. She tried to fight back. Someone was calling her name. Jonas?

But it was too late.

She could feel the momentum of the car as it rolled down the ramp, then plunged into the water.

TWENTY-NINE

Jonas heard "I need you" and then nothing more from Madison. Waves of panic pounded as he made his way to the other side of the vehicle deck. He'd promised himself he wasn't going to let anything happen to her.

Because he loved her.

I love Madison.

He forced his mind to focus. There was no time to let his feelings or fears seep in and color his judgment. Not now. Because if he did, he was going to panic. Instead, he had to focus on finding her.

"Captain." He spoke into the radio as he ran toward the other side of the deck. "I'm out of communication with my partner, and I think she's in trouble. Tell the Coast Guard I need them here now and send security down to the port side of the vehicle deck immediately."

"Roger that."

He could hear the shouts of a crowd that had gathered above him on the passenger deck by the time he got to the end of the port side. A horn blasted as the ship came to a stop. He could see a car bobbing on the surface of the water. Surely she wasn't in the vehicle. He moved down the ramp, closer to the bobbing vehicle, and saw a flash of pink through the window. Madison was in the car.

He neared the end of the ramp. He knew they had man overboard drills in place. But he couldn't wait for them. He ripped a fire extinguisher off the wall as the car continued to sink. He had seconds at most to pull her out. He caught the movement of a small boat that was speeding away as he dove into the water.

He had to focus on his mission, but he couldn't hold back his disgust at their plan. Madison had been their distraction.

Clasping the fire extinguisher, he managed to swim toward the car that was still bobbing on top of the water. But it wouldn't stay that way for long. Reaching the vehicle, he smashed the extinguisher against the back window. Nothing happened. The car shifted as he searched for movement inside and saw Madison's pink fleece again. He fought the currents as he slammed the extinguisher into the window a second time. Spider cracks spread out from the impact. A third time and it shattered. The fire extinguisher sank as he smashed away the remaining shards of glass, then reached for her hand.

Just another few seconds, God. Please.

She gasped for a breath as he dragged her out through the window. An orange rescue boat sped up behind him as he was finally able to secure her in his arms, struggling to keep them both above the surface of the water. At least she was still alive. Someone pulled her into the rescue boat, then helped him up. He lay on his back at the bottom of the raft for a few minutes, trying to catch his breath and slow down his heart rate.

He heard directions being shouted. Someone crouched down next to him.

"How is she?" he asked, forcing himself up.

"I think she'll be fine, thanks to you. Give yourself a few minutes to recuperate. I need to check your arm. You're bleeding."

Jonas glanced at it. "It's nothing. Just a scratch. Glass from the vehicle. I need to see her."

"She's got quite a goose egg on the back of her head, but her vitals are steady. We're heading to the island now and will have an ambulance waiting at the dock. I want you both checked out."

"The other boat," he managed to say. "The one with our fugitives?"

"The Coast Guard is looking for them now."

He moved to the other side of the boat as it headed back to the ferry. "Madison . . ."

Someone had pulled off her jacket and wrapped her in an emergency blanket. She looked up at him. "Are you trying to make this a habit? Rescuing me?"

He shot her a smile, relieved to see for himself that she was okay. "It's not a bad habit."

"What about the suspects?"

"The Coast Guard is looking for them."

"Jonas, I managed to dump my phone in Nadia's bag while they were shoving me into the car."

His mind scrambled to understand what she was saying. "You what?"

"Track my phone, and we can find them."

"You're a genius." He leaned down and kissed her full on the lips, before pulling back. "I . . . I'm sorry. I have no idea what came over me."

"Just go. Get them."

The next few minutes sped by. The Coast Guard picked

him up from the rescue boat, while he worked with Michaels to pull up the tracking information on Madison's phone. The moment they were able to locate it, the hovercraft sped toward the signal, heading north of Friday Harbor.

Jonas stood beside the captain in the large craft, his gaze focused on the speedboat ahead of them. "Where are they heading?"

"Looks like the Haro Strait and the Canadian border, but don't worry. We'll get them."

The hovercraft accelerated, ready to intercept the smaller boat. The captain's voice boomed over the speaker system, demanding that the speedboat stop. The second boat skidded across the water for a few more moments, then slowed down in surrender. Jonas blew out a sharp breath as the speedboat came to a halt. Whoever their fugitives had hired to pick them up clearly hadn't got paid enough to defy the Coast Guard.

He shouted directions as he jumped onto the smaller boat ahead of three Coast Guard officers, demanding the fugitives surrender their weapons and put their hands in the air. Jesse hesitated.

"Put it down," Jonas said, steadying himself as the boat bobbed in the waves. "It's over."

✳ ✳ ✳

Jonas headed toward the medical center in Friday Harbor after receiving the news that they'd just released Madison. It was the second piece of good news he'd gotten today, but this one was even more important to him personally than the recent arrest of their fugitives. The two suspects had been passed off by the Coast Guard to the local sheriff's department and were now waiting to be escorted back to Seattle. But Jonas wouldn't be taking that trip with their fugitives. His only job right now was to get Madison back safely, something he had every intention of doing.

He found her sitting on a wooden bench outside the emergency entrance, surrounded by manicured lawns and tall evergreens. Someone had scrounged up dry clothes and shoes for both of them, but she still looked cold and tired. His gaze rested on her face, and he felt his heart race. What had he been thinking? He never should have kissed her.

He slid onto the bench next to her, aware of the relief flowing through him that she was alive, which outweighed the guilt of his impulsive action. "Sorry I didn't get here sooner. I was finishing up at the sheriff's department."

She smiled up at him. "You're fine."

"How do you feel?"

"A little tired and still cold, but the sunshine feels good. The doctor said I don't have to be admitted, though I think I might take a day or two off after all of this."

He chuckled softly. "That's probably a good idea. And how about some more good news?"

Her eyes widened. "You found them?"

"Thanks to your quick thinking, yes. We were able to pick them both up through the GPS on your phone."

"It all happened so fast." She shook her head. "It was just an instinctive reaction. I'd grabbed for my phone after losing my radio, thinking I could call you, which would have been impossible, but her bag was hanging beside me, so I just dropped it inside."

"I'm just glad you're okay."

"Me too," she said. "So now what?"

"I talked Michaels into letting us spend the night on the island so you can rest."

She nodded. "I'll do anything as long as a hot shower and a meal are involved."

"All of that's arranged," he said, noting the fatigue in her eyes. "I booked us a couple rooms not far from here. Michaels just wants an update from us, though I'm sure he'll have a pile of paperwork waiting when we get back."

"But at least we got them before they got away."

He reached out and squeezed her hand. It was shaking. "You *are* cold."

"I'm not the only one who got soaking wet. Thank you for saving me."

"Of course. That's what partners are for."

He pulled his hand away, unable to dismiss the currents simmering beneath the surface. No matter how much he'd trained to handle days like today, separating his emotions was proving impossible when it came to Madison.

"Are you ready to go?" he asked.

"Yes," she said, standing up. "And thanks for talking Michaels into letting us take the slow way back. A flight out of here might have been faster, but I need a chance to catch my breath."

Jonas pulled the keys for the loaner car from the sheriff's office out of his pocket as they headed toward the parking lot. "Are you up for a short detour before we head to the hotel?"

"I think so. What did you have in mind?"

He shot her a grin. "Hop in and I'll show you."

✳ ✳ ✳

The sun was sinking toward the horizon when they arrived at Lime Kiln Point, a rocky outcropping on the western shore of the island. From the information he'd read online, the rugged coastline was one of the best places in the world to view wild orcas and other whale pods, as well as porpoises, river otters, and bald eagles.

"I remembered you saying that this had been your favorite place to come with your father," he said, breathing in the smell of saltwater and wet cedar as they exited the car and headed for the trail. "I thought you might want to see it again."

"Wow. This place is even more beautiful than I remember. And it brings back so many memories." She zipped up her coat and her smile widened. "Thank you."

They walked the short trail through towering trees and passed the vintage lighthouse before reaching the rocky bluff overlooking Haro Strait. A few families sat at picnic tables, hoping to spot a whale, while kayakers paddled off the shoreline.

"To the west is Vancouver Island," Madison said, pointing toward the water. "And to the south you can see the silhouettes of the Olympic Mountains."

"You were right. This place is incredible." He scanned the blue waves for a spray of water as they sat down on one of the rocks, hoping to catch at least a glimpse of one of the whales. But more importantly, hoping he could muster up the courage to say what he needed to say to her.

He didn't have to touch her to feel her proximity to him. "I didn't bring you here just for the scenery. I need to talk to you about something."

Her brow furrowed. "Okay."

"I'm sorry about the kiss," he said finally. "I was out of line, and that never should have happened. I don't have an excuse, but seeing you out in the water . . . I thought I was going to lose you." He paused. "I don't want it to come between us."

"You . . ." She lowered her gaze. "You just took me off guard."

"I thought you were dead."

"I know," she said, looking into his eyes. "But I'm here and I'm okay. It's over."

"I'm not sure you understand." He fumbled over his words, trying to get across his meaning. "It was like the day you were shot. I remember forcing my way into your house. I saw you lying on the kitchen floor, and I was so afraid I'd lost you."

* * *

Madison blew out a slow breath, trying to calm her frazzled nerves. She'd tried not to allow anything romantic toward him to develop. He was her partner. The person she vented with when she was frustrated with a case and needed a solution. But even she hadn't missed the familiar feelings that had been slowly settling in between them lately.

"Another close call with death wasn't exactly in my game plan for this trip, but it's over," she said, "and I'm okay. We're okay."

"Are we?"

She glanced up at him again, not sure what he was trying to say. "What do you mean?"

He looked down at his hands. "I never meant to feel this way, but after you were shot, I found myself coming by and checking on you a couple nights a week." He paused for a moment. "At first, I saw our Friday night dinners together as just something between friends—"

Her breath caught in her lungs. "And now?"

"One day suddenly it wasn't."

An eagle flew overhead as Madison worked to sort through what he was saying. Hearing his words had put the situation out in the open to a place neither of them could ignore. There was no question of the pull she felt toward him. She trusted him completely and knew he always had her back. He knew how to make her laugh and was always there for her. But falling in love again? That was something she'd tried to avoid thinking about by simply not allowing it to come into the equation.

But love wasn't a math problem to be solved, or a case to be unraveled. It was two people, pulled toward each other.

"I'm guessing you don't feel the same way," he said, breaking through her thoughts.

She looked up at him and studied his face, his words a statement rather than a question. "I don't know."

His shoulders drooped. "I've always respected you. You're good at what you do and have always impressed me, even from the first time we met back at the shoot house in Nashville. You're the best partner I have ever worked with. But that kiss . . ."

She sat still next to him, waiting for him to continue while her own thoughts wrestled inside her.

He shoved his hands into his pockets. "It took me off guard, seeing that car sinking into the water. Knowing you were inside. Then finally realizing you were okay."

She closed her eyes for a moment, trying to figure out what to say.

"What do you feel, Madison? About me. About us. Or is it just me who's conflicted?"

Tangled emotions swirled tighter. How was she supposed to answer that question when she'd not allowed her heart to go there? When it had seemed easier to keep her emotions at arm's length instead of exploring what could be between them? Because that place, a place of loving and losing, wasn't where she wanted to be. It made her feel vulnerable and exposed, and that was terrifying.

"Honestly, I don't know. It's been too easy to convince myself that I don't need to fall in love again." She swallowed hard, trying to string enough words together so that she made sense. "I'm so afraid of losing my heart to someone, and then losing that person."

Someone like you.

"What if you took fear out of the equation?" he asked. "None of us have any guarantees of what is ahead but letting that stop our heart from feeling—we have a choice."

She clasped her fingers together. She faced fear every day in her job and chose to move forward anyway. Why was it different when it came to love?

"Have you even thought about it?" he asked. "About falling in love again?"

"I've thought more about trying to protect my heart. If I don't love again, I can't become vulnerable."

Her words sounded raw, but they were honest.

"Maybe I'm pushing too hard. Stepping where I shouldn't—"

"No." She read the worried look on his face as her gaze swept his profile. Her sister had called him drop-dead gorgeous with dreamy eyes, and she didn't exactly disagree. She looked away, trying to pull her unsteady thoughts back together. "It's been five years. Danielle keeps telling me I should be open to a new love in my life."

"If you're not, that's okay."

"The thought of stepping out in faith and opening my heart terrifies me. I need time to process things."

"Okay."

She couldn't say she'd never thought about what might

happen with Jonas if she decided to crack open the barrier around her heart. But every time those thoughts had started to germinate, she'd shoved them away. If she never let them take root, she'd never have to worry about another shattered heart.

A boat sped past them on the rough strait, catching her attention. This area was beautiful. Weathered. Rugged. Unpredictable. In the short time she and Jonas had worked together, she'd come to both respect and rely on him when life became unpredictable. He had, in fact, become a constant in her life. A voice of reason, and an anchor that kept her grounded when she couldn't make sense of what was going on around her. The bottom line was if she ever did open her heart again, Jonas would be someone she could see herself taking that journey with. But was that something she was ready for? What about the need for closure on Luke's death?

Maybe the more important question was what if that closure never came? Because what if in the process of looking for it, she missed what was right in front of her?

"I don't know if I can untangle what I'm feeling," she said finally. "Before I was shot, I remember feeling like I was almost to the place where I could let Luke go and move on. I still felt a strong desire to know who'd killed him, but I'd also come to the realization that I might never know, and that was okay. Because it had to be okay. There could be no going back and changing things. No do-overs or replays. I had to consciously make the decision to go on with my life, even if all the loose ends were never wrapped up in a tidy ball at the end."

Wind whipped around them, sending shivers through her and almost negating the warmth from the setting sun as she fought to push back the emotion and order her thoughts.

"Then someone showed up at my house and stole that sense of security from me. Ever since then, I've found myself slipping into that space I tried to avoid for so long. The panic and the fear . . . things I believed I'd almost finally conquered were suddenly back."

"We haven't stopped looking, and we won't," he said. "Not until we find whoever is behind his death."

Madison caught the intensity in his voice. "I know, but all I have is a bunch of dead ends." She struggled to put her thoughts into words. "I'm no closer now than when Luke was killed. How's that possible? But closure . . . I know I might never get what I've been looking for, but it's easier to talk about it than it is to actually do it." Madison waved her hand, suddenly feeling guilty. "I'm sorry. You've focused so much on me these last few hours, but you've been through a lot this week too."

"My situation's a little different. Felicia and I were never even engaged, and she walked out on me a long time ago. We didn't have anything near the history you and Luke had."

"It doesn't matter." Madison shook her head. "It still hurts, and just because my pain is different, it doesn't diminish yours."

"Maybe that's part of what draws me to you. You have that ability to take on any challenge given you and face it head-on, and yet there's a vulnerability that lies under the surface. You push me to be a better person, Madison. That's part of why I'm in love with you."

In love with her?

She worked to fight back the growing fear. Maybe when all of this was over, when they found the person who shot her and Luke . . . But she knew that the right timing might never come, and she couldn't expect him to simply wait for her to make up her mind.

"Jonas . . ."

The rounded head of an orca broke the surface of the water twenty feet from the shoreline. Seconds later, two more rose, their black dorsal fins trailing behind, before all three vanished.

Her shoulder brushed against his. The beauty of the surroundings wasn't enough to distract her from his nearness. A part of her wanted to throw her arms around him and tell him that she felt the same way. That she was ready to take a step forward together and see where that took them. The other part of her simply wanted to run.

She caught the hesitation in his eyes before he looked away.

"There's something else I need to talk to you about. Michaels had some other news for me when I spoke with him earlier."

She zipped her fleece coat up higher, thankful for the change in subject. "Okay."

"I've been invited to interview with SOG."

"Wait a minute." Her eyes widened. "The Marshals' Special Operations Group?"

"Yeah. It's an idea I've toyed with for a while. If I successfully complete the training course, I'd return to my regular duties, leaving only when my team was called to deploy or for routine training sessions."

"Wow." Her feelings of pride over his accomplishment trumped her own personal turmoil for the moment. "That's fantastic, and a huge honor."

"Well, I'm not there yet. If I make it through the selection process, I'd be looking at a month of sixteen-plus-hour days training, and academic studies on top of that. If I decide to go, that is."

"What do you mean, *if*?" she said. "You'd be perfect for the assignment."

"Maybe, but my timing with you would really be off. I'd be gone for a while."

"I'll still be here."

His phone buzzed, and he pulled it out of his pocket. He glanced at the message and frowned.

"Is everything okay?"

Jonas dropped his phone back into his pocket. "Let's go get some dinner. There's something we need to talk about."

✳ ✳ ✳

Jonas had refused to share his news until they made it to the restaurant. Once they were seated, he looked at her and began. "I have a retired buddy who spent forty years on the police force. His name is Edward Langston. I didn't want to get your hopes up, but he has a thing for cold cases. It's something he does in his spare time, and he's good at it. Really good. And as you can imagine, after forty years on the force, he has connections with everyone."

A memory surfaced in Madison's mind. "You mentioned his name when you borrowed that file transcript from me a couple weeks ago."

"Yeah. I showed it to Edward, and he was immediately interested. He remembered hearing about the shooting when it happened, and for some reason Luke's case stuck with him. He'd like to sit down and talk with you about it. He has some questions."

She pressed her hand against her chest, willing her heart to slow down. "He found something?"

Jonas nodded. "He thinks he found a lead on your husband's murder."

THIRTY

Madison filled the coffeepot in her kitchen while trying to unravel what she was feeling. Despite the success in bringing down their fugitives, the past few days had been exhausting, both physically and emotionally. The one bright side was that all four of the fugitives were now being held without bail. The DA wouldn't have any trouble putting them away for a very long time, along with Barton Wells and Adam Cain for their involvement. As soon as it was clear all the suspects had been arrested, they'd turned on each other like a ravenous pack of wolves.

Jonas had suggested they postpone tonight's scheduled meeting with Edward Langston if she didn't feel up to it, but she'd insisted she was fine. Or at least as fine as she could be. She'd convinced herself of the same thing after Jonas had talked to her at Lime Kiln Point about how he felt about her. She'd thought that all she wanted was a friendship.

Wasn't it?

The oven timer beeped, and Danielle rushed into the kitchen to check the cherry pie she'd made for tonight. Leave it to her sister to sweep in and pick up the slack even when she had her own family to take care of.

"I can't thank you enough for coming over and making me dinner, plus the pie," Madison said, pulling out mugs for coffee and small plates for dessert. "You didn't have to."

"It's the least I could do after everything you just went through." Danielle closed the oven door, then set the timer for three more minutes before turning back to Madison. "How are you feeling?"

Madison turned on the coffeepot and leaned back against the counter. "About the fact that I almost drowned, or that we actually might have a lead on Luke's killer?"

"Either." Danielle shrugged. "Both."

She met her sister's worried gaze. "I'll be fine. You can stop worrying about me."

"I know you will be fine, I'm just worried about your meeting tonight and the emotions that it's going to dig up."

"I appreciate that, really, but I need to do this. I know I have to let go and let God take over," Madison said. "At least, that's what I'm trying to do, but surrendering has never been easy for me. I like being in charge. I like figuring out solutions to problems, but sometimes"—she let out a whoosh of air—"sometimes that desire isn't enough. The truth is, I'll never be able to change what happened, no matter how much I want to."

Danielle raised an eyebrow. "You've learned you're human?"

Madison chuckled. "A human with more limitations than I wish I had."

"And if you never find out who murdered Luke? What happens then?"

"I'll have to make sure that doesn't stop me from living. Because while this isn't the route I expected to take in life, I'm tired of living as if I died that day as well. It's just so . . . so hard sometimes."

"Sounds to me like you've taken another step forward." Danielle rummaged through a drawer for a pie server and pulled one out. "What does that mean for you and Jonas?"

Madison shrugged. "Honestly, I'm not sure. I'm still trying to figure out how I feel."

Danielle furrowed her brows. "It seems pretty obvious to me," she said. "I know I've teased you a lot about him, but how could I not, with your standing Friday night dates?"

Madison snatched a washcloth off the sink and started scrubbing down the already clean counter. "He kissed me on the rescue boat."

"Wait a minute." Danielle set the pie server on the counter and stepped next to Madison, forcing eye contact with her sister. "He kissed you?"

She nodded. "After he pulled me out of the water."

"And?"

She closed her eyes for a moment, wishing she hadn't brought up the kiss. Wishing she could forget it herself. "He's in love with me."

A wide smile spread across her sister's face. "Then what's the problem?"

"Working together and trying to juggle a relationship is more than I'm ready to take on."

The timer went off on the oven, interrupting their conversation for the moment. Danielle grabbed the pot holders, then pulled the pie out of the oven.

"You know I support whatever you decide," Danielle said. "I just want you to be happy, but something tells me if you're honest with yourself, you feel the same way he does."

"Maybe, but I can't think about Jonas right now." She leaned against the counter while Danielle turned off the oven. "Right now, I'm just trying not to get my hopes up that Edward really found a break in the case. Because every day I look in the mirror and see the scar on my abdomen. I don't know how to get past that."

"Do you know anything about Edward?" Danielle asked.

"Not really. I'm picturing Columbo with a trench coat."

"I'm just praying he's able to bring you the closure you need."

"Me too."

The doorbell rang.

Danielle squeezed Madison's hand. "I'm going to slip out the back, unless you need me to stay."

"No, get back to your family." Madison pulled her sister into a hug. "Thank you."

"I'm always here for you."

"I know."

Madison smoothed down her pants with her hands, then headed for the front door.

Edward Langston definitely wasn't what she'd expected. The older man looked like he worked out on a daily basis. Definitely not a frumpy detective in a trench coat.

"I'm glad to finally meet you, Madison," he said after she'd invited him and Jonas in. "Though I wish it was under different circumstances."

She smiled. "Thank you for coming."

"Are you kidding me? I think I'm getting the better end of the deal. Dessert and conversation with an interesting woman. At least, that's how Jonas describes you."

She drew in a deep breath, trying to ignore her racing pulse. "You might have to share what else he's said about me."

Edward laughed. "You might be more interested in the stories I could tell about him."

"Edward . . . ," Jonas warned with a grin.

The tension in her shoulders eased slightly. Not that the rest of the evening was going to be easy, but maybe she would be able to unpack some of the stress she'd been carrying while also finding some answers. Maybe she'd be able to find a way to put the past behind her and move forward with Jonas.

She led them into the living room. "Jonas did tell me that you were quite the jokester."

"My late wife used to tell me I didn't have a serious bone in my body, but reality was I needed something to help me shed the stress of things I saw every day." Edward sat down on her couch. "You know how it is with this job. With all we see, sometimes those one-liners are the only things that keep you out of the funny farm."

"I understand all too well," she said, sitting down on a chair across from him. "I suppose we all have to find our own ways of coping with what we see. And I'm sorry about your wife. I didn't realize she'd passed away."

"Three years ago this fall. I miss her every moment of every day, but we had forty wonderful years together. At least I did." Edward let out a low chuckle. "She had to put up with me for all that time."

Madison smiled. "I doubt that was the case."

"Oh, I know I drove the woman crazy. She always told me I needed to think about retiring or starting a new career, but I told her I'd never find another job where I'd get paid to drive fast, shoot guns, and play hide-and-seek."

Madison cleared her throat, her gaze shifting to the file he held. "I thought we could talk in here. And once it cools down, I've got a fresh cherry pie waiting for us."

"If it tastes as good as it smells, I'm in. Though you didn't have to go to any trouble."

She waved away the compliment. "The pie's my sister's donation to the cause. I'm always amazed how she finds time to bake with three kids in the house."

"Women are amazing creatures. I know my wife was," Edward said. "Though your partner here isn't too bad either. I heard the two of you just brought in a couple wanted felons."

Madison looked up at Jonas, hoping the awkwardness between them would eventually disappear.

"They almost made it to the Canadian border," Jonas said, shifting forward in his seat at the other end of the couch. "And not without a couple close calls along the way."

"But that's not why we're here," Edward said.

Madison clasped her fingers together on her lap. "I don't know how much Jonas has told you about my husband's case other than the files he gave you."

The atmosphere in the room shifted again, bringing back some of the tension she'd felt earlier.

"He gave me the CliffsNotes version of your story. Said you'd been working for five years to solve your husband's murder, then you were shot three months ago, presumably by the same person."

Madison nodded.

"I truly am sorry for your loss, and for everything you've gone through," Edward said. "I know what it's like to lose someone you love, though thankfully, my Sadie went peacefully in the night. I'll always be grateful for that."

Edward cleared his throat, then pulled out a pen and a

yellow ledger with notes scribbled across the front. "I know the last thing you want to do right now is relive that moment, but I do have some questions I'd like to work through."

Madison rubbed her palms down her legs nervously. "Of course."

"I'm wondering about the ring found near your husband. According to the case file notes, it wasn't his."

"Correct." Madison nodded. "They never could establish if it was a part of the crime scene or just lost by someone else in the parking garage."

"That makes sense. What did you find out about the ring?"

She took a deep breath. "Um, it's one worn by gamers, something my husband definitely was not. And it was custom made."

Edward wrote a few words on his legal pad, then looked up at her. "From what Jonas has told me, you've always believed that Luke was killed because of one of his patients. And that his death was staged to look like a robbery."

"There have been numerous theories, but that's the one I always go back to." Her gaze dropped to her hands. "I guess I've never wanted to believe he was just killed over the twenty dollars in his wallet."

"I can understand that. And something had to have motivated the shooter's behavior for them to have come after you again." Edward paused. "Can you tell me what you'd been working on related to your husband's case just before the break-in here?"

"I'd been frustrated, actually. For a long time. I felt like everything I did was simply spinning me in circles. So I would start going through everything again, starting with the ring."

Edward leaned forward. "That's interesting, because it's the ring that has kept niggling at me."

"Why?" Madison asked.

"I'm not sure. People lose rings every day, and it's not too far-fetched to think it was simply too loose and fell off while someone was getting out of their car or something." Edward sat back on the couch. "But neither do I believe in coincidences."

Jonas shifted in his seat. "So maybe Madison was getting too close to the truth."

"Maybe," Edward said. "I started going through the list of people who died in the hospital who had received care from Luke. Tried to find a connection to the ring. I interviewed a woman who makes custom rings for gamers. It's a small but viable niche. She gave me the names of a dozen other designers who also make them, but I wasn't able to track down conclusively who made the ring. At least not yet."

"I came to the same dead end," Madison said. "That specific piece of jewelry is from a video game called Night Crawler, but I was never able to track down the owner or the seller."

Edward blew out a short breath. "I need to ask you one more question."

"Okay."

"Did you ever consider the possibility that your husband wasn't the target?"

Madison fidgeted with the ring on her right hand, suddenly feeling like her nerves were being stretched tighter than a rubber band. She didn't like the change in the conversation, because as much as she wanted answers, the truth could also be terrifying. That was a road she didn't want to go down.

"Yes. It was something we looked at, but it just led to more dead ends."

"In the file notes, it mentions that Luke was driving your car that day."

"He was. His was in the shop. I had my partner pick me up." Madison hesitated. "You really think I could have been the target?"

Edward nodded. "Thanks to a friend of mine who owes me a few favors, I was able to get a list of your case files."

She pressed her lips together. "Okay. What did you find?"

Edward paused before speaking. "One of them stood out. I'm sure you remember Thomas Knight?"

Madison nodded. She'd arrested Knight for murder, and in turn he was sentenced for life. He was only eighteen years old. She'd never been able to shake the frustration of what happened that day. At eighteen, Thomas had his whole life ahead of him, but his freedom had been wiped out in a series of bad choices.

"I did some research on Knight." She mentally flipped through her old memories of the case. "He was a gamer, and he dropped out of school his senior year."

Edward nodded. "Do you know anything else about him?"

Her mind brought up the information automatically. "His mother was out of the picture. Negligence, from what I heard. He had a sister, but she was younger and lived with an aunt. He'd been on his own since he was sixteen. The whole situation was tragic."

Madison struggled to put the pieces together. Had she been so close to the situation that she'd missed going far enough down that road? "So you think that whoever shot Luke was trying to, what . . . punish me for arresting him?"

"I think this could be about more than just his arrest. Thomas Knight was killed in prison. I think you were targeted because you were the arresting officer and Luke's murderer blamed you." Edward leaned forward again. "I can't prove any of this yet, but did you know that the video game Night Crawler uses a black rose as a symbol of death?"

Madison's insides turned cold. She glanced at Jonas, whose expression looked as conflicted as she felt. "No."

"They are placed on the graves of victims," Edward said.

Her mouth went dry as her mind fought to move in that direction. "If your theory is true . . . Luke should still be alive. I should be the one who died that day."

Edward held up his hand. "I know what you're thinking, Madison, but I don't want you to go there. None of this is your fault. You have to know that on some level. There are things in our line of work that we can't control. This is one of them."

She nodded, but the sick feeling that had settled in her stomach only continued to spread. "So what do we do now?"

"Let me keep searching. See if I can find out more."

"I'll go get the pie," Jonas said, standing up abruptly. "You two sit here and keep talking."

She noticed a look pass between the two men, but there were too many other things swirling around in her head at the moment.

Edward waited until Jonas had left the room before he spoke again. "You know, I've solved a couple dozen cold cases over the past few years, and I've sat across from people who, like you, hope to find out the truth. And what you need to know is that when that day comes, no matter how hard you've fought for it, or how bad you wanted it, the truth will both bring closure and stir up the pain again. Unfortunately, that's normal."

"I know." Madison leaned against the back of her seat, pulling her legs up beneath her. "Just when I think I'm about to move past it, something seems to bring things to the forefront."

"Like the break-in?"

She nodded.

"I truly am sorry for the loss of your husband, and for what happened to you, but no matter the outcome of this investigation, I don't want you to blame yourself."

"Easier said than done."

Edward set his notebook on the end table next to him. "When Sadie died, I kept going over every detail round and round in my head. What if we'd gone to the doctor sooner, or gone to a different doctor? What if I'd made sure she ate better, or took more supplements? But the truth is, as intentional as I was about taking care of her, there was nothing I could have done that would have prolonged her life. Sometimes, we just have to thank the Good Lord for bringing blessings into our lives, and then when it's time, we have to let them go."

Tears filled her eyes. "Sometimes I feel like I've managed to move on, and then out of the blue there will be a reminder, and I feel like I'm reliving that day all over again."

"I understand. I truly do. But I know this too: whatever the truth is about your husband's death, it wasn't your fault," Edward said. "I also know that eventually, if you don't let go of the guilt, you might one day regret missing what's right in front of you."

Madison glanced toward the kitchen. "Jonas."

Edward nodded.

"What did he tell you?"

The older man grinned. "Nothing, but I see the way he looks at you. And at the same time, I know how hard it can be to move on. About six months ago, I took an old friend out to dinner. She and I have known each other for thirty-odd years, and yet I never once imagined myself loving anyone other than Sadie. It took me weeks to come up with the courage just to ask her to dinner."

"And?" Madison asked.

"Turns out I haven't laughed that hard in years. I realized I was smiling again, and it was okay. So while I'm not going to presume to know what you feel about Jonas, I can tell you that loving Ruth doesn't change my love for Sadie. I know it's what she would have wanted. In fact, I can't help but think she's smiling down at me, because I've finally decided to start living again. It just took me a long time to figure it out." Edward lowered his voice. "You can't let what was taken away from you stop you from living again. Bottom line is that I've learned that life doesn't always give us what we expect, but God does heal the brokenhearted. And even if Jonas isn't the one for you, don't stop holding on to that promise."

THIRTY-ONE

Jonas parked his car at the bottom of Kerry Park where Madison had asked to meet him, then started up the stairs, wishing he didn't feel so nervous about seeing her again. The last time he'd seen her was three days ago when she'd kissed him on the cheek, thanking him for introducing her to Edward, then said good night. He'd gone home, unsure of what she was really thinking. Or if he'd managed to completely overstep the boundaries he'd worked so hard to keep between them.

But his heart had crossed the line, and there was no going back.

He knew that talking with Edward had been difficult for Madison. Her mind had to have been swirling with memories of Luke and what had happened the day he was killed. Which was why he'd promised to give her time. If he really loved her, he owed her that much. He'd been worried about her reaction from the first moment he'd spoken to Edward, but he also knew that each step closer to finding closure meant her finding healing as well. And that was all he hoped for. Not just because he wanted a chance at a relationship with her, but because he truly wanted her to find healing.

Which was why he'd decided to turn down the offered training with SOG. He'd passed his interview yesterday, but the timing seemed off. He wanted to be there for whatever Madison needed in the coming days and weeks, and that wasn't something he could do if he was off the grid training for the next month. There would be another chance to volunteer for duty with the Special Operations Group. Now just wasn't the time.

She was standing on a patch of grass, overlooking the iconic view of downtown Seattle with the Space Needle as the sun set and the city lights began to appear. A ferry was crossing Elliott Bay, and the late-evening sky was clear enough that they could see the silhouette of Mount Rainier. A perfect background. Perfect night.

Perfect woman.

At least for him, she was.

"Wow. I haven't been up here for years. I'd forgotten how stunning it is," he said, walking up to her. He tried to take in the view spread out in front of them, but all he could see was her.

"Thanks for coming up here," she said, still staring out across the city. "It's one of my favorite places."

"I can see why," he said.

"Being here always makes me feel closer to God." She sighed. "It reminds me that he sees everything that's happening with every single one of us. And that always gives me enough hope to keep going. Something I've needed lately." She turned to him, but the smile he was expecting had vanished from her lips. "Edward called me this morning."

"And?"

"He did some more digging and has evidence that the ring they found by Luke belonged to Thomas Knight. Edward found a photo of him in his school yearbook wearing the ring."

"Which would confirm you were the target," Jonas said.

"Or they meant to shoot Luke in order to hurt me. It would explain the flowers at his grave, constant reminders of his death. They didn't want me to forget. They killed Luke because they wanted me to suffer." She blew out a sharp puff of air. "But either way, if whoever shot Luke believes we're together, you could become a target."

"Wait a minute." Traffic passed behind them, and a siren whirled, but he shut out everything except for her. "You don't know that."

"Why not?" She threw her hands up. "They murdered my husband. They broke into my house and shot me."

"Madison—"

"Wait." She shook her head. "I need you to understand something. I thought I could move on with you even if I never found out who murdered Luke, but knowing I was the target . . . his death will weigh on me the rest of my life. I can't ignore that and put your life in danger. I won't go through that again."

He wanted to pull her into his arms and show her exactly how he felt, but instead he shoved his hands into his pockets. "You're missing the point. I want to do life with you. You and I can face this together. You don't have to do it alone."

Her lips were pressed together as if she'd been rehearsing what she was about to say. "I know, and I appreciate your being patient with me. I might seem unflappable on the outside most of the time, but this whole scenario . . ."

"I get it, and that's okay. There's no time frame on us moving forward, but don't let this situation stop us from at least trying to see what might happen between us."

She gazed up at him. "I can't make any promises. Not now. Not until I know for certain that I'm not putting your life at risk."

He wanted to argue with her but knew he wouldn't be able to change her mind. "None of this changes how I feel about you, but you need to know that I didn't come to you with expectations. My biggest fear was that having this conversation would change things between us. But I can't let my fear of what might or might not happen keep me from saying something. That if there is a chance for something between us one day, I'm willing to wait."

"And if I don't know when that day will be?"

He drew in a deep breath. "I'm learning that life isn't all black and white, and you can't always fix everything. It's messy, and there isn't an answer that fits every situation. But that's okay. I'm hoping life keeps moving us forward together. Forces us to stop hiding behind our pasts. But I won't try to push things forward. I've tried that and it doesn't work. I tried to fix Felicia, but the truth was, she didn't want to be fixed or need me to fix her. And I won't do the same with you."

"I want you to move forward with the Special Ops Group—"

"There will be other opportunities."

"No." She shook her head. "The timing will never be perfect. You need to do this. For you."

"I don't know—"

"Promise me, Jonas."

He caught the determination in her eyes and nodded.

"And if we still can't figure a way out of this jumbled mess?" she asked. "What then?"

He drew her into his arms, relieved when she nestled against his chest. "We'll figure this out, and in the meantime, I'll always be here for you. That will never change, no matter what happens."

Because some things in life were worth waiting for.

Loved this book from Lisa Harris?
Read on for a Sneak Peek
of the Epic Series Conclusion,

THE CATCH

COMING SPRING 2022

PROLOGUE

He'd lied to her again.

It was her fault for believing him in the first place. For trusting the slew of promises he never kept. He'd told her he loved her. Told her he'd leave his wife for her so they could be together. Becca played the fool and believed him. She knew now that he never intended to stay with her, and as far as she was concerned, he wasn't capable of being faithful. Today was no different, and yet he called and she came running.

She sat in her car, trying to gather her own frayed nerves, as she stared at the gated house where he lived with *her*. While she'd never been inside the five-thousand-square-foot house, she knew it included a chef's kitchen, a vaulted back porch, and a three-car garage. The apartment she shared with their son was less than a thousand square feet. Robert paid for the majority of her expenses, but it was never quite enough, so she continued to work at the café and relied on his handouts and promises that he'd leave his wife for her.

She gripped the steering wheel and frowned. The reality was that she didn't care about the big house. She wasn't even sure she loved him anymore. She only cared about their son.

Her son.

She drew in a deep breath as she got out of the car and headed up to the front door. It was strange that he'd asked her to come here. He'd never done that before. The closest she'd gotten to the front gate was when she'd driven by one time on her own. She'd wanted to know where he lived and spent his time when he wasn't with her. She'd felt guilty about their arrangement since the beginning, but Robert had swept in and given her the feeling of family she never had. Saying no had been impossible until she realized that this life was nothing more than a fairy tale that could never have a happy ending.

Still, as much as she wanted to, she never found the courage to walk away.

Until now.

Today, all of that would change. No matter what he said, she was going to tell him that she was leaving him. She was tired of playing his games and always losing. Tired of the tangled web she'd found herself in as the scorned mistress that could never show her face at his office or at one of his political fundraisers. She'd seen the photos of him and Myra on the news last night, smiling into the camera as if he didn't have a care in the world. She'd actually believed that could be her standing next to him one day. His expression told her otherwise. He would never give up his life for her.

Becca put her hand on the brass doorknob, then stopped. Was she supposed to walk in or knock?

She didn't have to answer the question as the door swung open.

Myra stood in the doorway, a smile plastered on her face from too much Botox. "Becca Lambert, it's nice to finally meet you in person, though I guess you weren't expecting me to be here."

LISA HARRIS ——— 311

"I don't understand." Becca studied the woman's pencil skirt and button-up blouse that likely cost more than what she earned in a month. "How do you know me?"

"I'm not nearly as clueless as Robert thinks I am. I'm the one who sent you the message from his phone. I thought we could . . . talk."

Becca took a step backward, fighting every instinct in her body that told her to run. "I'm not sure that's a good idea."

"It won't take long. Just a few minutes. It's time you and I got to know each other."

She didn't want to talk to Robert's wife. Didn't want to be in the same room with the woman.

"Where's Robert?" Becca asked.

"At work. Or so he says. He's always working, but you don't really think you're the only pretty girl who's caught his eye, do you?"

Becca blinked back tears as she tried to stuff down the guilt. She and Robert had met by chance at an office building in downtown Seattle. He was handsome and charismatic, and he paid attention to her. She'd grown up in foster care, and for the first time in her life, she felt loved by someone. Special.

Then she found out she was pregnant.

After that, there was nothing she could do to change their agreement. He promised to pay the bills as long as she promised to be quiet. His wife was never to find out. None of his associates could be confided in either. No one could know he was the father of her baby.

Becca shook her head. "I need to leave—"

"I wouldn't if I were you. I know everything about you and Robert, including the fact that you had his son."

Becca's mouth went dry. "Robert told you that?"

Myra motioned her inside. "It didn't take much detective work to find out where he really spends his time away from me."

"I made mistakes," Becca said, stepping through the imposing entryway to a boldly decorated living room that was far too gaudy for her tastes, though the red and coral theme seemed to fit Myra perfectly. "But you have to understand that I didn't know he was married when I first started seeing him."

By the time she found out the truth about Robert's marital status, she'd already lost her heart. Guilt pressed against her chest. How many times had she told herself she needed to walk away? How many times had she chastised herself for not taking her own advice?

Myra's smile disappeared as she turned around. "Don't play innocent with me."

"I'm not—" Becca stopped. She had no idea what this woman wanted from her, but she clearly wasn't interested in a string of apologies.

"Here's the bottom line," Myra said. "I have the ability to make your life extremely miserable, but . . . I'm going to offer you a one-time deal."

Becca's fingers clinched her purse strap. "What do you mean?"

"I will give you enough money to leave Seattle and start over. I don't care where or how, as long as it's far away from here."

Becca forced herself to relax her fingers, but she couldn't absorb what she was hearing. "You want to pay me off?"

Myra leaned against the desktop, then crossed her ankles. "You make it sound so . . . so illicit."

"Isn't it?"

Myra's gaze seemed to pierce through her. "No more illicit than sleeping with someone else's husband."

Becca's gaze dropped to the expensive rug on the floor, following the dark orange squiggly pattern along the edge. Nausea swept through her, making her want to vomit. She should have known this day would come. Nothing good ever came from keeping secrets.

"The bottom line is that you don't have a choice," Myra continued. "You're going to walk away and never contact Robert again. And"—she tapped her manicured fingers together—"you will sign over your parental rights to Robert."

Becca's head shot up. "You can't do that."

"You don't seem to understand how things work. Without money and power, you're nothing but a waitress working overtime for tips. If you try to fight me, you'll lose."

"No." Becca straightened her shoulders, determined to dig up enough courage to fight back. "You can't buy me off."

"Then you're more foolish than I thought," she said, her voice cold. "Robert doesn't love you, Becca. He never did. Not really. You've been nothing more than a temporary distraction."

"I'm not taking your money."

"Then I'll need to find something else to persuade you."

"What do you mean?"

"I know you left your son with his sitter this morning," Myra said.

Becca's heart pounded in her chest. If Myra did anything to hurt her son . . . "What did you do?"

"It's not what I've done, it's what I will do if you don't cooperate. You will sign the papers I've had drawn up, giving Robert full custody of the child, and you will walk away with the money."

"No—"

"You seem to think you can fight this, but you can't. I will hire the best lawyers in the city, and in the end, you will still give up the rights to your son. Now it's just up to you to decide if you take the money or end up losing everything."

Becca stumbled backward. "No. I'll never give up my baby."

She grabbed a handgun out of her purse. The one that, ironically, Robert had bought her. There wasn't time to think through the consequences. All she knew was that she wasn't going to lose her son.

Lisa Harris is a bestselling author, a Christy Award winner, and the winner of the Best Inspirational Suspense Novel from *Romantic Times* for her novels *Blood Covenant* and *Vendetta*. The author of more than forty books, including The Nikki Boyd Files and the Southern Crimes series, as well as *Vanishing Point*, *A Secret to Die For*, and *Deadly Intentions*, Harris and her family have spent over sixteen years living as missionaries in southern Africa. Learn more at www.lisaharriswrites.com.

How Do You Catch a Fugitive Who Has Nothing to Lose?

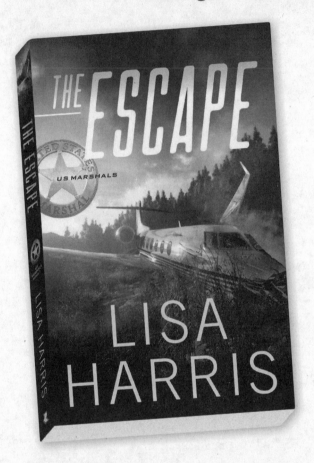

For US Marshals Madison James and Jonas Quinn,
a desperate murderer and a downed plane
turn a routine prison transfer into a hunt
through the rugged Pacific Northwest.

meet
LISA HARRIS

lisaharriswrites.com

@AuthorLisaHarris

@HeartOfAfrica